Saint Carlen

of

Silver Falls

Volume 5
of the Silver Falls Series

Rebecca Woods

Dedicated to my husband, Kirk
Who saves me from all things computer.

This is a work of fiction. The characters, names, incidents, places, and dialogue are products of the author's imagination, and are not to be construed as real.

ISBN-10: 1517148499

Cover design by Savannah Armstrong

Printed in the United States of America

Table of Contents

Chapter One

Saint Carlen

July 1917

Pounding a nail into yet another shingle, Carlen began to wonder if it would be sufficient to stop the leak in the kitchen ceiling that had tested his wife's patience all through the spring. Off in the distance, he could hear the ocean roar as though a storm was on the approach, battering waves against the cliffs. And yet, above his home the sky was clear and the sun shone pleasantly on his efforts. The verdant green hills and valleys of the Silver Falls district all but filled his senses with peace.

"Hello, Reverend Sanderson," a small voice called to him.

Carlen glanced around the yard below from his perch on the roof, earnestly looking, but failing to find the source of that greeting.

"Up here," the voice called again.

Up? Turning his gaze to the sky, he saw Meredith Layne, drifting slowly toward him in a thin wooden chair, held aloft by several large and brightly colored balloons.

Alarmed at the sight, he called out. "Meredith! Just what do you think you're doing?"

"Daddy ordered balloons for the fair tomorrow and I wanted to see what it would be like to fly."

"But how do you propose to come down?" the reverend asked as the little girl drifted closer.

"I brought a pin," she smiled, holding up the small deflation device. "I'll pop one balloon at a time, so I don't come down too fast."

Carlen shifted nervously as the girl slowly drifted even with the preacher's house.

"Meredith, you do realize that you're drifting toward the ocean? I think it would be best to come down right now. Do your parents even know what you're doing?"

Merrie shook her head. "No, they don't, but it's so interesting to see everything from up here; I feel like a bird, flying free in the sky." Looking off in the distance, Merrie Layne's brows began to knit. "It *is* getting close to the cliffs. Will you help me down, Reverend Sanderson?"

Carlen scooted to the edge of the ridgepole and made a large sweeping grasp for the chair leg steadily floating away from him - and missed.

"Pop the balloons, Merrie!" he called out. "You're headed straight for the cliffs."

Looking off toward the ocean, suddenly aware of the danger, the little girl froze, her eyes large with fear as she gripped at the chair seat. Carlen scooted back across the roof to the ladder and quickly scurried down the rungs as fast as he could manage. Soon, he was rushing through the yard and into a pasture, running in pursuit of the floating chair and its paralyzed, young hostage.

"Pop the balloons, Merrie! I'm right here below you; I'll catch you! Pop them, now!" he shouted.

"I'm afraid to," she called back.

"Find your courage, Merrie. You must pop them before it is too late!"

"I dropped my pin!" she screamed back. "Oh, Reverend Sanderson, can you find it?"

"No, Meredith, there's not time. Can you untie the balloons?"

The little girl shook her head, her hands now gripping the chair so strenuously, they were turning white.

"Reverend Sanderson, I'm frightened! Will you save me?"

Carlen looked right and then left, scanning the field for anything he could find to stop the chair from drifting closer to the ocean and certain death, but all that lay near him were waving fields of grass. Finally, he spied a tree not far away with several dead limbs. Running ahead of the child, he reached the tree and began breaking off pieces, hoping to fashion a spear from the dead wood. Finally, rushing back, he called out.

"Cover your face, Merrie. I'm going to try and hit the balloons."

Hoping to strike high, he thrust the stick into the air but completely overshot them by several feet. Still, the chair drifted closer and closer as he continued to throw what sticks he had until, at last, he hit and popped one of the balloons, bringing it to drift ever so slightly lower toward the earth. Unfortunately, Merrie was still too high for him to reach and inching dangerously closer to the cliffs.

"Oh, dear Lord, help me save this child," he whispered, as he ran back to the tree for more sticks. "Hang on, Merrie!"

The chair was passing the tree now, a good hundred yards to its northern side and less than a quarter mile from the ocean. Running back to it, Carlen thrust stick after stick at the balloons and though many of them were a square hit, they merely bounced off and fell back to the earth. The chair was, however, getting closer to the ground, and closer to the edge. There was nothing more to do but follow her, hoping she would lower to within reach before it was too late.

Standing below, a mere fifty feet from the precipice, he noticed that the balloons began to increase in their forward motion, less than ten feet above the minister's outstretched arms.

"Listen to me, Meredith, you must jump! If you go over that edge and out to the ocean, it will be certain death. Jump to me!" he shouted.

The child could not move from her terror, but sat with her fingers clenched tightly to the seat.

"Jump, Merrie! Jump now! JUMP!" he yelled as commandingly as he could.

Carlen watched helplessly as her wide eyes looked down toward him, filled with fright. "Save me, Reverend Sanderson!"

He ran a few more feet, and leapt with all his might toward the chair legs before they moved beyond the grassy edge. Tragically, he hadn't come close to touching them.

"Save me, Reverend Sanderson!" Merrie cried as she drifted out over the water. "Oh, please, save me!"

*

Carlen sat up with a start, heart pounding, the words still ringing in his ears, as he realized it had all been a dream; a very disturbing dream! Despite the lost apparition, the panic he had felt for the little girl's welfare still gripped at his senses, as though he were yet in the midst of the trial. Linda was asleep at his side and the boys had yet to stir. Quietly, leaving his bed, he left to the front of the house and stepped outside.

The sun was barely rising, and a mild breeze, almost undetectable, swept gently over the hills and off toward the ocean. The ladder he had been using the day before in an attempt to find and repair an elusive hole in the roof still balanced against the eastern wall of the house. The morning birds called out to each other across the fields and trees.

Stepping back into the house, a firm determination settled over the man as he quietly dressed for the day, left a note in the kitchen, and began his walk over to the little stone house beyond the brook. It was a day before the town fair and Carlen remembered hearing Nathan speak of selling balloons at the festivities. Surely, it wouldn't hurt just to check and be sure. The Laynes lived barely more than a mile away.

Walking down the drive beside the brook and below the shimmering silver maples, Carlen noticed first the wagon with hydrogen canisters sticking out above the sides. Next, he saw Nathan sitting on a stool just beyond, methodically filling balloons and attaching them with strings to the wagon's sides.

"Good morning, Nathan," he greeted.

"Good morning, Reverend!" Nathan was clearly surprised at the minister's presence. "What brings you out so early today?"

"Just satisfying a curiosity," Carlen smiled. "Is your little Merrie up and about yet?"

"No," Nathan laughed. "I'm afraid I'm the only one awake at this hour. We're selling balloons for the fair tomorrow and I thought I'd try them out ahead of time to see how they'll do. Hopefully they'll stay aloft for the better part of a day."

Carlen tugged at one of the balloons, surprised at the tension. "They have remarkable lift, don't they?"

"Yes, but I'm pretty sure they'll not carry a whole wagon off. Please, sit down and we can visit while I work."

Nathan retrieved a chair from the other side of the wagon, the same thin chair from Carlen's dream.

"How many balloons did you order for the fair?"

"Only a hundred; I thought we should try them first before investing too much time or money."

"What were you planning to do with these?"

Nathan shrugged. "Leave them tied to the wagon, I suppose. I want to see how sturdy they'll be and how well they hold the gas."

"Ah, yes." Carlen nodded. He then looked over at the house for a few minutes before venturing his next thoughts. "How many of these balloons would you estimate it would take to get a child airborne?"

"I have no idea. Why do you ask?"

Carlen shrugged, deep in thought. "They're very large; I'd guess twenty or so might get someone of Meredith's size off the ground in this chair; wouldn't you say?"

Nathan scowled as he studied the reverend's face.

"That might be enough." Sighing deeply, he looked back at the wagon and counted what he'd filled so far; there were seventeen colored orbs tied to the side rail. "You know, I hadn't thought of that particular scenario, but it would be just like her to try such a thing."

Carlen smiled. "Children will be children."

"Well then, I suppose we don't need any more to encourage the situation along, do we?"

Carlen laughed and shook his head. "Probably not. In fact, would you mind if I took a few home for my boys? I can report back to you on their sturdiness and function."

"That's a fine idea," Nathan nodded. "Why don't you take several? Just let me know how they do."

"I will; and you'll watch that little Meredith of yours closely today?"

"That I will," Nathan promised, as he gathered the floating orbs and tied them together. "Can I talk you into staying for breakfast?"

Carlen glanced toward the house and smiled before declining the offer. "I have a lot requiring my attentions today if we're to be free for the fair tomorrow, a stubborn leak in the roof not being the least of them. I should get back home. Tell your family hello for me."

"Yes, I will."

Nathan smiled and waved as Carlen clasped the clump of strings attached to the inflatable wonders and started back toward the road. Turning one last time, the reverend called out.

"Thank you, Nathan. I'm sure my boys will be delighted!"

"You're welcome!" he nodded, loading the canister back into

the wagon and securing the gate. "Come again."

As he walked on, out of the drive and on his way through the countryside in the general direction of Parrish Road, the reverend bowed his head and whispered quietly.

"And thank you, dear Lord, for saving Miss Merrie. Amen."

Chapter Two

Remember the Lusitania

July 1917

Emma Larssen sat in the back of the Layne's festive wagon, clapping and singing her happy songs with the three oldest children, while Annie squished as close to her as she could manage. All around the sideboards, eighty-three gala balloons bobbed and swayed in the ocean breeze as the Belgians hauled the rumbling dray toward town. Chase rode up front between his parents and all of them were dressed in the finest fair-going outfits they could contrive.

Due to his position as fair manager, Hayden's presence at home had been scarce over the past month, working sun-up to sun-down, trying to get everything ready for the great day. Meanwhile, in an attempt at filling her own empty hours, Emma had sewn a new dress and primped herself to as beautiful a state of perfection as was possible. Truth be told, she was especially excited to arrive at the fair, join her husband for the day, and show off all of her efforts.

Coming closer to town, handbills for the fair began to show up on the telephone poles, intermittently mixed with campaign posters reading, "Vote for David Harrison - Mayor of Silver Falls." Occasionally, there was a drawing of him mixed in with the other posters, though having to be hand-made, these were fewer and farther between. Coming up on an especially large poster, picture included, Nathan looked at it admiringly.

"You know, Hannah, you did an especially good job on that one. It looks just like him."

Hannah smiled and wrinkled her nose at her husband. "With all the fuss, you'd think it was a tight race."

"Who's running against him?" Emma asked.

"No one," Nathan replied.

"Then why go to all the effort of campaigning?"

Nathan only smiled. "Because it is David Harrison; he's probably hoping the handbills will just remind people to vote today while they are at the fair. I imagine he'll have the entire countryside whipped into shape within the first year."

Emma knitted her brows, thinking about it further. "Don't you have to live in town to be mayor?"

"Well, that used to be the rule," Hannah replied, "but Davy had the charter changed to include anyone within four miles."

"Why four?"

Nathan laughed. "Because his house is just a hair over three."

Fingering the strings, Emma brought an orb down to examine it more closely. "I like the balloons. What are you going to do with them?"

Hannah glanced back. "The children are selling them for spending money."

"That sounds like an adventure," Emma laughed.

"They're a nickel apiece if you want one," Meredith announced. "You could be our first customer."

"I think I will," their cousin agreed.

"Whoa!" Nathan pulled on the reins to slow the horses. "What's going on here?"

They had barely pulled into town, though the ruckus could be heard far beyond the area of the booths. Men in uniforms stood out in front, megaphones poised to their mouths, calling to the crowds.

"Protect our freedoms! Defeat the German forces invading France," shouted one man.

"Enlist now; America needs you!"

"Remember the Lusitania!" yelled another. "Never forget, the Germans sunk the Lusitania!"

"Your country needs you! Sign up now!" another called through his blow horn.

Rising to her knees and looking past Chase to get a better view, Emma shaded her eyes with her hand.

"What's going on?"

"Apparently the war has reached our little town," Nathan mused. "And they're using our megaphones from the fair."

"What's the Lusitania?" Melanie asked.

"Do you remember the Titanic?" Emma asked.

"The ship that sank?"

"Yes. Well, the Lusitania was a ship just like that which the

Germans sank a couple of years ago."

"How?" Andy asked.

"I'm not sure," Emma replied, "but there were lots of Americans on it."

"They used torpedoes from a submarine," Nathan put in.

"Did they capture the Americans?" Annie wanted to know.

Emma shook her head solemnly. "No, most of them died."

"I think war is terrible!" Melanie declared.

"Me too," Emma agreed. "And why drag our young men into it? It's not our war."

Hannah drew her hand to her mouth. "Nathan, Look! Jason and Jonathan are in line at that booth. You don't suppose they would leave, do you? How would Davy ever handle the farm without them?"

Nathan's brows knit as he tried to make sense of the situation. This wasn't at all the scene of joviality he had expected to see. Pulling over to the bank, he jumped down and tied his horses to the hitching post, before quickly walking to the area of the booths.

"What's going on here?" he asked one of the men.

"Are you in charge of this town? We'd like to know why you have so many able bodied slackers when they are so desperately needed overseas."

"Slackers?" Nathan asked. "We're a quiet farming community; the men here work as hard as anyone. They can hardly be called slackers."

"Who are you? Are you in charge here?" the man demanded once again.

"Nathan Layne," he answered, extending his hand to the officer. "I'm president of the bank and responsible for the overall environment of this fair. This is a day of festivities for our town; not a time to be recruiting for war."

"We have our job to do," the man answered, then turning to the crowd he yelled. "Sign up here to serve your country!"

Nathan calmly lowered the megaphone. "Not in our town and not at this fair."

"You can't shut us down," the man argued back.

"I'm afraid I can and I will." Collecting the devices, he calmly informed the men. "These are needed and intended for someplace else. I'll have to ask you to desist."

The men stopped their clamor, but continued filling out forms as quickly as they could.

Megaphones in hand, Nathan pulled the Harrison boys aside. "You boys aren't enlisting, are you?"

"Yes," Jason answered. "Our country needs us to defeat the Kaiser."

Nathan looked skeptically back at the booth. He hadn't heard much of anything about the war before now, no one in Silver Falls had, and he was highly doubtful as to the legitimacy of the situation.

"What about your father? Does he know what you're doing?"

"Yes," Jon answered.

"And he approves?"

"Pretty much; he said we could sign up as long as we didn't leave until after the harvest."

Nathan could hardly believe his ears. What was David Harrison thinking? Jogging back toward the wagon, he deposited the megaphones inside and spoke to his wife.

"Hannah, will you stay with the children and help them sell their balloons? Emma, I need you to find Hayden; I need to speak with him right away. I'll be over at the restaurant; maybe Janette will know more of what's going on."

*

The restaurant staff was very busy preparing for the day and the many customers they would accommodate. The Falls was always busy, but never so much as on the day of the town fair. It took a while in the mayhem for Nathan to locate Janette, but he eventually found her directing a crew as they set up tables on the terrace outside.

"Hey, do you have a minute?"

"Hi, Nathan. I'm pretty busy; what do you need?"

"What's going on with the recruiters out there? I hardly think that our town fair is an appropriate venue for them. It's not like it's our war."

Janette immediately lowered her eyes as a look of guilt swept over her face. Shrugging, she directed Nathan to a table, away from the commotion of workers.

"Maybe you'd better sit down."

"Why?" he shrugged. "How is this even an issue?"

"We *are* at war," she whispered. "Wilson declared war on Germany a few weeks back."

Nathan shook his head. "I don't believe it; we haven't heard anything about it."

Janette sighed in defeat. "Wait here; I'll be right back." She disappeared for a minute and then returned with a small stack of newspapers. "I've been keeping these from the town. Our customers frequently bring the Portland papers with them to read on the train, leaving them in the restaurant."

"Yes," Nathan acknowledged. "We've often gotten our news that way; but why would you hide them?"

Janette winced. "The war has been escalating and I didn't want it to trouble our customers. Also..." she hedged, "I didn't want it to affect our town. It just seems so senseless; our young men going off to die, and for what? Another country's cause? It's not like it's on our shores, Nathan. Oh, I know it sounds unpatriotic, but I'd do it all over again. I'm sorry that those men have found us even now."

"How bad is it?

"Take a look. You're free to read the papers; just please don't pass them around. In Portland, they're holding all sorts of war parades and signing up whatever men they can. It's like an infection of sick enthusiasm. The boys have no clue what they're headed into and act as if it will be their one great chance at becoming a hero."

Nathan shook his head as he leafed from page to page. "Have you seen Hayden? Is he aware that those men have taken over one of our booths?"

"He set them up with it." Janette put her hand on her cousin's arm. "That's not all, Nathan; he was the first to sign on."

Nathan looked up from the papers, stunned at her words. "Without speaking to Emma?"

"I assumed Emma knew." Janette blew out a heavy breath. "I doubt she'll take to that news well."

"No," Nathan agreed, "she won't at all. It would be a blow for a seasoned adult, and she is barely out of her childhood."

"I'm afraid it has ruined our fine town fair before it has even begun," Janette lamented.

Nathan shook his head. "I closed them down, but they haven't left yet. Still, it's going to stop. It's not acceptable to recruit here – not today. They'll have to find another place, or come back another day." Nathan gathered the papers together and folded them into a neat bundle. "Do you mind if I borrow these to catch up on the events?"

"No that's fine; just return them when you're done. I need to get back to work." Janette stepped away from the table, but then turned back. "I don't know what can be done, but thank you. Maybe it will redeem the day."

Janette walked away to supervise the workers while Nathan left to the door and headed back outside. The officers were gathering to the train platform, all while the ocean breezes wafted gently through the town. The happy chatter of excited children and families came back to the streets as a normalcy returned to their day of intended celebrations. Off in the distance, he could see the empty family wagon, already bereft of the gaily colored balloons.

Nathan heaved a sigh, and went in search of his family, wondering who else had enlisted and what more could be done. Perhaps it was worry over nothing. The people around him all seemed unfazed.

Looking over the brick paved road, his eyes landed upon Emma, who had obviously just found Hayden. Giving a twirl of her new dress, she stood on her tip toes to kiss him. In another moment, they turned and were off to the grandstands of the arena.

Hannah turned back, saw her husband and waved, accidentally letting go of the string to a final, unsold balloon. Up and away it floated, rushing into the vast expanse of sky.

"Maybe it's just me," Nathan whispered to himself. "Surely, this will work itself out."

Gathering his energy, he broke into a jog to join his family while, far above them now, that final festive orb drifted away into the unknown, a tiny red spot against the blue and white of the sky. Off and away it floated, into the unknown, on this Fourth of July.

Chapter Three

Emma

August 1917

Eyes red-rimmed and brimming with tears, her heart filled with fear, Emma sat on the bed, helplessly watching her beloved Hayden pack his bag. This was it, the final act to confirm that he was actually going to leave her. She had cried so much over the last four weeks that she wondered how there could be any tears left to shed, and yet they kept coming.

"You can't leave. You mustn't. What if you get killed? Oh, Hayden, I am so frightened for you! Please don't go; please!"

"I have to," he stated impassively. "I've already enlisted."

"Then unenlist!"

"It doesn't work that way."

Hayden was busy packing what few things he thought he would need into a bag, trying to leave with as little conflict as possible. His plan was to catch the evening train out of Silver Falls and report for duty in Portland the following morning. Emma, on the other hand, grew more desperate with each action.

At first, she didn't believe it. Hayden didn't mention it for days; others had, but Emma had shaken it off as impossible. Surely, her husband would never do such a thing They had waited too long and too faithfully to be together. She was certain he would never do anything so rash as to jeopardize the entirety of their happiness.

While enlisting had seemed like a noble action to Hayden at the time, it didn't take long to realize that he had acted in haste. Consequently, it took a while for him to work up the courage to inform his wife, and when he finally broke the news, Emma's entire world crashed down around her. In all the years of longing she had waited, it was always with a bright hope of promise at the end. Now, he said that he would be leaving for war, to face straight into the guns of an enemy, a danger so real, that he may never come back.

He hadn't chosen those exact words, of course. In fact, he had broken it to her in the gentlest language he could manage, but that was all Emma heard. He was leaving her alone while he went off to die, leaving her to suffer and languish in heartbroken misery for the rest of her life. She had cried and pleaded then, nearly as much as she had done since, but the effect was always the same. After some initial regret, Hayden clenched his jaw and continued on.

Walking to the bathroom now, he heaved a sigh and looked around at the newly finished walls and fixtures. They had only lived in this house a scant two months in its completed state and he, too, wondered how he would leave it all - his young wife, his own home. Shaking his head at the thought, he gathered his comb and shaving supplies from the shelf and brought them back to the bed only to find that his bag had disappeared.

As soon as he had left the room, Emma removed his clothes to the dresser, hid the bag, and then stood at the window, looking off across the valley toward Silver Falls.

"Emma, where are my things?"

Squaring her shoulders, trying to summon any courage she had left, she answered. "I'm not going to let you leave."

"What?!"

"This is not love, Hayden. You promised to love me, to protect and take care of me. You promised!"

"Emma, I have to go. If I don't show up, they will throw me in jail. Do you want me to go to jail?"

"I'd rather you went to jail than died."

"Oh, Emma, do stop behaving like a child. Now, where is my bag?"

Emma just shook her head. "No, this isn't right and I'm not going to allow it."

Hayden was beyond his wits' end and weary of the entire conflict. Duty had swelled in his heart that day, causing him to sign up without pause. He never thought it would end up like this. The truth was, he hadn't thought it through at all.

Impatiently, he looked around the room, under the bed, in the armoire, through the drawers, and under the pillows; the bag was simply not to be found. Suddenly, in a fit of frustration, he grabbed his young wife by the shoulders and began to shake her as he yelled.

"Blast you, Emma! You will obey me! *WHERE IS MY BAG?*"

Of course, his rash actions didn't help; she was already in a fragile state and the angry outburst only upset her all the more. Wrenching herself from his hands, she ran from the house, out the door, and up the hill, beneath a tree. Here, she fell into the grass, crying at the brutality of the whole situation.

"Emma!" she heard him call from the door. "Emma, where are you?"

The grass was tall and she was not about to move from her place and risk being found. Rather, she brought her hands to her face in an attempt to quell the fear and quiet her sobs. Despite the anger, she was still so in love with Hayden, she didn't know how she would so much as breathe with him gone. She was terrified at the danger he would face and the entire plan seemed nothing but pure insanity. Beyond that, she was heartbroken. How could he just leave her?

Soon, she heard his footsteps approach and then felt a gentle hand on her shoulder.

"I'm sorry, Em. I should never have done that back there. I should never have yelled or treated you roughly. Will you forgive me?"

Emma scarcely waited a moment before sitting up from the grass and welcoming his arms around her. "Yes, yes; I forgive you; only, please don't leave me, Hayden. I can't live without you. I don't know how I will go on alone."

"Listen, I'll still be taking care of you; the pay is thirty dollars a month and I'll send nearly all of it home. I'll only keep enough for what I absolutely need. Do you know how much that will be for you, Em? And we have money in savings. I'm not leaving you destitute."

"But you are!" she cried. "It's not the money, Hayden; how could you do this? It is the cruelest decision you've ever made. I think that's what hurts me the most; I could never have done this to you for as long as I loved you, for as long as I lived."

Hayden was at a loss, feeling tortured with regret, tortured for losing his patience, and tortured for ever making this decision in such an arbitrary way. In less than four hours, he would be boarding the train to leave and he did not want to do so under such an unhappy cloud.

"I should have talked to you first, I admit, but I can't undo that error. I'm sorry for all of it; but, Em, please don't make me leave you like this. You must summon some courage."

Emma looked up at him with pitiful, pleading eyes and shook her head. "You can't possibly love me and do this."

Hayden looked up at the sky and then over the valley below their home, wondering what he could say. "I do love you, Emma; but it is my duty. I have to go." Filled with sorrow, Hayden held her tightly and spoke a new promise. "I will make this up to you, somehow; I promise. I will do everything in my power to come back and I will never leave you again."

Everything in his power? His power!

Emma marveled at the futility of such an oath. The whole point of her anguish was that nothing would be in either of their power. At that moment, something inside of her snapped. With the last of her hope extinguished, her will to fight suddenly died. He was going to leave, no matter what she said or did. In the moment that he spoke those words, the young girl who had loved so ferociously and hoped and prayed and longed for so many happy dreams to come true, vanished. In its place, a very sad and defeated person stepped in.

Feeling soul-broken and numb, she walked back to the house and did as he wished. Spending the last few minutes exactly how he wanted, she gave him a hug and a kiss and the bravest farewell she could manage. There would be no more tears shed for him - not until after he was gone.

From her heart, through to her spirit, something inside of Emma gave up and died. There was nothing more she could do, nothing more she could say to change his fate. In that moment, she understood that the only thing left was to say goodbye, as bravely as she could. And that was just what she did.

Chapter Four

Pastoral Plans

September 1917

Carlen and Linda stepped through the doors of the restaurant and marveled anew at the beautiful and luxurious surroundings. Though they had been here many times, the fancy waiters in their coat-and-tails never ceased to impress them. Now, as if that wasn't enough, in addition to the fern covered lattices and climbing vines, there were other newer features in the establishment as well.

During the spring and early summer, Janette had added an entire indoor balcony around the peripheral walls, filled with skylights and windows overlooking the ocean. Beautiful curtains of flowing material started at the ceiling and gracefully drifted downward to the carpeted floors. It afforded a well-lit environment and plenty of fresh air to waft through the building. The whole atmosphere whispered of gentle ocean breezes and the background ambiance of waves upon the shore.

Soon, James approached the couple. "Good evening, Reverend Sanderson, Mrs. Sanderson." He smiled so pleasantly as he bowed a genial greeting. "The Stephens are waiting to receive you, if you'll follow me."

Linda smiled at the action. It was lovely after all, such a welcomed and refreshing change from the dreary rigors of her home duties. As they passed a table on their way, however, the pungent smell of steamed clams drifted to her nose, causing her to gasp for air and pass in haste.

"Are you all right?" Carlen asked.

"Yes," she whispered. "Though it appears I can no longer abide the smell of clams."

Carlen smiled and squeezed her hand softly. "Fortunately our table is near an open window."

"Well, there you are," Dane announced as Carlen helped his wife into her chair. "We were beginning to wonder."

"Are you kidding?" Linda answered. "It is like stepping into heaven here; we would never miss an opportunity to come."

Janette smiled at the comment. She had worked hard to create such an environment, even seeking Dane's input as to what he thought heaven might be like. It was more work to maintain, but well worth the effort. While The Falls had ever been a place of refinement and dignified pleasure, the latest improvements came close to making it ethereal.

James passed menus to each of the guests and then stood patiently, white towel over his arm, to receive their orders.

"Four fruit flurries," Janette called out, as their waiter nodded and left. "You'll love this drink."

"What is it?" Linda wanted to know.

"Mm!" Janette closed her eyes and savored the memory of flavor. "Mangoes and pineapple pureed and mixed with a sweet iced confection that is nearly as light as snow. It's brand new. You'll be one of the first to try it."

"What's a mango?" Linda asked.

Dane laughed. "Fruit of the gods."

Janette nodded. "They might as well be; we had them shipped up from Mexico. I'm sure you'll love it. What would you like for dinner?"

"Apparently anything but steamed clams," Carlen smiled. "Linda is finding their aroma difficult to appreciate in her current condition."

"Condition?" Dane asked.

Janette gave a quiet nudge. "I think that means she is expecting."

"Well, congratulations! Good thing we're near an open window then."

"Yes, a very good thing," Linda smiled. "How are your children doing?"

"The girls are just fine," Janette answered, "and little Luke is already a baby saint. He's barely two months old and already sleeping through the night. Honestly, he has the sweetest disposition. He must get it from Dane; I'm certain I was never that pleasant."

"How old are the girls now?" Linda pursued.

Janette smiled. "Lucy is eight, Leah Marie, seven, and Lizzie turned three this last March. It's hard to believe how fast they've grown! If only I can make them slow down for a while so I can enjoy it more. Who's watching your boys?"

"We dropped them off with Hannah on the way in," Carlen answered.

"They love playing with her children," Linda added, "and I think Chris might have a mild crush on Annie."

"Really?" Janette laughed at the idea. "I guess they are about the same age, aren't they?"

"Close," Carlen agreed.

"Well, Annie is a beauty, to be sure," Janette nodded. "Does she like him too?"

"They play well together for a couple of seven-year-olds," Carlen answered. "Let's hope that's all it amounts to for quite a few more years."

"Well, it's cute; that's what I say," Janette declared.

In another minute their drinks arrived and their orders were taken, allowing the group to sit back and enjoy the moment.

"To the future," Dane exclaimed, raising his glass in the air.

"To the future," they all agreed.

While they sipped at the richly aromatic concoction, Carlen began to wonder at the purpose of the toast.

"Exactly to what about the future are we toasting?"

Janette and Dane both grew sober at the question. They had hoped to finish dinner and perhaps a dessert before bringing up the actual business of this meeting. After all, undesirable news was generally best presented on a full stomach rather than the ill comfort of hunger.

"It can wait until after dinner," Dane replied.

"No time like the present," Carlen persisted.

Janette cringed. "Not in this case."

"I'm guessing there's bad news to share?"

"Yes, well, maybe..." Janette hedged, "but not before dinner. It's certainly nothing that will change in that amount of time."

Carlen took another sip of his tropical drink and wondered over the options. Janette's life was completely consumed in the daily maintenance of her business with the restaurant. Surely, there was nothing that would be changing there, and Carlen couldn't think of a single circumstance with her that might involve unwanted dialogue between them. It had to be something with Dane. He thought about it a little longer. It probably involved the ministry, but how? Dane seemed happy with his duties; his sermons were fine and uplifting. What could the source of their discomfort possibly be?

Presently, another waiter brought a basket of rolls to the table, along with a plate of appetizers for the group.

Carlen took yet another sip of his drink, almost lost in his thoughts. "Can you give us a hint of the news?"

"What do you think of the war?" Janette asked, though Carlen only shrugged.

"It is complex and tragic. The church can never condone war, as it goes against nearly every principle of the gospel. And yet, the complexities of the cause make it impossible to dismiss with any degree of simplicity."

"What about the soldiers?" Dane persisted.

"They are, most of them, unwitting servants for a higher power in the governments of the earth. The soldiers cannot be condemned; but they will be hard pressed to escape the ravaging scars of combat upon their bodies as well as their minds. I can only thank heaven my boys are too young for this conflict."

"I agree and feel the same for my son." Dane nodded at the words. "But when you consider, as a principle, the terrible evil and tyranny involved in this present engagement, do you not feel some sense of responsibility to do what you can to stem the tide?"

Carlen shook his head. "not abroad."

Meanwhile Janette, glancing back and forth between their guests, tried to smooth over the moment. "Carlen, won't you have a roll? They are buttery and so utterly delicious."

"Thank you," he answered, taking one and placing it on his plate. Unfortunately, he was beginning to lose his appetite at the prospects of where he thought the conversation was headed.

"Dane," he paused a moment before finishing his thoughts, "you're not considering enlistment, are you? You're well beyond the age they're looking for; besides you have your family and the ministry to consider."

Dane nodded. "You're right, and I have no plans to suit up as a soldier, so let's enjoy our dinner for now and we can talk about this later."

Carlen let it go from the conversation at that point, though not from his thoughts. He had a sinking feeling that Dane would yet announce a departure from Silver Falls. He tried to feign enjoyment after that, but he could hardly wait for the dinner to end and the discussion of business to begin. As the dessert plates were finally cleared, he tried to think of a tactful way to pursue it.

"Thank you, Janette; it was a lovely meal," Linda offered.

"You're welcome and be sure to order desserts for Hansel and Chris; they'll be disappointed if they miss out."

"I hope you can forgive my impatience," Carlen began. "I don't want to bring a cloud over the evening, but would it be possible to discuss the previous topic? Dane, are you planning to leave Silver Falls?"

Dane lowered his eyes. "Yes; I feel I must do something for the cause. I'm planning to enlist as an army chaplain."

"What about your family?" Linda asked.

"Mrs. Taylor still helps out often, and Janette has considered hiring a nanny, at least while I'm gone. My larger concern is the work of the church here. I realize it's too much for one man, Carlen, and I want to be sure we make arrangements for help before I leave."

"There are no extra pastors coming out of the seminary," the reverend announced. "With the advent of war, suitable men are scarce. The possibility of a junior pastor would be next to nothing."

"No; but what about choosing an assistant from among our faithful members?"

"Who?"

Dane shrugged. "We thought we could discuss the possibilities tonight. There's David Harrison; he has always attended faithfully. With the boys gone and their house empty, he might have the time to take on such a responsibility."

Carlen shook his head. "David would seem an obvious choice, but he is the town mayor now. Many would see it as a conflict of interest."

Dane nodded. "I'd forgotten about that. Well, what about George Layne, or John, or even Nathan. I know his family is still young, but they never miss a Sunday. You and he are friends as well. He might be someone to consider."

Looking across the table, Carlen wondered more. "How do you feel about all of this, Janette?"

"About the assistant pastor?"

"No, I was thinking more about the situation of your husband leaving."

Janette shrugged and shook her head. "I don't like it; but I see now that something must be done. Just because it is overseas doesn't mean that it can't spread this way. Think of the Lusitania, Carlen. More than a hundred passengers were Americans who died at its sinking. Oh, I tried to stop it from ever coming to Silver Falls, but it has come, and there's nothing to be done about it now. I can't sit idly by while Germany terrorizes Europe and the open sea. I detest the war and dread Dane ever leaving, but having him serve as chaplain would surely help. It will be a sacrifice, definitely, but he wants to do his part to end this conflict."

Carlen nodded, though he said nothing. Meanwhile, Linda wondered how it would be possible for her husband to handle the load of two congregations by himself.

"What if you asked for volunteers?" she suggested.

"No, dear; it needs to be someone we know we can trust and depend on. They will be dealing with the distribution of church funds and privy to sensitive information."

"I see. Well, I can help, and I will if you'll let me."

This time Carlen laughed, and heartily so. "Oh, trust me, Linda, you will be asked to help beyond your heart's content, but it still won't be enough. The church has grown to the point of full-time work for two men. I don't know of anyone in the area who has the time to replace Dane for all that he does. I can shoulder a little more of the load, but it will require a lot of work and dedication out of whomever we ask."

"Then let's make a short list of possibilities," Dane suggested.

"Yes," Carlen agreed, "and pray for them. Surely, the Lord will help us in this."

Looking off out the window at the vast ocean beyond, Carlen tried not to let his expression betray him. Dane leaving? How would he manage two congregations alone, and on foot? The very thought of it was overwhelming to consider. Finally turning back to the group, he gathered his courage and mustered his most convincing smile as he spoke.

"Surely, He will help us find a way."

Chapter Five

Eavesdropping

September 1917

Hannah, Susie, and Alannah all sat with their tea and cookies at the kitchen table, leafing through the several catalogs from page to page as Susie tried to decide on the things she would need to finish off her home. As Hannah and Alannah had both been through this before, she was hoping to glean from their experience. Those were the pragmatic reasons, but more than anything else, they were all just enjoying an excuse to hover over the pages and dream of the luxuries within.

The morning sun filtered here and there through the trees to the row of windows, as the ever present ocean breezes tossed the leaves from the silver maples back and forth. Nathan was still out in the barn, finishing the last of his morning chores, and the children were playing in the front yard within the protective confines of the picket fence.

It wasn't that the older children needed the fence at all. Maggie and the triplets were now ten years old; even Annie and Ben were seven and fully capable of staying out of mischief. Chase and Rose, however were still only three, and it was decided for their benefit that all of the children would stay in the yard for their play.

Looking up from the book and out the windows, Susannah ran her hand over her rounded middle.

"I feel it moving. Oh, I can hardly wait to have this baby, Auntie Hannah. It seems as though it will never come! I'm filled with curiosity. Will it be a girl or a boy? Will it look like me or Grant? What will its personality be like? I do hope it's a pleasant child, not like the twins. Jase and Jon were always into so much trouble."

"I remember," Hannah smiled. "I guess boys will be boys."

"Yes, and girls will be boys too, if you let them."

This last comment was from Alannah, who found the whole concept of a double standard of behavior between boys and girls hypocritical and offensive. There were no differences for expectations in her home. Her son's poor behavior was as quickly corrected as her daughters', and Ben was well-behaved indeed. But then, Alannah only had one boy, and he was of a mild disposition at that. She had yet to try her hand at a child like Chase, one who tried the limits of every boundary and naturally seemed to find more mischief than all of the other children combined. If he touched it, it frequently broke. If he cried, it was always as loud as possible, and heaven forbid if he should become bored without supervision!

Just then, Nathan came in through the side door. "Looks like the local women are having a fine time."

"Oh, but we are!" Susie exulted. "You should join us."

"Thank you, but if you'll all excuse me, I think I'll go wash up and stay as far out of your way as possible."

He was gone in another moment, leaving the women to resume the pleasant quiet of their dreamy purpose.

Glancing at Susannah's fond caress, Alannah couldn't help but smile. She, too, had a secret waiting to share, but a certain part of her was curious as to just how long she could get away without anyone knowing. It had been over four months since she'd discovered the fact herself, though no one had yet noticed. She found it partly amusing and partly distressing, wondering if after only three children, she'd lost all her girlish curves. Susie was due in January and Alannah in February, but while Susannah openly touted her wonder and expectation, her neighbor held the secret close to home, as she wondered how long it would go on.

"Oh, forget the curtains!" Susie announced. "Let's look at the baby things again."

Flipping back several pages, she happened to land at the section bearing information on kitchen appliances. It was here that she paused instead.

"This is the stove I want," she announced, pointing to a drawing on the page. Looking around the room, she began to muse out loud. "Why haven't you gotten your electric stove yet, Auntie Hannah? It's been years since you said you would."

Hannah looked around the kitchen at her appliances. The wood-burning stove was still fully functional, but it was true that she had longed for something that didn't make the house so hot in the summer. In fact, she had wanted it for many years.

"I don't know how we'd heat the water if we got rid of the stove."

Susie tapped the page of the catalog. "Right here, Auntie Hannah; they sell them with water heaters, and the water stays warm whether you are cooking or not."

Alannah was surprised at Hannah's response as well. Hannah knew that the new stoves had reservoir options. Why would she answer that way?

"How long has it been," Susie continued; "four years, or five?"

"More like seven," Alannah corrected. "Why hasn't Nathan bought you the stove yet?" she asked. "Or a refrigerator, or an iron, or any of the other things you've asked for over the years?"

Hannah sighed, looking around the kitchen. It was true. He had promised her any convenience that she wanted, but most of them had never actually materialized.

"We do have electricity," she pointed out, "and lights. We're not completely without conveniences. Besides, we've had running water and flushing toilets longer than anyone in the area."

"True," Alannah agreed, "but you've been asking Nathan for an electric stove for seven whole years, if not eight. Why has he never gotten it for you? And don't give me that whole 'he loves this lifestyle' routine. It seems to me that his lifestyle preferences have taken priority over your toil and discomfort for a very long time."

Unknown to them, Nathan had finished washing up and was unabashedly eavesdropping on the conversation, pleased at Hannah's defense of him and more than a little curious at Susie and Alannah's presumptions to the contrary.

Finally, Hannah let out a sigh. "I suppose you're right," she announced, making her husband all but fall to the floor in surprise. "He's known how much I've wanted them, but I guess he's a little short on follow-through at times. It is very uncomfortable having to toil at that hot stove all summer long, though it does keep the house warm during the winter."

"Yes, but they sell electric heaters that warm the house up evenly," Alannah rebutted.

"And the house isn't freezing by morning either," Susie put in. "It stays nice and toasty all through the night and day. The cost is minimal when you consider the comfort; and no chopping wood to have it."

Hannah sat back in her chair, trying to think of a way to defend Nathan. She had always tried to be content with what they had, but now she rather wondered exactly why he would think that she should toil as she had for the simple pleasure of his resistance to change. Honestly, when they put it that way, it did seem a bit selfish of him. It wasn't like they couldn't afford it. Not only did they have a very large balance in their account at Silver Falls, he had an even larger balance at Adam's bank in Colorado. They could buy any appliance they wanted with nary a dent to their savings.

At last, she looked around the table and shook her head. "You are right; I don't know why he won't get them."

Once again, Nathan stood in quiet surprise at her refusal to point out his justifications. The fire was so pleasant during all other times of the year, and why should they pay exorbitant electric bills when wood was completely free? Besides, he enjoyed the chopping!

"What would you get from the catalog if you could order anything yourself?" Susie asked.

Hannah's brows rose as she contemplated the options. "Well, for starters, this stove right here, with the extra-large holding tank." Looking over the pages, her heart fairly flying at the freedom those conveniences offered, she continued to point to items right and left. "I'd like an electric icebox too," she announced.

"Oh, they are nice, Hannah," Alannah joined in. "If I could do it over again, I'd get one that is larger though, like this. It's wonderful being able to put your leftovers away and use them again without the worry of sausage poisoning, and it keeps the milk fresh for days."

"And our eggs stay fresh for months at a time!" Susie added. "You can save them up in the spring when the hens are laying heavily without having to paraffin so many of them. Honestly, I can't imagine living without one."

"How is Grant able to afford all those luxuries on his teacher's pay?" Hannah asked.

"He's saved well over the years and recently sold his house in Portland, so we have plenty. He told me to pick from the catalog whatever my heart desired and he would get it for me."

"Ah, young love," Alannah teased.

"He's just that way," Susie defended. "He would do whatever he could to lighten my load and see that I was as comfortable as possible."

"Until he leaves for the war," Alannah countered.

"Oh, he won't leave; I can rest assured of that. He doesn't believe in war, at least not this one. He said it is Europe's war to fight, not ours. He was quite upset that Hayden signed on and tried to talk him out of it; they almost came to blows over it. I'm afraid it's put a damper on their friendship. Hayden said that Grant was completely unpatriotic and a coward."

Hannah and Alannah were surprised at Susie's words. "What did he say back?" Alannah asked.

"Nothing about that; he only told Hayden that he hoped he would return safely and that he would try to keep an eye out for poor Emma in the meantime. I think it rather stung Hayden's pride. Emma was so upset with him over the entire thing."

Alannah nodded. "I guess he and Nathan are a little alike that way, not always considering their wife's well-being."

Hannah thought about that. If he were younger, would Nathan march off to war without asking her first, without knowing if she was willing to let him go?

Her silence further surprised her husband, who was being proportionately punished for the flagrant transgression of his eavesdropping. After all, she should know he would never leave her like that, never do something so rash without talking to her first. He waited for the solid defense of his character which he was certain would follow... and waited, and waited, while the women sat in silent thought around the table.

"I'd like this too," Hannah finally announced, pointing to a large and ornate chandelier on the page.

Alannah laughed. "It's huge! Where would you put it?"

"I don't know," she smiled, "but since we are only dreaming and Nathan will never buy any of it, then what does it matter? I suppose I can want it simply because it is beautiful."

All three of the women laughed at that, and in the noise of their mirth, Nathan decided that he had heard enough. He was hurt and disappointed by their words, but perhaps he was even more disappointed with himself. It was an acknowledgement that hadn't fully risen to the surface of his conscious thought yet, that one place where the truth hurts most.

Nathan was good to Hannah, very good, but it was true that over the years he had put his preferences above her comfort, requiring, as she had said, more sweat and toil than was necessary. He wasn't the one standing at a blazing stove all summer long while she labored to store their harvest, cook their meals and wash their clothes. No, he was outdoors, with the ocean breezes to refresh him and waft at the wetness.

All these things rather taunted him now, but only in that unconscious place where he struggled to acknowledge the guilt. Susie and Alannah's words had stung him, but Hannah's refusal to defend their lifestyle had cut him to the core. In her silence, he had felt betrayed.

"Fine," he told himself, as he emerged from his clandestine place of surveillance, "if she wants it that badly, then I will get it for her. *ALL* of it!"

"Ladies," he acknowledged, as he headed back out the kitchen door.

When the screen door closed with a bang, Hannah cringed and watched until it was clear he was out of earshot.

"You don't suppose he heard us?" she asked the others.

"I don't think so," Alannah volunteered. "Besides, we only spoke the truth, and he should know that it's wrong to spy on a lady's conversation."

They all looked at each other and smiled after that, eventually going back to the pleasure of leafing through page after page of wondrous amenities; though Hannah worried a little at what she knew might have been hurtful to the man that she loved.

*

"Nathan! Come in, come in. How are you doing today?"

David Harrison welcomed his brother-in-law through the front door, wondering only mildly at the unannounced visit. He could have used the phone to save himself the walk, but it was more like Nathan not to avail himself of the convenience.

"Fine; how are you?"

The words were pleasant enough, though David detected irritation behind them.

"Is everything all right over at your place?"

"Yes, it's fine. Hannah, Susie, and Alannah are all catalog shopping. Is Grant not working on the house today? I didn't see him out there."

"Yes, we're all just taking a lunch break. He's in the kitchen; did you need to speak with him?"

Nathan shook his head. "Actually, I came to see you. I want to buy Hannah a motor car, and I don't know the first thing about how to get one. I was wondering if you would help."

Had he thrown a bucket of cold water into David's face, his brother-in-law could not have been more surprised.

"Finally had your fill of mucking out the barn?" he chided, as he worked to regain his composure.

"No, it's only for Hannah. You know I'd never give up my horses."

David nodded, having detected that tone of annoyance again. It was a very curious thing. Why would he buy a car for Hannah? She rarely went anywhere without him and never anywhere in a hurry. David was clearly intrigued, wondering how far he might push for details.

"What sort of car does she want?"

"Oh, I don't know," that irritated tone remained. "I've never looked into them. Are there many to choose from?"

"Well, yes," David laughed, "a very great many. There are different styles, colors, and brands. Does she want a used car, or something that will be more reliable?"

"New; she needs to have the best there is."

"Well then, why don't we talk to her and get her ideas on it."

"No, you need to keep this to yourself; I want it to be a surprise. How long does it take to get one?"

David rubbed his chin, deep in thought at Nathan's words. An angry surprise? Just what was going on between them?

"It depends; do you want to buy what's available or order something special? There's a place up near Council Crest with a good selection. We could check it out one day, if you like."

"I'd like that. When can we go?"

David leaned his head back and laughed. "Something tells me you're in a hurry. I suppose we could go tomorrow if you like. Would that be soon enough?"

"Yes; only promise you won't breathe a word of it. I don't want it getting back to Hannah before it's here."

"Why all the secrets?"

Nathan shook his head, and David saw that look of irritation anew. "I just want her to have the things that she's desired."

"Hannah has asked *you* for a car?" David was clearly incredulous.

"Well, no," Nathan hedged, "not exactly; but she has admired them and spoken of Janette's many times."

"Very well; I'll pick you up tomorrow morning. We can take the nine o'clock train out to Portland; unless you'd rather ride your horse and meet me there," he teased.

At last, Nathan broke into a smile and shook his head. "Your car will be fine."

Something was up; David was sure of it! He figured the truth would come out sooner or later, but considering Nathan's obvious annoyance, he thought he'd better be patient and wait for the latter. He would probably learn more tomorrow. Either way, it promised to be an interesting trip!

Chapter Six

Telegram

October 1917

It had taken Nathan nearly a month to get everything ordered, gathered and stored at the Harrison's house so that Hannah wouldn't discover it before the right time. He planned to give it to her all at once, for her birthday, and have Susie and Alannah over for the festivities. A certain part of him wondered if they would ever again accuse him of making his wife suffer, or depriving her of anything.

However, Nathan wasn't really capable of holding an effective grudge. By the time it all arrived, the entire issue seemed ridiculous and overstated. The gifts were there, and because of that, he gave them to her for her birthday, all of them, but it ended up being awkward and far too overdone. By the time they got to the car, Hannah was mystified. Regardless, David taught her the basics of operating it and she occasionally took the children for drives into town or over to their grandmother's house, just for fun.

It was a beautiful car, a shiny, yellow sedan with soft leather seats and a removable top. After running out of gas a few times and having to walk the rest of the way to wherever she was going, she eventually got the hang of maintaining it in an acceptable working order. Not that she ever drove it much; there was very little need to go places, but when she wanted to get somewhere quickly, it was there.

Inside the house, the stove, icebox, heaters and several other luxuries proved to be far more useful. Nathan mourned quite a bit at the abandonment of his old favorite things; he even rerouted the chimney pipe and moved the stove to another room, certain they would need it, someday. However, everything worked very well and the whole family, ultimately, lived in much greater comfort than before.

Hannah especially loved her new stove. Much to the delight of her family, including her husband, it seemed that she could hardly stop baking long enough to do whatever other chores were required. It was where she stood one evening when a tiny knock sounded at the kitchen door. Answering it, she found her niece on the other side.

"Emma! Come in and sit down. I was just pulling some muffins out of the oven. Are you hungry? Would you like some?"

"I don't think so, Auntie Hannah; my stomach is all tied in knots. I don't think I could eat anything." Sinking into a chair at the table, Emma raised her hand to her forehead. "Hayden is missing," she stated quietly.

Hannah took a seat next to her. "Are you sure?"

Emma had been frequently emotional since Hayden's departure, but this latest development was more startling than the rest and appeared to be driving her ever nearer to an emotional cliff.

"What else could it be?" she cried. "He said he was going to have things changed so his paychecks would be sent directly home, and now I haven't heard anything more from him and the paychecks have stopped completely."

Hannah frowned. "I don't know why he didn't just have the other arrangement to begin with."

"He said he wanted to be sure he'd have something pleasant to send in his letters. He didn't think it would be a problem."

"But the change could take a while, Em. Why would that make you think he's missing?"

"Ben and Lauren did the same thing and theirs has already changed. I haven't heard from Hayden in over three weeks and..." she hedged, trying to control her worry, "oh, I just feel it in my bones."

"What did his last letter say? Wasn't there something about not being able to write as often?"

"Yes, but that was nearly a month ago. He was going into a different division because of his French; he was supposed to be coordinating some sort of underground mission between the American soldiers and the French. Oh, Auntie Hannah, what if he's been killed?"

Hannah put her hand over her niece's and gave it a reassuring squeeze. "Now, Emma, try to calm yourself; there's no sense jumping to such drastic conclusions and fretting like that if you don't have to. It won't help anyone or anything. I'm sure he's fine. He said he wouldn't be able to write as often; surely that's what has happened. He's probably involved in some sort of secret mission over there, that's all. Have faith that he'll be alright. You have an address, don't you?"

"Yes," she whispered.

"Then just keep writing to him. Surely he'll answer eventually."

Hannah was doing her best to be supportive and reassuring, but nothing she said convinced the girl or seemed to offer any comfort at all. Instead, Emma stood from the table and started for the kitchen door.

"I guess I'll go home," she whispered. "I don't want to burden you."

"Emma," Hannah called after her, "it's no burden; you don't need to leave. Why don't you stay a little longer and we'll talk about something else."

Emma burst out in staggered sobs. "I don't want to talk about anything else. My husband is missing!" With that, she turned and ran up the well-worn path between their homes.

Hannah frowned with concern before going to the phone. Soon, she asked to be connected to the doctor's office in town.

"This is Dr. Layne."

Hannah heard Peter answer, along with the "click, click, click" of multiple earpieces picking up in the background.

"Peter, it's Hannah; is Caleb there today?"

"He's out on a call. What's up?"

"We're having a problem over here; I think someone needs to come by."

"What sort of problem?"

"Not over the phone," she hedged.

"Well, I'm about to close up for the day. Can it wait another half-hour?"

"Possibly; I'll be at Emma's. Can you meet me there?"

At the mention of Emma, Peter quickened his pace. "Yes, I'll be there, as soon as I can."

*

"Emma, I'm going to give you some medicine that will help you relax, but you need to stop fretting so much. It will ruin your health."

"But he's missing," she whispered between staggered breaths as she sat on the edge of her bed.

"We don't know that," Peter spoke in soothing tones. "There could be any number of reasons that he hasn't written. Here, I want you to take one of these; I'll leave the rest with Hannah in case you need more, but try to get some sleep, Em. You're going to be all right; we'll all make sure of it."

Emma took the pill and a drink of water to wash it down and then, with hands clasped together at her chest, she laid back on the pillow, trying to stifle her anxious sorrow. Taking a brave, deep breath, she held it in and then blew it back out, before her face screwed up in grief and she sat back up, the tears flowing once more.

"Emma," Hannah hugged her and kissed her forehead, "you must try not to worry. Try to believe that it will be okay."

"It's all right, Auntie Hannah; you can leave now; you can both leave. I don't want to bother anyone; I think I just want to be alone. I'm tired," she said, lying down once again. "I think I should just go to sleep."

Pulling Hannah outside and securing the door behind them, Peter handed her the bottle of pills.

"Keep these away from the children in a safe place and keep me informed. She's suffering from hysteria; the medicine will calm her down, but it can be habit forming; don't give them to her unless you have to. Other than that, bland foods will help and try to keep her quiet or from being overly stimulated."

"Are you sure, Peter? It seems like she needs the opposite of being left alone right now. If it were me, I would want my family around me. I would want to get out in the fresh air and do cheerful things."

"All in good time; right now we just need to get her through this."

*

The weeks of silence dragged on for Emma, as the season descended into the ebb of winter. Finally in December, just before Christmas, she received some news, an official telegram. It was every wife and mother's dread to get such a piece of mail. Most of them opened it unsuspectingly, only to be devastated by the news within. Emma, however, knew better. She had been expecting it for months.

In a state of numbness, she trudged the path between the two homes to knock on the Layne's kitchen door.

"Emma, come in!" Nathan welcomed her, before looking anew at her face. "Are you all right?"

She didn't say a word, only dropped down in a chair at the table and handed the telegram off.

"I can't read it," she whispered, her eyes fixed on the floor at her feet. "Please, will you read it for me? I don't think I can bear it, even though I've expected it all this time."

"This is a telegram, Emma. They don't inform people of deaths in a telegram. They're supposed to send a soldier for that."

"No." Emma's voice was so hollow, it hardly sounded like her at all. "If it was a large battle with lots of deaths, then they'll only send a telegram. I read of it at the end of summer."

With great trepidation, Nathan opened the letter and read the contents to himself. By now the entire family had gathered to see what was happening in the kitchen.

"He's missing in action, Emma. That doesn't mean he's dead."

Emma looked up with cautious hopefulness. "What does it mean?"

Nathan read the letter aloud:

> Dear Mrs. Larssen, we regret to inform you that your husband, Pte. J.H. Larssen, is missing in France. We have kept an ongoing search for him and his comrades over the past several weeks, but have not been able to locate any of the group. We are listing them as missing in action. Pte. Larssen was of great assistance in moving the position forward and always diligent in his duty as far as he was able. Our sympathies are extended to you at this difficult time.

"Oh, Emma!" Hannah exclaimed. "That means he's probably alive!"

"I don't know; I don't think so."

"But you can't give up hope. I wonder if there is a place to write, a place where you can send him letters. Think what it would mean to him."

"Maybe," Emma nodded. It was all she had strength left to do. Could there honestly be a chance? Should she dare to hope? "Thank you," she finally whispered.

Collecting the letter from Nathan, she turned and trudged her way back outside, over the yard, up the hill and into her own home.

Hannah watched from the doorway for several minutes as her husband came to stand behind her. They heard the door close, though a light never showed through the window in the house on the hill.

"She needs her family, Nathan. I'm afraid it will destroy her to stay in that house by herself any longer."

"I agree with you. Let's talk to her parents and see what can be done."

*

At the doctor's office, Caleb paused in his cleaning to speak. "I need to talk to you, Pete. Do you have a minute?"

"Sure, I'm all yours. What's on your mind?"

"I'm going to sign on with the war. Emma is so heart-broken; I've got to do what I can to find Hayden."

"But Caleb, you're in your forties."

"It doesn't matter; they're so desperate for doctors, they'll be glad to have me. I'm going to request the French front; I figure it will give me the best chance of finding him. I can't just wait around anymore while Emma is slipping away. If she knows that I've gone to look for him then maybe it will give her some hope. If nothing else, I'll be helping the war effort while I'm at it."

"What does Marian think?"

"She mostly wanted assurance that I would be safe. Once I explained the situation and how doctors weren't in danger, she agreed. I hope you'll understand; I know it will be a lot of work for you, but I don't know what else to do."

Peter nodded. "I do understand."

Truly he did; something needed to be done to find out what had happened to Hayden. If he was dead, then so be it; everyone would at least know and be able to move on. This limbo, however, was enough to make them all crazy. While the Larssens believed he would eventually surface and greeted each day with that hope, Emma had not dealt well with it from the beginning. Her constant worry for him had descended into fear, and then depression, spiraling even further into anxiety and despair.

"When will you leave?" Peter asked.

"Soon; I was hoping within the next few weeks. Are you sure you can handle the workload alone?"

Peter only shrugged. "We can all only do what we must. There aren't many other options."

"Alright then; I guess that's that."

Taking a deep breath, Caleb turned back to his duties. France! He'd never been farther away from home than Colorado and, truly, didn't want to leave now. Only the day before, he had read about the need for doctors at the front. The work was rigorous and the workers rarely lasted long; still, he felt he must go. It would hopefully provide some sort of opportunity to locate his son-in-law, and it wouldn't be on the front line of battle; that part should comfort his family.

Something had to be done and, as a door opening from a dark room to the light, he felt this would be his only chance.

Chapter Seven

Examination

November 1917

Meredith Layne climbed up onto the hitching post, threw the reins over the horse's head and, grasping the saddle horn, carefully stepped one foot off the post and into the stirrup. Fred was very tall, and she was not; however, with a little ingenuity and quite a lot of training, she had figured out a way to climb onto something else she could reach better and coax the gelding to sidle up. It was a perfect solution.

From there, amid a glorious carpet of drifting, yellow maple leaves, she and Fred started their ride down the quarter mile lane toward town. Meredith's young body relaxed in the saddle as she looked up into the trees, smiling her happiness. School was out for the day, and just now, between the golden leaves drifting down over her face, she could see through to a magnificent sky. The brilliant blue was there in small patches, right between that yellow canopy still clinging tenaciously to the arching branches above.

It was a perfect day, and she was on her way to achieving a perfect, and very long awaited goal.

*

"Okay, Uncle Peter, I'm ready."

"Ready for what?"

"To be a doctor."

Meredith had tied her horse at the hitching post, and walked confidently into her uncle's office.

"You will teach me, won't you? Like you did with Uncle Caleb? You said that if I read all the books you would teach me, and I have; I've read every one of them."

"Is that right?"

"Yes, and you can even test me on it. Ask me any question."

"You've really read them, already? All of them?"

Peter was genuinely impressed. Shaking his head, he walked to his desk and took a seat on the edge, folding his arms across his chest while Merrie came to stand before him, ready for the examination.

"Alright, well, let me think here for a moment."

Peter rubbed his chin, trying to remember what particular information the volumes of medical journals had to offer.

"What can you tell me about tuberculosis?"

"Tuberculosis… um… can you spell that?"

Merrie, who had gained all of her knowledge through nothing more than reading, had many a creative way to say the conditions she'd never heard spoken. Thus, the pronunciation of this particular disease had somewhat thrown her; but only momentarily.

Peter jotted the word out on a piece of paper and then slid it in her direction.

Merrie took a quick peek and a look of complete recognition spread over her face.

"Tuber… how did you pronounce that again?"

"Tuberculosis."

"Right; I'll not forget it, you'll see."

"I'm sure you won't," Peter laughed. "Now, tell me what you know about it."

Merrie squared her shoulders, raised her chin, and looked straight forward, as if answering for the school spelling bee, reciting what she knew.

"Tuberculosis, also known as consumption, is one of the most common diseases of our time. It results from contagious bacteria which typically attacks the lungs, but can also affect other parts of the body. The most common symptoms are fever, a chronic cough, sometimes with blood-tinged phlegm, and weight loss. Treatment is rest and fresh air and, in some cases, surgery... but can I just say that I think the whole surgery idea seems drastic, especially since it rarely works for long, if at all. In fact, there isn't really any effective remedy for it."

To say that Peter was impressed was an understatement! Presently, he stared at his niece in astonishment.

"I know you're going easy on me. Tuberculosis was such an obvious thing to ask. Try something harder, won't you?"

Peter only laughed and shook his head. "If I can think of anything else. Let's see... what about rabies? What is rabies, and how do you treat it?"

Meredith smiled and wrinkled her nose. "You've chosen bacterium again. Don't you want to ask me something more difficult?"

"Just answer the question."

"Very well."

Merrie squared her shoulders as she once again looked forward and recalled the information.

"Rabies is a bacteria carried in the saliva of infected animals and frequently spread through a bite. It is common in raccoons and skunks, but the most common case in humans is through the bite of an infected dog. The first phase of symptoms is fever and a headache, also itching or prickling around the wound. The later phases progress to delirium, drooling, hallucinations and death. Treatment: first, shoot the dog."

Peter's brows rose high on his forehead.

"I'm kidding," Meredith laughed. "It's just that they never say to kill the animal before it bites someone else. To me, that would be the first thing to do. Anyway, if caught early, it can be treated with the rabies vaccine. If not, then death will surely bring an end to it." Meredith looked suddenly thoughtful. "Uncle Peter?"

"Yes?"

"You know that whole story about vampires?"

"What about it?"

"Well, you know how it says they bite people and then the people turn into vampires?

"Yes."

"Have you ever wondered if they just had rabies and people didn't understand what was wrong with them, so they made up stories about vampires instead? And then there's the vampire bat, and what if it had rabies and bit a person and then the person started biting people and they all started biting other people, just because they all got rabies?"

"I suppose that could make more sense of the story."

"I think so. But anyway, ask me more questions. I'm still waiting for a hard one."

Peter did ask more. In fact, he asked all the questions he could think of, and Meredith answered them perfectly, albeit requiring that he spell out several of them on paper.

"Oh, Uncle Peter, I'm afraid it will take me some time to learn the proper pronunciations, but if you'll be patient with me then I really think I'm ready to be a doctor."

Peter laughed again at her enthusiasm. "What will your Uncle Caleb think? He hasn't even been gone a week."

"Well, you don't have to tell him, you know. Besides, he's on his way to Europe and you need help."

"What would you do if someone got sick? How would you go see them?"

"I have Fred."

"Your horse?"

"Yes; he'll take me wherever I need to go."

"I see. Well," Peter pulled out his watch to check the time, "it's getting quite late, and I still have rounds to make before I can go home. We probably ought to call this pleasant, little interview to an end."

"Can I go with you? On your rounds, I mean."

"What about Fred?"

"Oh, he knows the way home. Daddy always says that if we get lost, all we have to do is give the horse his head and he'll bring us safely home, because a horse won't forget the way back to his oats. I can tie up his reins on the saddle and he'll go right home."

"Well now, that's probably true, though I've never tried it."

"Daddy said that there was a livery in Colorado that advertised one-way horses. He said you could rent the horse to get where you needed to be and then just tie up the reins on the saddle horn and turn them loose. They always went home to their oats lickety-split. So, can I go on rounds with you for part of my training?"

"Don't you think your parents will be worried if Fred shows up at home and you're not with him?"

Merrie wrinkled her nose and smiled again. "We *could* call them on the telly to let them know."

"Very well; it sounds as if you have it all planned out."

*

The sun was setting over the ocean as Peter drove down the lane and stopped before the hitching post. Through the kitchen windows, he could see Hannah at the sink and wondered if she was fixing dinner or cleaning up from it. Either way, he thought he should see his little prodigy safely inside.

"Peter! Hello, come in. We're just finishing up dinner; can I get you something to eat?"

"No, thank you. Alannah will have dinner for me as soon as I get home."

Nathan winked and nodded toward his daughter. "How did our little doctor-in-training do?"

"She is a veritable fountain of knowledge. Which reminds me; Meredith, we need to settle on an agreement that you won't contradict me in front of my patients."

"Oh dear; what happened?" Hannah asked.

"Uncle Peter made a wrong diagnosis and I corrected it," the little girl stated proudly.

"About that…"

"Well it was wrong; you even said so yourself," Merrie continued.

"Yes, but how does it look if a little girl seems smarter than the doctor who has been to school all those years. Now, I'll only train you and take you with me if you promise to never embarrass me like that again. Is it a deal?"

"Deal!"

Merrie shook her head full of curls, grabbed a roll and then scampered off to tell her siblings all about how she was right and Uncle Peter was wrong.

"I hope she wasn't too much trouble for you," Nathan offered.

"Yes, and thank you for humoring her," Hannah added. "She's had her nose completely buried in those medical books for the last several months. I'll be glad when she gets this out of her system and returns to a normal childhood."

Peter looked at his sister-in-law curiously. Did she really think that Meredith had done all that study just to return to playing with dolls?

"Well, don't be disappointed if she wants to continue on. I'm afraid she has a head full of knowledge that isn't soon to go away. She's an amazing child. How does she remember it all?"

Hannah shrugged. "I'll never understand it, but Grant did some tests with her at school and says she has a photographic memory. He said that she can look at a page and then picture it in her mind and read the information from it that way."

A look of recognition crossed Peter's face. "So, that's what she was doing? You know, I couldn't even trip her up with trick questions. It was as though she was reading it right out of the book. What an amazing gift."

"Well, it's certainly an amazing something," Hannah concluded. "Thank you again, Pete, and thank you for bringing her home."

"Did Fred make it okay?"

"Yes," Nathan smiled. "He came right home to his oats."

The doctor laughed. "Of course he did."

Standing to leave, Peter waved his goodbyes at the kitchen door. Many things were on his mind, not the least of which was his niece, her newfound knowledge, and just how he was going to handle the "training" she expected to receive. He really must be more careful of his idle promises in the future. She was far too young for his patients to take seriously - and yet, she held such promise!

Walking out to his car, he paused to look around. Fred stood with a menagerie of other horses in the pasture, clipping at the grass in an effectual attempt to appease his hunger. Across the brook and over the way, the lights to his own house shone out in the approaching darkness. Alannah and his children, including Maggie, would be busy in the kitchen.

Peter thought about that. Though they were close in age and the best of friends, Maggie and Meredith shared little else in common beyond their family ties. The young doctor raised his brows at the thought. None of his children excelled at such things the way Merrie did.

Looking back at the stone house across the brook, he smiled and shook his head. It was the same at Nathan's, and every other house in the countryside. No other child could compete in that intellectual realm. But then, life was not all about intellect. Kindness, honor, and good form were equally important, and Maggie was ace at those, while Meredith could often make use of much improvement.

They were all children of great promise. Still, Merrie possessed a mixture of intellect and judgment that was often astonishing. Climbing into his car and starting the engine, Peter shook his head, as he thought about the prudence reflected in her answers, wisdom that went well beyond the book-learning of standard schooling. Finally, he laughed and mumbled to himself.

"When it comes to rabies – First: shoot the dog!"

Chapter Eight

A Letter from Caleb

January 1918

January 19, 1918

My dearest Marian,

I have reached France safely, but there is a dreadful flu going around. It is heavily infecting the newest troops that have arrived, and it is a virulent, nasty thing. I caught it almost the first day we made shore and lost my rational senses for several days. The doctor quickly became the patient, I am sad to say, which was humbling, if not humiliating. Thankfully, I recovered quickly enough. Not all its victims were so fortunate.

I am currently stationed at the American hospital in Reims. Each day the train brings new soldiers from the front, mostly with war related injuries, though with the advent of this new illness, we've had many more soldiers rolling through than usual, coughing up or nearly drowning in their own gory flux while they cling to life as best they can. After they're stabilized, the first thing they generally want to know is where we are from, hoping to hear something about home. So many of them are desperately homesick and we do our best to share what we can. Since I am one of the newest here, they often seek me out, hoping for fresh news from America.

My shifts are very long and I easily see more than fifty patients each day, but this isn't something I feel to complain about, for it allows me to see many more soldiers than I had dared to hope. Tell

Emma that I ask each one who is able to speak if they know Hayden or anything about his regiment.

Occasionally, I hear some small bit of news about his group, but so far no one has known him personally. It sounds as if they were captured. Some of the prison camps are more civilized than others, even allowing their prisoners to send brief postcards home to let their families know they are still alive. I feel much more hope for his safe welfare being here than I did while at home. Tell Emma to keep her chin up. We'll find him eventually.

And now I have a word for Alice, who had contemplated helping in the war as a nurse. She could not have a more noble desire for service, as nurses are in an impossibly short supply. If she is still inclined to offer of herself in that way, I would most heartily encourage it.

I've seen Paul once already since I've been here. He is working safely behind the lines and looks wonderfully well. He said he would be writing home shortly; hopefully you've already heard from him. Did you know that Maria Larssen is writing to him? The things we parents never find out are astounding at times.

Well, my dear, it is time to close; I long to see you again. Please write as often as possible. You can't imagine the cheer your letters bring.

I am, as always, your devoted husband.

Caleb

Chapter Nine

Last Will and Testament

March 1918

"Mother, Merrie is sick and needs you."

"Huh?"

Hannah attempted to focus her eyes, trying desperately to clear the sleep from her mind. As she rolled over to see who was speaking to her, she met the concerned face of Melanie in the limited light of an early morning dawn.

"She said she's dying," Melanie urged in a whisper.

"Dying? Mel, what are you talking about? She can't be dying; she was fine just last night."

"She's the doctor and she says she has dengue fever. She said it was deadly and she's been calling for you."

"Dengue?" Nathan mumbled, stirring to consciousness. "Isn't that a jungle disease?"

"I don't know," Hannah shrugged. "I don't think I've ever heard of it, but if she's sick then I'd better see to it."

Reaching for her robe, Hannah stumbled from her bed as Melanie took her mother's hand and began to pull her in the direction of the dark, winding stairs.

"Mother…" Hearing the footsteps approach, Merrie called out in as pitiful a voice as she could manage. "Mother... is that you?"

"Yes, Merrie; I'm right here. What's wrong?"

"I'm very ill… I… I don't think I'm going to make it."

Hannah put a hand to her daughter's forehead. "You have a fever, Merrie; that doesn't mean you're going to die. It is a little high though; I'm guessing around a hundred and one."

At this, Melanie piped up. "It's one-hundred-one-point-six; we already took it."

Still trying to clear the sleep from her mind, Hannah began to check over her daughter.

"Where else do you feel badly?"

"I have a horrible, bad headache."

"Maybe we should wake up Annie and get her out of here. You're probably contagious."

"Dengue fever is not contagious," Merrie whimpered.

"I don't think you have Deng… whatever it is."

"Oh, but I do! Fever, severe headache, and my body hurts everywhere. I expect the bleeding to start any time now."

"Bleeding!" Melanie gasped in horror.

"Bleeding?" Hannah asked skeptically.

"Yes," Merrie managed in a sickly whisper, "from the nose and mouth, possibly under the skin."

"Just how does one catch this illness?" Her mother was clearly not convinced.

"From a mosquito bite."

"Meredith, it's March sixth; we're just coming out of winter. I hardly think we need to worry about mosquitoes."

Merrie shook her head. "I heard one buzzing in the room last night and look at this." Pulling her sleeve from her elbow, she pointed to a small red bump.

"What is that supposed to be?"

"A mosquito bite."

"Well, if you think you can make it downstairs for breakfast, I'll cook your favorite applesauce pancakes with fruit and whipped cream on top; maybe that will make you feel better."

"Applethauth pancaketh?" Andy was up and wide awake at the mere mention of food, stretching and then rubbing his eyes.

Meredith whimpered with a little more emotion. "Mother, I'm dying! I can't possibly be expected to go clear down to the kitchen. I'll need to take my meals in bed."

"You're not dying, Mere," Hannah repeated, standing and stepping toward the door.

"Oh, but I am!"

"I can bring breakfast to her," Melanie volunteered.

Hannah looked at her daughter. Sweet Melanie, so adorable, kind, and helpful, was far too gullible to her sister's pranks.

"I'll call Uncle Peter," Hannah stated as she walked out the door and started for the stairs. "In the meantime, there will be pancakes in the kitchen if you're hungry."

"I am *dying*," Meredith called after her.

"Well, don't die until after you've had your pancakes," Hannah answered back.

"I don't think she believes you," Melanie whispered as their mother left the room. "Are you sure it's dengue fever?"

Merrie put a hand to her forehead and pinched the bridge of her nose. "Either that or malaria; they're both mosquito-borne illnesses. What else could it be? Oh, but my head hurts!"

Downstairs, Nathan could hear the conversation on the phone from the kitchen clear to the bedroom, all while Hannah mixed pancake batter in a bowl. After a lengthy discussion, she thanked Peter for his time, apologized for waking him, and finally returned the ear piece to its cradle. Grabbing his clothes, Nathan quickly dressed for the day and joined her at the stove where she ladled pancake batter into the skillet.

"Was Peter not up? It's nearly eight."

"No, but he thanked me for waking him. Apparently, he overslept."

"It is rather dark out with all the clouds. So, what's going on with Meredith?"

Hannah laughed and shook her head. "She's convinced that she's dying of some mosquito borne fever."

"What did Pete have to say?"

"Besides diagnosing her as a complete hypochondriac? He said it was possible to get encephalitis from a mosquito bite, but not overnight, and highly unlikely at this time of year. He also said that dengue fever has an incubation of four days from the bite to the onset of symptoms and that it's a tropical disease; it's not likely it would ever appear here."

"So, there's no way it could be that?"

"No," Hannah smiled, "nor malaria, which he said would probably be the next thing she'll claim. Malaria is typically ten to fourteen days after the bite and never in this area."

Nathan sat at the table and shook his head. "What are we going to do with that girl? It seems the study has only given her a complete knowledge of all the things that can possibly go wrong with her body."

Hannah smiled. "Oh, I don't know; she occasionally comes up with something useful. The other day, when Chase cut his finger, she had it cleaned and completely closed before I could even get into the house, and it has healed perfectly free of infection.

Besides, she is sick with a hearty fever; I have to give her credit for that."

"But dying?" Nathan persisted.

"Well, she's always had a flair for the dramatic."

Nathan nodded his agreement. "That she has."

"Peter said it was more than likely just a bad cold. Apparently, Maggie, Ben and Rose are all complaining of the same affliction, and Meredith has been playing with them all week."

A moment later, ten-year-old Melanie appeared in the kitchen, stood before her mother and squared her shoulders, a look of mild indignation on her face.

"You should listen to Meredith, Mother. She *is* a doctor and she knows what she's talking about. I don't think it's very kind of you to treat her so lightly when she is so obviously and desperately ill."

Hannah ran her hand along the side of her daughter's face and smiled. "Oh, Mellie, she's not a doctor yet and she's *not* dying. Uncle Peter said it was just a cold. Maggie has it as well and they were playing together all last week."

"But what about the mosquito bite?" her daughter rebutted.

Hannah shook her head. "Dengue is a tropical fever. We don't get it here and especially not at this time of year. Uncle Peter also said we don't get malaria here, ever, if she happens to think she's dying of that next. Besides, they both have lengthy incubation times, nothing even close to overnight."

Melanie's brows knit. "It hardly seems she would be faking it; after all, she does have a fever."

"Yes, she does have a perfectly legitimate fever, which is why I've made her favorite pancakes. Do you want to take a plate of them up to her now?"

"Yes, thank you."

Melanie took the plate and left to share the bad news about malaria with her sister.

When they were once again alone, Nathan leaned back in his chair and smiled. "So, are we all in danger of the 'dengue' as well?"

"Peter said it's mostly children that he's been seeing for it, not adults. He thinks it's a bug that made the rounds a few years back and that the children just aren't immune to it yet. He said the others would likely get sick, but we should be fine."

"Well, that's good to know."

Once again, Melanie appeared at the kitchen door. "Merrie said her neck is hurting and that her mosquito bite has gone into meningitis. I told her about the incubations and she said it was the only other thing that could explain her symptoms."

"Oh, good heavens," Hannah looked up as if seeing through the floorboards to her daughter's room and shook her head.

Outside, the misty rains of the season dripped placidly from the roof, collecting in puddles and making conditions quite wet and uncomfortable for anyone with a remote desire to stay dry. It would be a long day of house confinement for them all today.

"Breakfast is ready; applesauce pancakes!" Hannah called from the kitchen.

Nathan grinned at the commotion of footsteps thundering down the stairwell as Andy, Annie, and Chase all hurried to get their fair share of the delectable morsels, eventually making good time at the task of getting all those piles of pancakes to disappear from the platter.

Before long, Melanie was back, pleading her sister's case. "Merrie said that meningitis is very dangerous and she'll need to be treated right away or she will die."

Hannah shook her head. "She's not going to die, Melanie. You need to not let her get you so worked up."

"Is Merrie sick?" Annie asked.

"Yes she is," Nathan affirmed, "so you need to stay away and leave her alone to rest. She has a fever and headache and you'll catch it too if you get near her."

"I don't want to get sick," Chase complained.

Nathan ruffled his hair. "I don't want you to get sick either, so stay away from Merrie and let her rest, alright?"

"Okay."

At the conclusion of breakfast, the children scattered off to find something to play with while Nathan donned his coat and headed for the door.

"I'll be mucking out the barn today," he announced to his wife. "Call me in if you need anything."

Hannah nodded and stood at the sink, nibbling at the last applesauce pancake before slipping more dishes into the soapy water. Soon, he was out the door and jogging through the rain, down the path and into the barn.

About then, Melanie reappeared in the kitchen with her sister's tray of dishes. "Merrie said that her arms are hurting and she's very weak. She said that her eyes are hurting too. I really think we should call Uncle Peter again. She looks dreadfully sick."

"I'll check on her again; will that make you feel better?"

"Yes."

Hannah dried her hands and started for the stairs once again. She could hear the other children playing quietly in the boys' room, keeping a safe distance from their afflicted sibling.

When she arrived, Meredith lay quite still in her covers, a note of paper in her hand.

"Oh, Mother!" she complained. "Please make them stop talking! It's hurting my head even worse. Does no one around here have any respect for the dying?"

Hannah tried to stop herself, but the laughter at that last comment couldn't be helped. "What can I do for you, my love? Melanie said you now have meningitis?"

"It must be; my neck and head hurt so badly that I can hardly think."

"Let's try the meningitis test Grandma taught me when I was young. Can you touch your chin to your chest?"

Merrie bent her chin down as far as she could. "Yes," she moaned. "See, I told you I had meningitis. Grandma must be smarter than I thought."

"Actually, if you had it, you wouldn't be able to touch your chest, and you did it so easily, I'm sure you are meningitis free, at least for today."

Meredith tossed her mother a look of grave disappointment. "Grandma is not a doctor," she announced.

"No, but she's pretty good at figuring out what's wrong with a child."

Putting a hand to her forehead, Meredith began to whimper. "Please make the noise stop!"

"All right, children, take your toys downstairs to play and let's give Meredith some peace and quiet so she can rest." Turning to her daughter as the children left the adjoining room she asked. "Is that any better?"

"Yes... except that I'm dying. It's so fitting that it is raining today... as if the heavens are weeping for me. Drip, drip, drip; the angel tears are falling from the sky."

Hannah stifled a smile. Pulling the covers up a little more, she brushed the hair from her daughter's forehead. "Is there anything else I can do for you?" she asked.

"Yes; will you ask Reverend Sanderson to pray for my soul?"

"I'll see what I can do."

"And where is Melanie? I want her here with me in my dark hour of need."

"I'm right here," the little girl answered.

Meredith breathed out a heavy sigh and raised the paper from the bed. "I have my last will and testament, Mel. Since I won't live to be a mother, I want you to take Matilda and give her to your first born daughter in remembrance of me. Andy can have my marble collection and I want my perfect sand dollar to go to Annie, but make sure she's careful and doesn't break it. It's not often you can find a perfectly whole sand dollar..."

Hannah bit her lip and turned away, trying to stave off any further mirth as she stood to leave.

*

The horn honked three times in the drive as the late Model T sped the final distance to the house, skillfully dodging the ruts and potholes of winter, finally pulling to a stop at the hitching post. Grandmother Sarah barely allowed the car to halt before her feet hit the ground and she scurried up the path holding a covered pot in both hands. Hannah met her at the kitchen door, wondering at the visit and welcoming her mother-in-law in.

"How's she doing?" Sarah asked.

"Meredith? I think she's sleeping at the moment," Hannah answered with a shrug. "Why?"

"Why? Melanie called me not half an hour ago to say that she was dying of meningitis and could I help. I brought a batch of garlic chicken soup and a garlic wrap for her neck."

Hannah smiled and closed the door. "Oh, that will cure her, for certain."

"You don't seem very upset by this. Is Nathan sitting with her now?"

Hannah shook her head. "No, he is out cleaning the barn.

Peter said it was just a bad cold."

"But Melanie was so upset. She said her sister was dying and that you weren't doing anything about it."

"Really, Mother; if Meredith was dying, don't you think I'd be the first one to call you?"

"Well, yes, I suppose. Do you mind if I see her?"

"I don't mind at all; she's upstairs in her bed."

Hannah gave a final stir to the pot of stew and checked the bread in the oven before deciding to follow Sarah upstairs. Truthfully, she wanted to see Meredith's face when the garlic wrap was applied, but she had not made it halfway through the living room when a knock sounded at the front door, turning her from her path. There she was met with a ray of sunshine from the recently parted clouds.

"Reverend Sanderson; how are you today?"

"Fine; I just heard about Meredith and came as quickly as I could. How is she?"

"Oh, let me guess, Melanie fetched you?"

"No, my neighbor had a phone call from your house saying that Meredith was near death with meningitis."

"Oh, this just gets better all the time," Hannah laughed. "I'm so sorry you had to trouble yourself. Peter has assured us that it is only a bad cold."

Carlen looked down at her with knit brows. "Are you sure?"

"Pretty sure," Hannah smiled. "Sarah is up there now, applying a garlic wrap and giving her garlic soup, laced with chicken."

Carlen wrinkled his nose. "I wondered at the smell."

"Oh, Grandma, no, *please, no!* It stinks so bad!"

The cries came pealing out from the room above in mournful, pitiful pleas.

Carlen smiled. "Maybe I'd better pray for her yet."

"Well, if she survives the garlic."

Hannah saw the reverend to the stairs when the phone began to ring in the kitchen. Turning around, she backtracked once again.

"Hello?"

"Hannah, what the devil is going on over there?" Peter asked. "Melanie called in hysterics to say that Meredith was dying, then I got a call from Mother, who was all in a panic over meningitis?

And if that wasn't enough, I just had a visit from the undertaker, asking about the size of casket we'll need for her."

"Oh dear, no, no, no." Hannah sighed. "Please tell him it was a false alarm. Somehow, Meredith has convinced Melanie that she is going to die. Mother is applying a garlic wrap as we speak and Carlen is up there as well, ready to pray over her supposed final breath."

Peter chuckled into the phone and then outright laughed over the news. "Serves her right, you know, scaring everyone like that. Oh well, the garlic can't hurt anything more than her senses. Have you given her any aspirin yet?"

"I gave her one this morning, but it hasn't helped much, judging by her complaints."

"Alright, I'll be leaving the office in another hour and will check her on the way home."

"Thanks, Pete. I'm sure she'll appreciate that."

"Right; you'd better find Melanie soon though and tell her to call off the hounds!"

"Auntie Hannah?"

The small voice came from the kitchen door, just as Hannah was replacing the ear piece to its cradle.

"Emma; how good to see you!"

Emma went straight to her aunt and threw her arms around her as she began to cry into Hannah's shoulder.

"I'm so sorry about Merrie! I was singing at the restaurant when I heard the news and came straight over. She was such a smart little girl; I'm going to miss her so much!"

At the end of her words, Emma began to sob out her heartache, while Hannah marveled at how far and fast the errant news had spread.

"Em, it's okay; Merrie is still quite alive."

Drawing back, with one hand to her mouth while the other wiped away at the moisture on her face, Emma shook her head.

"But it's all over town that she died today."

"So I hear; but it was just a rumor. She's very much alive. Do you want to go see her?"

"Is she going to die soon?"

Hannah laughed. "I don't think so, not today anyway. Peter said it was just a cold."

"A cold? That's so mean! How did a rumor get going that she was dead?"

Hannah just smiled and shrugged. "You can go on up and see her if you like."

Emma took another minute to dry her tears before leaving the kitchen and ascending the stairs to the sick room. Soon, Hannah heard the mattress creak as she settled at the end of the bed. This was followed by Emma singing a song, and then another, and then a third. Finally, after a time, they all came down, Carlen and Sarah and Emma, and bid Hannah a happy goodbye.

"Can this day get any stranger?" Hannah muttered to herself.

There had been a lot of commotion in the house of late, but looking around at the quiet now, she realized that she hadn't seen the other children for quite a while. Stepping outside to see if she could hear them, Hannah finally went out to the barn where her husband was finishing up with his cleaning chore.

"Have you seen the children anywhere?" she asked.

"I haven't; I've been working in here the whole time. It sounds like you've had a bit of company though."

"Yes, I guess you could say that. Somehow word has gotten out around town that Merrie succumbed to her illness and died today."

"What?!" Nathan was understandably shocked. "Is she all right?"

"Oh, I think she is fine. Peter should be here to check on her soon; I just can't find the other children. Have they been out here with you at all?"

Nathan shrugged and shook his head. "Maybe they're playing at Alannah's."

Scanning the horizon, Hannah let out a deep sigh. "Not likely; not with her children all sick."

"Well, they're surely somewhere on the farm then. I suppose as long as they're all together they'll be safe enough."

Hannah shook her head at that. "Melanie is on a mission to summon as much sympathy for Merrie as possible. It wouldn't surprise me if she's taken the others off to find more help."

Hannah stepped from the barn to the farm bell and rang it three times. "Andy! Melanie!" she hollered.

She was about to ring it again when she heard Peter's car at the end of the drive. It was a quarter mile away, but she could see that he was traveling with more than just himself. As he drew steadily closer, Hannah turned back toward the barn and called to her husband.

"Found them!"

Peter waved as he pulled up to the hitching post, opened the door and began helping the younger children out. Hannah was surprised to see that each one of them had their arms filled with flowers.

"What on earth?" she muttered to herself. "Where did you children find flowers in March?"

"Cousin Janette gave them to us; they are from the restaurant tables. We brought them for Merrie to enjoy until she dies, then we'll put them on her grave…" Mellie's voice broke from the sorrow of that thought.

"It wath the leathe we could do," Andy added sadly.

"Oh, please tell me that you didn't take all of the restaurant's flowers," Hannah begged to be relieved of the knowledge as her husband joined her from the barn.

"I'm afraid they did," Peter answered; "cleaned Janette right out."

At his words, Melanie rushed into the house before her mother could insist that they take them all right back where they had come from.

Carrying Chase in his arms, Peter approached his sister-in-law. "Unfortunately, I think you have one over-tired four-year-old on your hands here. Apparently the three-mile walk to town was a little more than he could take."

"I'm so sorry, Pete," Hannah offered as she reached out to take him from his uncle's arms.

"I've got him," Nathan said. "Hannah, why don't you go on up with Peter and check on Meredith. I'll get Chase in the tub and warm him up."

Hannah nodded at the suggestion and turned for the house.

As they climbed the narrow stairs to the top, Hannah was only half-surprised to see the rest of the children gathered around their sister's bed. However, once she came in full view, she was shocked to see Meredith, as if already dead, holding a bouquet of crocus blossoms at her chest with all the other collected ferns and flowers neatly arranged around her body.

"What the devil is going on here?" Peter exclaimed.

"Shh, you'll wake her," Melanie pleaded.

"And I intend to!" her uncle rebutted. "Now all of you move aside and give me some space. And clear all this confounded vegetation off the bed!"

"No, don't," Meredith called out, suddenly 'awake.' "It's so lovely that they brought me flowers."

Hannah went to the bedside and began clearing the flowers away to the end. "You know, Mellie, these flowers will last a lot longer if they're in a vase of water. Go downstairs and check under the sink. I'm sure we have at least two vases there. Andy, you and Annie bring up some empty canning jars and we'll see if we can't make arrangements for the flowers on the windowsill. They'll only wither away if you leave them in the air like this."

As the children trudged off to their errand, Hannah took a seat on the other side of Merrie's bed while Peter continued on with his examination.

"Can you touch your chin to your chest, Merrie?"

"I don't think so…"

"She did it earlier, and with ease, when she thought it would confirm meningitis," Hannah answered.

"Okay, good; I guess we can rule that out."

"Hey! I don't think we can," Meredith blurted out.

"You are not the doctor, little Miss Merrie; I am."

"But I'm dying," she insisted. "I can feel it in my bones and… and look, my skin is mottling, a sure symptom of the final stages of death."

Peter smiled at her resolution. "It's also the sign of a temperature change. I'm afraid the only thing you are dying from, little miss, is hypochondria. Do you know what that is?"

Meredith rolled her eyes in great disdain. "Of course I know what it is! I am a doctor, after all."

"Well, I hate to break it to you, but you *were* a future doctor in training. Unfortunately, I can't use an alarmist hypochondriac as a partner. It would ruin my credibility, as it has quite ruined yours. I'm afraid I'm going to have to sever our agreement to your medical education."

Meredith's eyes grew large at the pronouncement. Uncle Peter was ending her training? It couldn't be!

"But," Merrie cried out, "you can't just fire me, Uncle Peter. We're family!"

"That we are, child; and I'm not firing anyone. You were never hired in the first place; I only agreed to teach you a few things until you were old enough to go to school. So, let's get one thing straight right here and now that you need to understand. Reading a volume of books doesn't make you a physician any more than babysitting a group of children makes you a mother."

By now, the children were filing solemnly back into the bedroom. Taking the groups of flowers and ferns, they quietly arranged them into the containers of water.

"Did all of you hear me say that?" Peter called out to the others. "Meredith is not a doctor, not yet. When she gets old enough to know better, then she may go to college where she will learn what she needs to know to become qualified." Turning his attentions back to the child in the bed, he firmly continued. "And I don't want to hear you going around misdiagnosing anyone in the meantime, including yourself. Do you understand?"

Young Merrie's chin quivered under the weight of the reprimand, as her eyes filled with tears and her lower lip began involuntarily to protrude.

"And young Melanie," he continued, turning to his other niece, "you have the entire town worked up into a dither thinking that your sister is dead from nothing more than a cold. This is going to stop today; do you hear me?"

"Yes, Uncle Peter." Melanie bowed her head in shame.

"Do *you* understand, Meredith?" he continued.

"But you taught Uncle Caleb and he didn't go to college." Clearly, she wasn't about to abandon her hopes entirely.

"Uncle Caleb does not make up illnesses trying to get attention and worrying people over nothing."

"I did have a fever," Merrie defended one last time.

"And it is gone now, isn't it?"

"Yes," her small voice confessed.

"You have a cold, Meredith. I am the doctor and that is my diagnosis. This is nothing more than a cold and you will be up and about in good order within a few days."

Peter stood to leave as the children silently finished their flower arrangements on the window seat, all of them feeling duly chastened.

As she saw him down the stairs, Hannah touched his arm. "Thank you, Peter. It looks like you've cured more than the obvious today."

"That's all right," he whispered when they reached the bottom floor. "And Hannah, don't worry about the flowers. Janette called me when the children showed up with Melanie's tale of woe. She said she had fresh flowers coming in on the evening train. All in all, it saved her the trouble of throwing them out."

At that, Hannah breathed a sigh of relief. "Thank you again, Pete."

Peter shook his head and smiled. "All in a day's work; and when Merrie is feeling better, perhaps in time, we'll be open to discussing her training once again, at least if she can behave herself between now and then."

Hannah laughed. "I don't know. Maybe, after things settle down in town, and as long as we don't get a bill from the undertaker for a casket."

Peter laughed at that. "Don't be too hard on her; I think she's been punished enough, between the thought of losing her training and Mother's garlic wrap!" Peter laughed and shook his head. "Poor kid; she'll be smelling the effects of her chicanery for weeks."

Hannah nodded her agreement as she saw the doctor out and closed the door. The garlic wrap had been potent, one of Sarah's strongest. It was sure to permeate the entire house for days, let alone the area immediately surrounding Merrie's head. Though there was some sort of justice to it all, Hannah could only shake her head as she breathed in the pungent fumes. It was enough to bring tears to her eyes, and that was clear downstairs.

Poor child, indeed.

Chapter Ten

Candles and Comfort Cake

March 1918

The cold, misty rains of February had nearly soaked the reverend through his riding coat as he tied off his horse at the hitching post in front of the old art museum. Off in the distance, the rough sea could be heard more than seen, as it crashed upon the rocks and sand in violent lashings. The darkness of an early winter evening had crept over the countryside sooner than usual due to the thick cloak of the storm. It was a good night to be on land rather than at sea. It was an even better night to be tucked under a blanket in front of a warm fire at home.

Carlen gazed off in the direction of the beach. Usually this place was filled with peace and beauty; tonight, it was mostly just discomfort. Shaking the water from himself, he opened the door and went inside where he hung his jacket on the long row of pegs in the hallway and then searched, half by memory and half with his hands through the darkness of the corridor to the lamp on the table at the end. He felt for the drawer, withdrew a box of matches, and struck one to the side. In the blaze of light that followed, he quickly touched the fire to the wick of the lamp, gently illuminating the room.

The art museum had been a part of Silver Falls for nearly a quarter century. The door was never locked and people were free to come and enjoy the exhibits whenever they wished. However, the place was rarely disturbed anymore; consequently no one had seen the need to update it with electricity over the past few years.

Ancient lamp sconces still adorned the walls every few feet, but Carlen walked past them. Instead, he got the fire going in the wood stove, hoping it would quickly take away the chill. Finally, he went to the front of the room, knelt down on the hassock before a table and struck another match, lighting the taper in its holder. The scant light revealed a terracing stand holding dozens of candles in small votive containers. Lighting a candle, Carlen prayed for the first individual on his list, Hayden Larssen. A minute later, he touched the flame to another candle and said a prayer for Jimmy Layne.

It wasn't a part of his beliefs to light candles for prayer, but this night would include many people, not all of whom attended his church. It was to be, among other things, a prayer vigil for those many souls from Silver Falls who were engaged in the trauma of war. The flames were merely an outward expression of inner thoughts and faith that they had agreed on at the beginning. At the back of the room was a table adorned with even more sets of candles to accommodate the crowd.

David Harrison had started it all, of course. If there was ever something new in town, it was usually because their good mayor saw a need. In this case, he thought it would be beneficial for the town's people to gather and share the letters they'd received from their family at the front.

He had actually started it in his own home when his son-in-law, Ray Gibson, was sent home paralyzed from the waist down. They all began meeting at David's house to share news of the family and the war, free from the filters of the press. Ray frequently added missing details to the stories, due to his experiences at the battle front, which lifted his spirits and helped him feel more a part of something larger than his injuries. Soon, a neighbor joined them, longing for more news, and then another and another.

It didn't take long before the house was overflowing and David was out looking for another place to meet. As word got out, more and more people came. It wasn't enough to fill the theater, but for now the old art museum was just the right size. With the soft candle light and a few lamps, it provided a cozy atmosphere to gather around the wood stove and visit.

Candle after candle, Carlen prayed, kneeling at the front of the room. He preferred to be alone for this, which was why he arrived early each month; however, he soon heard footsteps on the boardwalk outside, followed by the cheerful voices of David and Laurel Harrison.

"It looks like Carlen has beaten us here again," David said to his wife.

Rounding the corner, they saw him rise from his knees to

greet them.

"Don't let us interrupt you," Laurel urged.

"No, it's quite all right; I was just finishing up. Did you see anyone else on their way? I'm afraid it's not a very cheery night for gathering."

"What's a little rain?" David mused. "I'm sure they'll come. Laurel made her famous cinnamon rolls and I brought hot chocolate; savory treats to sweeten the soul!"

Carlen smiled at the news. "Warm chocolate?"

"It's in the fireless cooker, wrapped in layers of blankets. I dare say, it should still be piping hot."

At this, David pulled it out and poured a cup for the minister.

"I'm impressed," Carlen agreed after taking a cautious sip. "It's enough to take the chill out of my bones."

David recovered the large pot and put a pillow back on top. "No sense leaving it to chill before everyone arrives. Alright, what needs to be done?"

"Not much more," the minister replied. "The stove is going and the candles are all set. We just need to light the wall sconces and get this place warmed up; it's still too cold for comfort."

"That it is," David agreed.

Soon, more footsteps could be heard outside, followed by the voices of Dan and Sarah Carroll, then Hannah and Nathan, along with David's daughters, Lillie, Janice and Susannah. They all rounded the corner, their arms filled with refreshments for the night.

"How is Mason?" Sarah asked Susie.

"He's doing great! It's my first outing since he was born and I have five whole weeks of cabin fever to cure."

"Grant volunteered to sit with Ray and help watch the children for us," Janice commented as she waited for a turn to light the candles. "Ray's feeling the weather a bit too much tonight to venture out. Oh, and Alannah had her baby this afternoon, so they won't be here either. Mother and daughter are both fine."

"Another girl?" Carlen smiled. "What did they name her?"

"Jennie Lynn," Susie piped in. "It will be an easy name to remember."

"There are more candles at the front," Carlen called out. "There's no need to wait in a line back there."

With the fresh lumen of each candle, the light in the room increased by that much more. David looked around at the effect. "You know, I doubt we'll need more than two lamps tonight."

Carlen nodded. "I think you are right; but with the numbers increasing as they are, we may have to set up another table of candles sooner than we thought."

The next few minutes brought an entire crowd, the Larssens and many more of the Laynes, the Bakers, Johnsons, Dorners and Van Dynnes, along with several others. It was five minutes past their official starting time and the main group was arriving in their customary tardiness. Finally, David cleared his throat, waved a welcome to the group and nodded to Reverend Sanderson to begin the meeting.

"As you know, I don't have any family in the war," the reverend began, "nor do I have any letters to share this time around, but I wanted to offer an observation. Each of you, as you came in tonight, lit a candle for your loved ones. When I arrived here earlier, the building was so dark that I couldn't see my way. Now, it is very light. Like our faith, the light of the candles shine. May we each remember that light as we go through the days and weeks ahead, knowing that our faith is joined as a heavenly force for the benefit of our loved ones." With that, he took his seat and David retook the floor.

"I have a letter here from Jase and Jon. If no one else wants to go first, then I'll share what they have to say." He paused to see if there were any objections. "Alright then, both boys are pilots and constantly fly together. Their commanding officers gave up trying to tell them apart and figure out which J. Harrison was which, so they solved the problem by lumping them together in pretty much everything they do. In some ways that's a great comfort to us; we can be sure that they'll look after each other, but when the transfer came, moving them from mechanics to pilots, our prayers for their safety redoubled. To lose one would be to lose both." David shook his head as he looked down at the letter in his hands. "Unfortunately, that's the way they write to us as well. One letter sums up both their thoughts. We can only hope that they will continue to write as often as they can and return to us safely." Unfolding the letter in his hands, he began to read parts of it aloud.

In November, as planes were becoming scarce, we began rebuilding them from scratch with whatever parts we could recover. This went on for a while until pilots became even fewer than the planes. It's unnerving to think that we are at such a disadvantage while in the very same sky as the Red Baron. We were warned in early November that he was spotted in the air once again. After so many kills and a head wound of his own, we had all hoped the German legend would stay put on the ground. We've been on the lookout for him ever since, though we've not seen him in this area. Still, it is enough to make the heart race when we hear a plane above us, being that it is his plan of attack, using the sun to blind his targets.

Despite that, it is an amazing feeling to be up in the sky, looking down on the earth. Sometimes Jase and I fly clear up to the clouds and from that high in the air it feels like you can see forever, out to the ocean or inland across the boundaries of country lines. It's quite an experience and, contrary to what you would think, feels safe and free.

Anyway, just wanted you to know we are still alive and well. Hope all is well at home. Tell the family to WRITE MORE LETTERS, please. We can never get enough news about the normal life of home.

Love, Jason and Jonathan

"That's all of my news," David announced. "Anyone else have letters to share?"

Kelly Layne raised her hand. "We still haven't heard from Jimmy; this is the second month now. No one has seen him, but they tell us that no news is good news when it comes to the war. Still, if you would keep him in your prayers, we would appreciate it. We do have a letter from Johnny, however. As you know, he is working with the cavalry, specifically tending the horses, so his position is a bit less dangerous than Jimmy's in the trenches." Kelly scanned over the letter and shrugged. "I don't know that this would interest anyone, really. Johnny is so fond of the horses especially, though he doesn't care as much for the mules. Their blacksmith was recently kicked by a mule, which broke the man's leg. While they were scrambling to find someone to replace him, Johnny stepped in and took over his job under the blacksmith's direction. He is now a full-fledged blacksmith as a result. His hours are much longer, since he didn't want to lose his position feeding and caring for the animals, but he is pleased with his new skill. He wrote that, in a few weeks when the blacksmith is back on his feet, he wants to help the veterinarian and see what he can't learn there as well. I think that's it for his general information. We're very thankful that he's safe, and for those of you who have remembered our family in your daily prayers, thank you so much."

As Kelly sat down, George Layne was the next to stand. "We have a recent post from our son, John. As you know he is a cook aboard one of the transport boats. We get to hear from him often and without the censoring black lines that you've all seen before. Last week, he accompanied a soldier on his way home from the front. The man was a captain and had been injured in a shelling. Here's what John had to say."

...Capt. Jordan's injuries were severe in the loss of one arm and two ribs, leaving him wholly disfigured. The hospital wanted to keep him longer, but he wanted just as badly to leave and finish his recovery at home. He was so happy to be on a ship making the two-week voyage for America; it made no sense with his injuries, but he was convinced that once he arrived back in our country it would somehow be all right. The farther

away we sailed from Europe and the threat of U-boats, the happier he became. He said there was rumor of the Russians signing a treaty and Czar Nicholas abdicating his throne. He said that the war has left Russia in a famine and the people in revolt. Capt. Jordan was very open about intelligence reports; he almost seemed to have a devil-may-care attitude for it, which I'm sorry to say, I've seen a lot among the returning wounded. Oft times the men feel betrayed that they have sacrificed so much for another country, only to return home maimed for life. While I can't think to condemn them, I am thankful for the others who hold their heads high and remain courageous in the face of their hardships. Courage is frequently emphasized when we are in danger, but perhaps it should be spoken of more to those who face the challenge of such extreme injuries. All of Silver Falls should know that Ray Gibson was one of those men who remained brave in the face of his trials. Janice should be proud. He was truly a hero in every sense.

The letters continued in like manner. Marian spoke of Paul working on the trains, transporting wounded soldiers from the front lines to the hospitals, and how he regularly got to see his father. She also spoke of Alice, who met a young soldier during her first week of nurse's training. Though he had left the hospital for his home in Oklahoma, he was writing to her regularly. Marian then read a letter from Ben, who was in the trenches. Each time the front was mentioned, it seemed more prayers were requested and offered. There would be no peace until all family members returned safely home.

Lillie, second daughter of David Harrison, read a recent letter from her husband, Mike Baker, who worked in the supply lines. On and on the letters went until the clock at the back of the room sounded at the top of another hour. It was then, as the Van Dynnes were finishing up a letter from their son, that the group heard the door open and wondered who was joining them so late.

"Emma!" Marian whispered, motioning to her, as the young woman rounded the corner at the end of the hallway, though Emma only paused, steadying herself with a hand against the wall as she brought the other to her head.

At the sight of it, Nathan jumped to his feet. "Are you all right?" he whispered, guiding her to his seat near Hannah.

"Yes," she answered; then, in an even quieter voice, she whispered, "I think I'm just very hungry."

As Mark Layne stood to report on his boys, Donnie and Drew, Hannah slipped over to the refreshment table to collect a few slices of sweet bread in a napkin, bringing them back to her niece. Marian, who was clear to the other side of the group, watched with grateful eyes.

"Thank you, Auntie Hannah." Emma managed before taking a nibble and trying to focus her attentions on the letter being read.

Soon, Dan Carroll stood and read a letter from his grandson, Ronnie, who worked with radio communications. Unfortunately, most of the letter was blacked out, though this didn't stop Dan, as he held it near a lamp trying, rather successfully to make out the censored post. There was something about the advancement of troops and a little more information on the Russian treaty and the Czar's family. Finally, he shrugged.

"I don't know what was so confidential about all of that, but that's what the letter had to say."

"Well then," David Harrison stood, "if there's nothing more, I suppose we'll conclude the letters and move on to the refreshments. It looks like Hannah brought her sweet breads." David gave a kindly wink to Emma.

Emma leaned closer to Hannah as he did. "Did anyone hear anything about Hayden?" she asked.

Hannah shook her head. "Not this time." Looking a little closer she smiled. "However, your color is starting to come back.

When was the last time you ate?"

Emma shrugged and shook her head. "I don't know; I think I ate yesterday. I wasn't even going to come tonight, but the rain slowed up and I was so famished. All I could think about were the delicious treats that everyone brings. I guess my hunger won out. Isn't that awful of me?"

Hannah laughed at the thought before giving her niece a hug. "Let's go get some more before it disappears," she whispered. "Laurel brought her cinnamon rolls and I don't want to miss out on those!"

Stepping to the back of the room, Emma paused at the candles and touched the taper to a wick, saying a prayer for Hayden, after which she caught up to her family at the refreshment table.

At the front of the room, Carlen quietly touched his taper to yet another candle and sent up one last heavenly petition before he was done that night – one final prayer, for Emma Layne.

Chapter Eleven

Marianne

June 1918

The atmosphere was tense as Peter sat in the darkened back room near the end of the bed. It was always this way, and until someone figured out how to take the natural pain out of childbirth, it would always remain so.

Looking around, he noted the old and worn furnishings. Had they been in better shape, one might have called them precious antiques, but here and now, they were just old and worn. The house was in a similar state, old... and worn, though the tenants didn't seem to mind, or even notice. It was a roof over their heads and they were happy with what they had.

"You're doing great, Mrs. Sanderson," he encouraged.

"Dr. Layne, could you open the curtains for me, please. I feel suffocated by the darkness in here."

"Yes, of course."

The curtains were drawn, allowing a roomful of summer sunshine to splash across the walls, after which Peter returned to his position. As he did, Linda bore down, again, hard. Though she had been remarkably quiet through the entire process up to this point, she began to groan now from the sheer exertion and intense pain.

"Breathe now," Peter urged. "Remember to breathe."

Almost immediately, the mother drew in a full breath and then went limp on the bed. She collected her senses and tried to relax, knowing that she would need the next few moments to rest and gather enough strength for the next round. This had been going on for hours, most of the night, and she was exhausted from the intense effort.

Weakly raising her finger, she tried to smile. "The baby is coming... nearly here."

Peter gave a quick look and then checked his watch. "You're right! Another minute to breathe and gather your strength. Steady. Are you ready now?"

Linda nodded as the pressure began to build once again around her middle. Taking another deep breath, she pushed with every ounce of strength she had left, and it was enough!

Peter quickly suctioned the baby's mouth and nose and then wiped the face before gently guiding the rest of its body into the world. As if on cue, the child let out a hearty cry.

"Congratulations, Mrs. Sanderson; it's a girl. Reverend Sanderson," he called out to the front room, "you have a little girl!

Not two seconds later, the door opened as a very happy and relieved father burst into the room.

"Oh, thank you, Peter! Thank you!" Carlen was all gratitude, as though the doctor had anything to do with deciding the child's gender. "Did you hear that Linda? We finally have our little girl. Now you will have someone to wear all those beautiful dresses you've made."

It was true. Linda had been a dressmaker by trade long before she married the minister, and while it wasn't any longer necessary to sew, at least beyond the needs of her family, she still loved to create beautiful things. The boys' clothes were as fine as they could be, and Carlen was always well dressed, regardless of his clerical garb, but for years she had yearned and pined to sew for a daughter of her very own.

During this last pregnancy, almost as though she couldn't control herself, she had sewn dresses and pinafores in nearly every size and color in the hopes that she might have a little girl to wear them one day.

Carlen had teased her about it, asking why she would sew them so large when she had her whole life to do such things, but Linda only reminded him that she had already sewn so many baby things during her other pregnancies. While the boys had used many of the items, there were yet too many packed away in her cedar chest that she had saved for that long-awaited little girl.

This time around, when Peter announced that the baby's heartbeat was faster than the boys had been, along with the possibility of it signaling a girl, Linda decided that she would apply her efforts to her desires. She assured Carlen that, even if they never had a daughter, then surely they would have a granddaughter someday. Carlen mostly found it amusing, until she started the wedding gown.

"Surely, there will be time enough in the future for these things, don't you think?" he had asked.

"Surely so," she had answered, "but I'm so excited; I can hardly stop myself."

"What if she wants a different style by the time she grows up?"

"Then I will sell this one and make another," Linda assured him. "She won't lack for a wardrobe as long as I am her mother."

They had both laughed over the idea then. Yet now, on this cool, June morning, as the doctor made the announcement, so many years of hope and longing were presented to the couple in the form of an absolutely perfect, little, baby girl.

Peter quickly finished with the essentials before wrapping the baby and handing her to her father.

"Oh, hey, that reminds me; I actually remembered to bring the scale this time. Let's weigh her and get an accurate number for her birth certificate."

"She's not very big," Carlen mused; "nothing like the boys."

Setting the scale up on the table, they placed the wiggling baby on the curved surface while Peter took the reading.

"Six pounds and two ounces," he called out.

"Six pounds?" Carlen laughed. "She is so tiny. Our boys were nine pounds if they were an ounce."

The doctor began filling out the information on the certificate before it could be forgotten. Going over the form, he asked. "Have you chosen a name yet?"

Linda looked up at Carlen and smiled. "Yes, her name is Marianne, for Carlen's mother, and Elizabeth for my mother."

"Marianne Elizabeth Sanderson," Peter repeated.

"Actually, there's more," Linda blushed. "Lucinda Jane, for my grandmothers and Naomi Ruth for Carlen's."

Peter's brows raised high as a smile spread over his face. "So, let me make sure I have this right. Marianne Elizabeth Lucinda Jane Naomi Ruth Sanderson?"

"Yes," Linda smiled.

"Did I spell it all correctly?" he asked, as he handed the paper over to the new mother.

Linda looked over the certificate and smiled. "Yes, that is

exactly right."

Peter laughed. "That's going to be a mouthful for you when she gets into trouble."

"You'll have to humor us on it, I'm afraid," Carlen agreed. "Linda is quite convinced that Marianne will be our last. She couldn't bear to miss out on any of the names."

At his announcement, Peter considered them both. Carlen was closing in on his fifties and, while Linda was ten years his junior, she was still fully thirty-nine at her last birthday. In all their twelve years of marriage, they'd had only the three children and Linda was probably right.

She had been up laboring all through the night and was understandably weary and worn, but at the news of her daughter's petite form, she rose up on one elbow and beckoned quietly to her husband.

"Carlen, please bring her to me. I want to see her and hold her for myself. Oh, how lucky we are to be a family!"

After another half-hour and seeing to the last of his responsibilities, Peter began to clean up and pack his things away.

"Well, everything looks right enough," he announced as he put the last of his instruments into the bag. "I suppose I should be on my way. Shall I send the boys in to see their little sister?"

Linda smiled. "Oh yes; if you would be so kind."

"Fine, fine then," the doctor agreed. Grabbing the scale and his bag, he made his way to the porch. "Chris, Hansel," he called out across the field to the boys who were presently trying to climb a gnarled pine. "Come inside and meet your baby sister."

"A girl?" Hansel's shout was all disappointment. "I wanted a little brother!" Running to the doctor as he was putting his things into the car, Hansel pulled on Peter's coat. "Doctor, can you take her back and bring me a brother instead?"

"Ha! I'm afraid a girl is all we had for your family today. Now, run along inside. Your parents would like you to meet her."

Peter shook his head and laughed at the idea before climbing into his car and starting it up. Looking back at the house, he laughed again. They were one of his favorite families, and all the more bursting with joy after today. It was the best part of his job, helping along such happy moments as this.

Listening to the morning birds all in a twitter through the trees around the Sanderson's home, Peter smiled and then put his car into gear, driving down the grassy lane and out onto the main road home.

*

Life carried on with all its normal business for six days more, until early into the next week when there was a knock on the door of the wood frame house beneath the large mulberry trees.

"Good morning, Alannah. I'm so sorry to bother you at this hour, but is your husband home?"

"Yes, of course; come in, Reverend."

Seeing the seriousness of his face, Alannah quickly turned to call her husband and nearly collided into him coming around the corner.

Peter was wiping the remnants of soap from his face. He had heard the urgency in Carlen's voice as well. Shaving for today would have to wait.

"Good morning, Reverend Sanderson; what can I do for you?"

"It's Linda; she's not feeling well. She's not one to easily complain, but she asked me to bring you as quickly as I could."

Peter grabbed his bag and began gathering details before they had even passed the threshold of the door.

"What can you tell me about it?"

"She has a fever and is very weak."

"Why didn't you come for me sooner?"

"It was all rather sudden. I wasn't aware that anything serious was going on or I would have. Linda rarely complains and she hasn't mentioned anything before this morning, but she woke up feeling terrible enough to send for you. I knew it had to be bad if she was willing to risk the inconvenience."

"Leave the horse!" Peter shouted, as Carlen headed toward his animal. "You can get him later. Right now, I need you in the car giving me all the information you can while we drive."

Climbing into the Model T, Carlen shook his head. "I don't know what else to tell you; besides the fever, she's just weak and feeling very ill."

"Has she been getting enough rest?"

"Yes; unlike with the boys, she's been very faithful in her confinement. We've done our best to care for her. I honestly don't know what could be wrong."

"Let's hope it's nothing serious."

They could hope all they wanted, but Peter knew better. For an infection to set in at this point, meant that something had been missed or not expelled at the birth. Either way, a high fever in a new mother was never a good sign.

Driving through the countryside as fast as he could, his passenger held onto the dash and door frame just to stay in his seat. The young doctor did his best to dodge the potholes and pine cones as he turned down Parish Road and sped past the church toward the plot of land which held the Sanderson's home.

Carlen had been deeply concerned over Linda's condition before, but seeing the doctor's panicked response only heightened his worry. Quietly, and to himself, he began to plead further with the Lord for her safety and well-being.

Soon, they pulled up to the little country house. The doctor grabbed his bag, and they hurried through the door to the woman on the bed at the back.

Peter took a deep breath and tried to collect his senses as he greeted Linda Sanderson with all the pleasant confidence he could muster.

"Well now, Mrs. Sanderson, what seems to be the problem here?"

Linda tried to manage a smile and at least a pinch of cheerfulness for their guest, but she was very weary.

"Something is wrong," she managed weakly. "I don't know what else to tell you." At those words, Linda faded off, apparently into sleep.

While Peter took her pulse and listened to her lungs, he caught the first whiff of rotted flesh. Not needing any further examination to know what course of action was needed, he turned to Carlen and shook his head.

"I can't help her here, I'm sorry to say. We'll need to get her to my office in town. She needs surgery, and right away." Turning to the woman on the bed, he tried to rouse her back to her senses. "Linda?"

"Yes," she whispered faintly.

"It appears we may have missed part of the afterbirth. We need to get you into town where I can do the surgery to take care of it."

Linda closed her eyes after the first few words and drifted back to sleep before Peter could even finish his sentence.

"Is my mom going to be all right?" Christian asked.

"We'll do the best we can to make it so," Peter answered the child, then to the reverend, he spoke more urgently. "Gather as many blankets as you can. We'll have to make up a bed in the back of the car to transport her."

"What about the children?" Carlen asked.

"We'll have to bring them with us; there aren't many other options."

"Come boys," Carlen called. "Help gather the blankets from your bed, and the pillows; let's make it as comfortable for your mother as we can."

After they had finished the task, Carlen lifted Linda from her covers and carried her out the door, while Peter retrieved the sleeping babe and loaded everyone in as best they could fit. Carlen took his daughter and held her closely in his arms while Hansel stood, squished between his knees. Christian sat on his outside leg, leaning close to his father's head, while keeping a vigilant watch on his mother in the back seat.

Starting out down Parrish road, Peter drove considerably slower this time, trying to avoid any unnecessary bumps or jolts. He drove past the bridge over Silver Brook and was turning to take the road into town when another idea came to him.

"Let's drop the children off at Nathan's house. With Caleb gone, I may need your help."

Carlen only nodded his agreement. To speak right now would betray his voice to the children.

Quickly driving down the lane, Peter nearly jumped from the car and sprinted to the side door where, omitting a knock altogether, he broke in on the family eating breakfast to speak his urgent request.

"Hannah, I have Linda Sanderson in the car with her family. She needs emergency surgery; will you watch the children for us?"

"Yes, of course!"

Hannah, alarmed though she was, left the table to see to the children outside while Peter headed for the phone.

"Yes, Operator, Dan's Carroll's residence." In another few seconds he was speaking again. "Mother, I need you at the office to help in surgery. How quickly can you meet me there? ...Thank you."

"There now, boys," Hannah soothed, as she tried to ease the tension of an obviously critical moment. "Have you eaten? No? Then climb up to the table for some potatoes and gravy. There are biscuits in the warmer and I can fry up more eggs here in a jiffy. Just eat up now."

In what seemed like one single action, she handed the baby to Nathan, helped the boys up to the table and began dishing up hearty portions of food onto plates for them.

"Thank you," Peter whispered as he gave Hannah's shoulder a squeeze before heading quickly out the door.

*

The white walls of the surgery were still cool from the night as Peter finished up and then turned to the sink to wash his hands. Sarah stood at the side of the table with their patient, monitoring her breathing and waiting for the anesthesia to wear off. Linda's condition had been very serious, though she appeared more stable now. Peter only wished they had come to him earlier. For now, he had done all he could.

Grabbing a towel to dry his hands, the young doctor entered the waiting room, where Carlen anxiously jumped to his feet.

"How's she doing?"

"The surgery was successful, but there's still a lot of infection in her system. We'll start her on a strong medicine for the septicemia; other than that, she'll just need to rest and heal."

Carlen breathed a sigh of relief as the knotting in his shoulders began to loosen.

"I'm not saying she's out of the woods," Peter Layne patted him on the back, "but with time and a good deal of rest..."

"Son!" Sarah called urgently from the back room.

Peter turned back. "What is it?"

"I think we're losing her!"

At Sarah's words, the two men rushed into the surgery, gathering at Linda's side. Carlen anxiously grabbed his wife's hand while Peter quickly re-took her blood pressure and tried to figure out what the problem could be.

"I'm not getting a reading," he muttered.

"Linda, you've got to hang on!" Carlen urged. "Can she hear me?" he asked the doctor.

"The anesthesia should have worn off by now," Peter answered. "Linda, can you hear us?"

It was hardly a response, but the woman's eyelids fluttered slightly. Removing the cuff, Peter changed his stethoscope directly to her heart only to hear the beats growing slow and weak.

"Linda!" Peter called firmly.

Stepping quickly to the end of the table, he threw up the blanket and began briskly rubbing her legs and feet, trying to stimulate her back to consciousness.

"Mother, rub her arms! Try to stimulate her."

Carlen could see his wife's lips turning blue, her skin becoming mottled. He had seen this before, many years ago, when his first wife had died. At the sight of it now, he began to panic. Speaking as gently as he could force himself to do, he ran his hand over Linda's hair.

"Linda, you must hang on. Think of little Marianne, my dear. You must hang on for her and the boys. They need you. Please, try to fight this, Linda! Don't give up. We all need you! Oh, my dear, please don't give up!"

With great effort Linda pulled her eyes half-open and met his gaze. She managed the slightest hint of a smile to her husband before her breath left her and the light dimmed from her eyes.

Carlen stood and stared at her in disbelief. "Oh, dear Lord!" he cried as he began to shake her by the shoulders. "It can't be possible. Linda! Linda! Breathe! You must breathe. Don't give up on us! Oh, dear God, don't let her leave us!"

Peter stopped what he was doing to come around to the head of the table. She was gone. Putting a hand on Carlen's arm, he ran his other hand over the woman's face, closing her eyes. Then, slowly, he pulled at the blanket, covering her face.

At the action, Carlen stumbled backwards in disbelief until he met with the surface of the wall. Peter had just said she was going to be okay; how could this be happening? How could it have changed so quickly?

"No, no; this isn't supposed to happen! Oh, dear God!" he

cried out, putting his hands over the sides of his head, his eyes wide in disbelief. "This can't be happening!"

The confusion of such a sudden turn in expectations completely stunned the minister. As he grappled to collect his very senses, his knees went weak and he slid down the wall to the floor, burying his face in his hands as he wept.

"Dear Lord, what will I tell the boys?"

Sarah went to Carlen's side and put a hand on his shoulder, kneeling beside him and trying to soothe with gentle words.

"I'm sorry, Reverend Sanderson; but there now; we will all help you. We will all help with the boys and Marianne."

It was an impossibly small attempt at comfort, and yet, what else was there to say? What more could be done in such a moment? It was as it always would be. Carlen would need time to absorb the facts, time to accept the truth, and then a while longer after that to gather up his courage enough to face the future that lay before him.

The clock on the wall continued to tick away; outside the birds continued to chirp and sing, blissfully unaware of the drama within. The breezes still blew and, off in the distance, wave after endless wave continued to roll upon the sandy shore.

In another realm, separated from this world, a woman stood quietly, filled with concern for the people she had unwittingly left behind. Soon, a portal of light began to open up in front of her and loving angels descended through it to bear her home through a veil of sorrow and off to a world of peace and joy.

The journey was over; her mission was complete.

Chapter Twelve

The Lord Will Comfort

June 1918

The reverend held his baby daughter and tried to balance the bottle in the way he had been shown. Marianne wasn't taking well to it and Carlen felt they were all barely surviving. As he struggled to care for his children, it seemed all he could manage was seeing only to their most basic needs. Balancing the demands of his calling to the community of Silver Falls was beginning to feel futile as well. His best was simply not enough, though there wasn't much else he could do.

Since Dane's departure to Europe, the entire load of two congregations had fallen fully upon his shoulders. It was difficult to manage under the most ideal of circumstances, but Marianne's birth and Linda's death had stretched him beyond his physical, emotional, and spiritual limits. The grief at his own loss might have consumed him had he not been even more concerned for his boys. Even at this moment, Hansel was pulling at his sleeve.

"When is Mommy coming home from the doctors?"

Carlen heaved a sigh and closed his eyes. Hansel had asked that same question every day since his mother's death. Carlen had explained over and over again that she wasn't coming home, and Hansel had listened carefully each time, only to ask the same question the next day. He was five years old now, nearly six, and it was clear that he was not accepting the situation as it was.

"Mommy has gone to live with Jesus," Christian answered sadly. "We'll see her again when we go to live with Jesus."

"Uh-huh," Hansel acknowledged, "but when will she be *done* living with Jesus and come home to us?"

Carlen only shook his head, hardly able to speak. It seemed all he could do anymore were the things that must be done. His body was consumed in fatigue and his soul buried in feelings of hollow, overwhelming sorrow. No matter what he did or didn't do, it was never good enough for each day.

"It doesn't work that way, son," he managed, "but we will see her again someday."

"Okay," Hansel answered, and then ran off to play. He had heard what he wanted. Someday his mother would come home, and until that day came, he supposed he would just need to let her have some time with Jesus.

The sound of a motor car outside sent the boys into motion while Carlen remained in his place, still encouraging Marianne to finish her bottle. Honestly, he barely cared who it was in his drive, though they would surely be at his door in another minute.

"Hello, Hansel," Carlen heard the cheerful voice of Janette call out. "How are you doing today?"

"Fine," he replied. "Mommy is with Jesus, but when she is done with Him then she will come home to us!" he responded happily.

"Oh," Carlen heard Janette reply, the apprehension in her voice plain to be discerned.

"I smell food!" Hansel continued enthusiastically. "Real food! Did Mommy and Jesus send us dinner?"

"Maybe in a way," she answered. "Is your dad around?"

"Yes; he's feeding Mommy's baby in the house. Are you gonna come in?"

Janette had spared no effort in the preparation of a hearty meal, and Hansel's nose had detected that fine fact. Having not enjoyed a proper meal in the last several days, he was in earnest hope that her pleasantly odoriferous creation would find its way to their own table.

"Would you help me carry the other basket?" she asked.

"Oh yes!" he answered. "If Mommy could smell this, she would come straight home from Jesus right now!"

"Oh... is that right?" Janette asked. Truly, she didn't know what else to say.

Coming in through the front door, she made a quick assessment of her surroundings. It was obvious that Linda's cleaning hand had not been near the home for a while.

"Hello, Janette," the reverend greeted, doing his best to muster a smile and some semblance of an attempt at standing to greet her.

"Don't stand, please. I just wanted to bring over some food.

Are you hungry at all, or is my timing not right?"

"We're starving!" Hansel replied in his father's place. "Mommy is cooking for Jesus now, so we have to stay hungry; but she will come back and we will see her again, you know, once she is done cooking for Jesus."

Janette looked at Carlen, who had presently closed his eyes against the words, slowly shaking his head.

"Alright, well, why don't you boys climb up to the table and we'll get you settled with something to eat. Would you like that?" Even Christian brightened at the invitation, as both boys quickly settled into their chairs.

Not knowing what to expect, Janette had brought one basket of food and the other filled with plates, glasses and utensils, and it was well that she did, for there wasn't a clean dish in the house. Quickly and quietly, she set up the table and served up three complete meals before turning toward the adjoining front room.

"Do you mind if I feed Marianne?" she asked.

"Thank you, Janette; you're very kind."

She had expected some bit of protest from the minister; after all, he was used to being the one ministering to others. For him to accept so readily could only be understood as a testament to their need.

"It's my pleasure," she smiled. "I haven't gotten to hold her yet at all."

Carlen stood to hand over the infant and was all but amazed at how deftly Janette drew her from his arms, without so much as a disruption to the suckling process. Clearly, she was more accustomed than he to the whole routine.

"Is she letting you sleep at night?"

"Occasionally," Carlen answered. With that, he took a weary step toward the table and unintentionally dropped into his chair with a thud.

Taking the boy's hands in his own, he offered a quiet and simple grace for their food and then looked over the spread, a little overwhelmed in relief, as his sons dove in. It was one chore he had fretted over half the day that he would now not have to perform. In fact, there was enough food to last them at least two days, maybe three.

Janette set the bottle on the counter and raised the infant to her shoulder to work the bubbles out of her system.

"She's beautiful. What do you boys think of your little sister?"

Christian looked at her sadly and offered a slight shrug, while Hansel worked hard at swallowing his mouthful of food so he could offer an actually solicited opinion.

"She's all right, but I wanted a brother. The doctor said we couldn't send her back, since that's the only baby we could get for now."

"I see," Janette smiled. "Well, it seems to me that she is a very fine baby!"

"Sometimes she smells bad," the little boy objected.

"Hansel!" Christian reprimanded him sharply. "She can't help it; she's only a baby and she's just what Mother wanted! She's all that we have left of…" the boy choked on the words and quickly put his hands against his eyes, as if pressing them would stop the tears from moving down his cheeks, while his shoulders shook under the burden of his sorrow.

"It's all right, Chris," Carlen consoled, putting a hand on the boy's arm and giving it a gentle squeeze. "He doesn't mean anything hurtful by it. Hansel, I think that's enough talk for now. Let's just eat our dinner and be grateful for such wonderful food."

The rest of the meal was passed in silence as Janette didn't dare to pose any more questions and Hansel tried his hardest to obey his father's wishes for more eating and less conversation. It was only after Janette handed the baby back and began to collect the empty dishes to their place in the basket that she attempted to speak again. The boys had gone outside, their bellies full and their hearts hurting slightly less at the remnants of cherry pie which lingered on their lips.

"Carlen, I know it isn't easy, trying and be mother and father both. Heaven knows, I've been doing the same since Dane left for the war, and I have family around to help. I'd like to offer the services of the restaurant to you and your family, at least until you can get through this."

Carlen shook his head. "I'm afraid I couldn't. It wouldn't be right."

"But it is right, very right. I know you aren't used to being on the receiving end, but it's time that you let others do for you and accept it graciously. Think of the boys and the joy they will find in it. All four of you are to be our special VIPs whenever you come. I've instructed the entire staff to see that it's so."

"Thank you, Janette. I do truly appreciate the offer."

"You mean, you appreciate the offer but you have no intention of taking me up on it?"

Carlen smiled. She had read him perfectly.

"I do truly appreciate the thought. Maybe we will come in."

"Well, if you don't, then you'd better expect that someone will be coming out here. I won't take no for an answer."

"Thank you, but that won't be necessary. We'll figure out a time to come in, soon," he added at the additional disapproving frown forming across her face.

"See that you do. You all seem very unhappy… well, with the possible exception of Hansel."

"We are very sad," he agreed, "even Hansel, in his own way; but the Lord will comfort us."

"I'm sure he will. In the meantime, let him comfort your children's hunger through us. Dane would insist on it if he were here. For all the good that you have done, Carlen, please let us return the favor. Even you, yourself, have preached that the Lord often answers our prayers through mortal angels. Let us be that for you now. The Lord is almighty, yes, but he can help you through us as well. There is no reason that your family should suffer with hunger."

Carlen lowered his head at the words. In all his years at the pulpit, he'd never once had his own sermons preached right back to him; he had never needed it - before now.

"Thank you, Janette. We will come," he answered. "Maybe once or twice," he thought to himself.

Janette nodded and smiled, as if she could read his mind. They were worse off than she had dreamed, but she did not have to accept this situation as it was; she had the means to do something about it. Callie Spencer lived nearby and had been recently hired on at the restaurant. Surely, she would be open to an occasional shift in her responsibilities.

Gathering her baskets, she gave Carlen a touch to the shoulder and a smile as she bid him goodbye. Dane would insist on no less than her best and whatever it took, Janette would see that it was done, especially at this time.

Chapter Thirteen

Harvest

July 1918

Hannah reached up to pull the white curtains over each of the kitchen windows in an attempt to block the morning sun and hopefully slow down the heating up process inside the house. It wasn't as bad as it used to be; her electric stove was nothing like the furnace she had been accustomed to using all summer long in the past. While they still frequently opted for cereal and sandwiches on warm days, such as this one promised to be, today she had prepared a fully cooked feast of fried potatoes, biscuits and gravy, griddle cakes, syrup, and scrambled eggs.

The cooking would not end there either, for the harvest had begun. David had sown a full two hundred acres of winter wheat the previous fall that now sat in the morning sun with heavy golden heads bent to the ground. The only trouble was that Jason and Jonathan were still off at war. David had been certain once the U.S. entered the conflict, that would be the end of it and his boys would be home in time to pick right back up where life had left off.

Unfortunately, that wasn't the case. With the prospect of two hundred acres to face on his own, he naturally turned to his family and neighbors for help. Laurel was preparing the noon meal and Hannah had volunteered to cover dinner. For now, the men were just getting started on the day. True, David had been out with his wonder machine since before dawn, steadily reaping away at the acres, but here at the Laynes, life wasn't in such a frenzy of activity yet.

"So, who exactly is planning to go out with me today?" Nathan asked as he spread a thick spoonful of blackberry jam on his biscuit.

"I will," Andy piped up.

"I will too!" Meredith volunteered.

"We'll need water," he persisted. "What about you, Mel? Are you interested in bringing water out to the workers?"

"I can do that," she smiled. "I'm sure Annie and Chase can help me."

"Sounds fine then; the whole family will be involved. I guess we'll be at Laurel's for lunch, Hannah; then here for dinner. It will be a smaller crowd than usual this year, just Grant, David and our crew."

"That's true, but ours are old enough to be more help than ever before. Just see that they don't get too hot." Turning to her children at the table, she offered a caution. "If any of you start to feel sick or dizzy, come into the house right away and cool off. There's no sense getting heat stroke over it."

It wasn't long before the older part of the family was off to the fields and Hannah began preparations for the evening meal. In truth, it was one of her favorite times of the year. The men were always so hungry after a full day's work, which made the food taste better than ever. The compliments usually followed in thick abundance, and there was never any lack of jovial conversation to go around. Was it the promise of another year's plenty, or something else? Whatever the reason, there was something in the spirit of community which increased the general feeling of cheer and good will each time.

Hannah decided to start on the pies first. There would be a latticed cherry, a deep-dish peach, and apple pies, all for dessert. Dinner would include rolls, roast, potatoes, carrots, and a special surprise treat of homemade root beer to drink. Nathan had started it the night before and not even the children had noticed it brewing in the corner of the kitchen. It was going to be such a delight!

As the sun crept a little higher into the sky and the shade from the trees began to cover the windows, Hannah loaded the pies into the oven and then reached to reopen the curtains, letting the light flow in on her work. It was at this point that she noticed more people outside than she had expected.

"Who is that out there?"

They were a good distance away and it took another minute of watching their actions before she recognized the long and graceful movements of the reverend. She presumed the children around him had to be his sons. Hannah smiled and watched a minute more, when one of the boys stopped working, then

Carlen stopped working, came to him and bent down low, apparently either listening or speaking to him. A few moments later, Carlen looked up and over to the single oak tree in the field. It was at that moment that she noticed something beneath it, something Carlen was hastily headed toward.

Hannah gasped. "Oh, my heavens, is that Marianne under the tree?"

It didn't take long to discover that it was when Carlen lifted the small bundle. There he stood, in the shade of the tree, an infant at his shoulder and a six year old crying at his side.

"Melanie?"

"Yes," she answered, appearing at the kitchen door.

"How would you like to watch little Marianne today?"

"The baby?" she asked excitedly. "Oh, yes!"

"See there, out in the field? Reverend Sanderson is trying to work with the men, but the baby is crying. Can you see it?"

"Yes, I see them."

"Why don't you run out and tell him you'll watch her for him. Ask if Hansel can come in as well. I'll bet the heat has gotten to him just from the walk over here."

Hannah smiled as she watched Melanie run from the house, across the bridge over Silver Brook, and through the field, at last arriving in the area of the tree. In another minute, Carlen gently handed the baby over to her, along with a bottle to Hansel. Soon after the boy skipped along at her side toward the house.

When they came in through the kitchen door, the dirt streaks down Hansel's flushed face confirmed the rest of Hannah's suspicions.

"Good morning, Hansel. Are you hungry?"

"Yes, we are always hungry since Mommy left us to live with Jesus."

"Is that so? Well then, why don't you climb right up to the table and I'll serve up some potatoes and gravy. Does that sound good?"

"Oh, yes; Mommy used to always make us potatoes and gravy."

"Poor child," Hannah sighed, wondering at how difficult their adjustment must be.

Looking out at the field again, she could see that Christian was clearly dragging at his work as well. She wondered how far she might push an intervention for his sake.

"Hans, do you suppose your father would mind if Chris came in and had a little something to eat as well?"

"He said we had to work with him and it would make us happy."

Hannah looked at the clock; it was a little after ten-thirty. Somehow, Christian's whole manner looked anything but happy.

"Mel?"

"Yes?" she called from the other room.

Hannah left Hansel in the kitchen and went to her. "Would you mind going out one more time to ask if Chris could help here in the house? I can finish feeding the baby."

"She's almost done," Melanie announced, carefully handing the infant over to her mother. "What do you want Chris for?"

Hannah wrinkled her nose and smiled. "I think I need his opinion on whether or not the root beer is ready, but don't tell him that or Reverend Sanderson might not let him come."

"We have root beer?"

"Shh… Yes, but it's top secret for now."

"May I try some too?"

"Yes, of course," Hannah smiled, checking the bottle and letting Marianne drink the last little bit. "Run along, and see if you can get Chris to come in."

Walking back to the kitchen window, she watched again as her daughter crossed the brook and ran out to the group working in the sun. She saw Melanie approach the reverend and point toward the house. Carlen stood to stretch his back, looking off in that direction and in the next moment, Hannah saw Chris join Melanie in the trek back. He did not skip along as Hansel had; rather his steps were as slow and heavy as Hannah supposed his heart must be.

Dishing up another plate of food, she placed it on the table with a tall glass of milk. "Grief is hard enough without adding hunger into it," she thought.

"Did you need me for something, Mrs. Layne?" the boy asked when they had come through the kitchen door.

"Yes, but it can wait. Are you hungry, Chris?"

The boy looked down at his shoes and shrugged, as if

ashamed to admit the fact.

"Eat up; I have a plate all ready for you and we can talk about that little job that needs to be done after."

"It's testing the root beer," Hans whispered across the table. "I heard her tell Mellie so!"

Hannah smiled at the lightened change in Christian's expression as he settled into a chair at the table.

"Mrs. Layne?" he asked.

"Yes, Chris, what is it?"

"Thank you."

"You're welcome, my love." Hannah smiled and tousled his hair.

At those tender words, Hansel sat a little taller in his chair. "You're the best mommy ever!"

*

Outdoors, beneath the bright July sun, the men worked steadily down the rows, gathering the wheat into bundles, tying off the sheaves and stacking them into shocks along the way. Soon, Nathan stood and stretched.

"I wonder if we'll be seeing a recession from all of this," he mused.

"From all of what?" Carlen asked.

"It's simple economics. With so many of our young men gone to war, there won't be enough help on most farms for a standard harvest. That means less grain on the market and higher prices, transferring over to more expense for the basics of life. If they are spending more for the basics, then people will have less money to spend on extra things."

"Do you think it could result in a famine?" Grant wondered.

"I doubt it. Certainly, we won't have the surplus we are used to, but David said that the prices in Amber Glen were higher than he's ever seen them."

"David appears to have a good crop," Carlen observed. "Are the same people coming through with the thresher?"

"As far as I know. Now, where is that water bucket?" Glancing over at the bright pink faces of his children, he called out. "Merrie, run inside and bring out some water, won't you?"

"I'll help her," Andy volunteered.

As they ran off toward the house, Carlen had to smile.

"It looks as though we've lost the last of our youthful help."

Nathan and Grant both nodded in agreement.

"Just as well," Nathan mused. "It's too hot for the children anyway."

"Speaking of help," Carlen began, "have you considered my request to be an assistant pastor?"

"I imagine the load has grown to be enormous," Nathan answered.

Carlen sighed. "Far more than I can do alone. The congregations have gotten so large, and now with the children... well, I need to have a plan in place. If I were to become ill or otherwise unable to preach a sermon, I don't know what we'd do."

"I'm sure there are others more qualified," Nathan hedged.

Carlen gave him a tired shrug. "I'd like to know who?"

"I can't think of any," Grant added. "I think our reverend has hit upon an excellent idea."

Nathan protested further. "I wouldn't know what to do. What about David Harrison? He has much more the flair for it."

"I thought of asking David, but he is mayor of the town. I doubt it would be wise to mix the two. I can have a sermon prepared and visit with you further on the format," Carlen continued, "if you'll consider it."

Nathan shook his head. "I really don't feel qualified."

"Well, think it over and we'll talk about it again a little later. I need to find help soon."

*

Back in the house, the young Sanderson boys were still busy filling the empty ache in their bellies, which in turn began to soothe some little part of the ache in their hearts.

"Have you had enough to eat yet?" Hannah asked them.

"Please, Mommy, could I have another biscuit with gravy?" Hans asked.

"She's not our mother," Christian corrected. "You're supposed to call her Mrs. Layne."

"Mrs. Layne, would you be my mommy?" the little boy asked.

"Hansel!" Christian reprimanded.

"It's all right, Chris," Hannah soothed. "He's just missing his mother." Turning to Hans, she smoothed the little boy's hair back from his forehead. "Maybe we can pretend, just for today. Would that make you feel better?"

Hansel puckered his lip and nodded as his eyes glistened with emotion. Chris glanced solemnly around the room, noting that they were alone with Hannah in the kitchen. Maybe it would be all right, just for a little while, just for today.

Hannah tenderly watched them a few minutes more, feeling compassion for their trial, until finally she felt it was time for another attempt at cheer.

"Alright then, if you boys are finished, I see nothing else to do but try out that root beer and see if it is ready. Do you think you can you help me with that?"

"Oh!" Hansel cried out. "You're the best mommy in the whole world!"

At that proclamation, Christian smiled too. Maybe, just for today, Hansel was right. A shred of joy began to seep into his heart, a glimmer of motherly love and goodness; it was something he'd not felt in months. Just now there was a hope that somehow, at least while they were here, the all-consuming pain of their loss might abate just a little, and for just a short time.

While the men continued to labor in the fields, sorrow began to ebb and happiness seeped into the kitchen of the stone house across the brook. Under the giant maple trees, two mothers – one of them seen and one of them not – smiled over a set of boys, their hunger appeased, their ache placated, and a glass of root beer raised to their lips.

It would have to be enough for all of them today.

Chapter Fourteen

Callie Comes for Help

August 1918

The knock at the door startled Hannah from her mending. She hadn't heard anyone in the lane. Rather, she had been thinking about Carlen and the boys. In reality, they seemed to consume her thoughts anymore.

Considering the strength and humility, she thought back to his composure as he stood before the congregation at Linda's funeral. The building had been filled to overflowing, and Carlen had preached the most powerful sermon anyone there had ever heard. He declared his belief in the gospel, his faith in the resurrection, and his absolute knowledge of the love of God for all of his children; all of this at the occasion of the funeral for his own wife. He had not been without emotion, but Hannah was more impressed with the intensity of his faith at the height of such a harsh trial.

Deep in her thoughts, she slowly shook her head in wonder, and that was precisely when the knock sounded at the front door.

Placing her sewing aside, she rose from the chair just as Andy reached the door and opened it. There on the other side was Callie Spencer, standing with Christian and Hansel, and holding Marianne in her arms.

"Is your mom home?" she asked; then looking up to see Hannah, she turned her worried eyes to the adult.

Hannah could only wonder what this was about. The Spencers were new to the area and Callie had been helping out with Carlen's children for little more than a month. They were familiar with each other only through their association with Janette, who had hired her, and she couldn't understand why the young woman would be standing on her porch now, or why she would have brought Carlen's children with her.

Seeing a movement at the end of her drive, Hannah looked

past Callie, just long enough to see Agnes Dane, standing idle at the edge of the road and straining to hear or see anything she could garner. She could only wonder what mischief Agnes was up to now.

"Come in, Callie. What can I do for you?"

The young girl nudged the boys at the shoulder to encourage them into the house. Though they were very familiar with the Layne's home, this time they seemed reticent at wanting to move.

"I need to talk to you," Callie motioned with her head toward the boys in a fashion so that only Hannah could see.

"Andy, why don't you take the boys upstairs to play while I visit with Callie? There are cookies on the table; take a few of them with you."

Once the children were safely out of hearing range, the girl began to speak in hushed tones. "I don't know what to do," she whispered. "Reverend Sanderson has been gone for days. There's no food in the house; I don't know where he is or when he'll be back."

"How long has he been gone?"

"Five days," Callie answered.

“Five days! Where is he?”

"I don’t know, but Mrs. Layne, I can't do this anymore. He said that if there was ever an emergency, I should come to you." Callie dropped her eyes at the declaration.

"Yes, that's fine," Hannah assured her. “What's the matter?”

Callie looked back over her shoulder and out the window. The old woman was still standing out at the corner where the Layne's drive met the road.

“She's still out there.”

“Who?” Hannah asked, looking past the girl and into the window. “Do you mean Agnes Dane?”

Callie shrugged. “I don't know her name, but she seems awful. She said you and Reverend Sanderson…” Callie lowered her eyes in shame as she let her voice trail off.

Hannah shook her head in mild irritation. It wasn't the first time that Agnes had done her best to blacken the reputation of others with malicious gossip, but this was the first time that Hannah had been her target.

"I probably shouldn't even ask," Hannah sighed, "but what did she say?"

"She said that you were the reverend's mistress and that the two of you have been carrying on in a sordid affair."

Hannah's gasped her surprise! "What?! You mustn't believe her, Callie; it isn't a bit true. She's just a miserable, old woman, judging the world through the eyes of her own experience." At about this point, another concern occurred to her. "Did the boys hear her say that?"

Callie shook her head. "I don't think so. She called me over, away from them, to ask what I was doing?"

"What did you tell her?"

"Just that the reverend wasn't back, so I was bringing the children to you."

Hannah closed her eyes against the words. It was all innocent enough, but Agnes would make the very worst out of it that she could. Ever since her daughter had disappeared, years ago, she had become more cantankerous and ill-natured than ever, always imagining the worst of the people around her.

"Try to avoid her, love. Her mind is in a dark and hopeless place right now; she will only make trouble for you."

Callie nodded her understanding. "I still don't know what to do about the children; I can't watch them anymore. I have to work and I need some rest. There's no food for them."

"Don't worry about it, Callie; Nathan and I will take over until he gets back."

A visible relief washed over the girl at her words.

"Let me get Nathan to take you home; he can leave a note for Reverend Sanderson and gather a few more of the children's things."

Nathan was just outside in the barn tending to the stock, but as Hannah stepped out the door to find him, she noticed Agnes, still loitering at the edge of their property.

"Tramp!" Agnes shouted in the distance.

In another moment, Nathan came out from the barn, to see what the ruckus was about. As he came to the house, Hannah closed the kitchen door behind them both.

Nathan smiled at her presence before noticing the look on her face. "What's wrong?"

"Where to begin?" she answered, shaking her head. "Agnes, or Carlen?"
"Agnes?" he asked.
"She's down at the end of the lane, shouting horrible accusations."
Nathan shrugged without giving it much thought. "I can't imagine you would let such a person bother you."
Hannah closed her eyes at the thought. "That's not all; Carlen is missing."
"Missing?"
"Yes, Callie just brought his children over; she said he hasn't been home for the past five days. It isn't like him, Nathan. Something must've happened. He wouldn't just leave his children. Anyway, I have them in the house, but Callie needs a ride home."
"Do you mean that she walked with the children all the way from her house?"
"No, they were at Carlen's, but she needs a ride home now, and we're going to need some of the children's things as well. You can leave a note for Carlen, in case he comes back, letting him know where they are. I'm worried, Nathan," she finished. "This isn't like him at all."
Nathan knit his brows. "No, it's not. Did she have any more information?"
"No, just that he hasn't returned and they are out of food."
"I'll see what I can find while I'm out."
Turning back, Nathan walked quickly to the barn to ready the horse and carriage.
Back inside the house, Hannah stopped in the kitchen for a small plate of cookies and milk. Bringing them to the front room, she traded them for the sleeping infant in Callie's arms.
"Eat up, dear," Hannah encouraged. "It'll be a minute before Nathan's ready." Looking down at the baby in her arms, she brushed her finger across the child's soft cheek. "She is a beautiful little thing, isn't she?"
"Well, she is when she's asleep," Callie complained. "She's been very cranky and not quite as lovely as you might think."
Hannah looked up in surprise and then back to the child in her arms. "She does seem rather tired."

Guilt swept over Callie's face at the words. "Yes, she's very tired, but at least she is quiet."

Thinking the comment odd, Hannah unwound the blanket to take a closer look; Marianne seemed to be all right, just unusually taken with sleep. She wondered if the child had cried herself into a deep exhaustion. She thought about questioning it more, but in another minute, Nathan was at the front door.

"All ready," he called.

Callie was up and gone in an unnecessary rush. "Thank you for the food, Mrs. Layne," she called out behind her as she closed the door and hurried to the buggy.

Hannah watched as Nathan helped her in, climbed in himself and then they were off, driving down the empty lane. Thank goodness Agnes was gone.

Figuring it would be a while before they were back, Hannah fully unwrapped the infant, resting Marianne in her lap while she examined her again. Something about the child's sleep didn't seem natural. Her diaper was mostly dry, but the baby's skin was loose, almost lifeless. Hannah watched her shallow breaths. The boys had been understandably sad since Linda's passing, but it wasn't likely that such a thing would pass on to Marianne. She was barely three months old and far too young to comprehend the events around her.

Hannah nudged the babe, trying to rouse her from her sleep, though Marianne gave no response.

"It's from the medicine," she heard a small voice announce.

Looking up, she saw Christian approach from the corner of the stairs. "What medicine?"

Christian only shrugged. "Mrs. Perkins brought it over for our babysitter because Marianne wouldn't stop crying. Callie has been giving it to her a lot. It makes her stop crying and go to sleep."

A look of recognition and then disapproval crossed Hannah's face. "Babysitter-in-a-bottle?"

Christian nodded. "I think so."

Hannah shook her head in disappointment; Carlen would never approve. The so-called "medicine" was purely alcohol, designed to knock a child out. No wonder Marianne was cranky, being fed liquor in place of milk and then coping with the after-effects she was surely suffering each time she awoke. Poor little thing!

"It'll be all right, Chris," Hannah soothed, running her hand over the boy's head. "I'll take care of Marianne now."

"Mrs. Layne," he began.

"Yes, what is it?"

"Where's my dad?"

"I don't know," she shook her head, "but we'll find him soon. I'm sure he has a good reason for being wherever he is."

Christian looked at her, searching her eyes for the truth before he turned and walked back up the stairs to join the other children.

*

It was nearly nightfall before Nathan returned. Marianne was still asleep, though she was beginning to stir and make small noises. All of the children were at the table finishing their dinner when Nathan walked in through the kitchen door, looking tired and disappointed. Not wanting to discuss unhelpful information in front of the others, Hannah began dishing up his meal instead.

"Here's your supper," she began before turning her attentions to the oldest child in the group. "Merrie, would you draw a bath for the younger boys. There are soap flakes on the shelf, behind the towels. Just a little bit though; remember it doesn't take much to make a tub full of foam."

Meredith left the table, and at the prospect of a bubble bath, Andy brightened measurably, a spirit which spread in some measure to the Sanderson boys. Even Chase began to wiggle in his chair.

Soon, the plates were cleaned and the boys excused to their bubbly bliss. Hannah began to clear the table around Nathan as he tried to make it through his meal.

"There's no sign of him, Hannah," he finally announced. "He withdrew a substantial amount of money from the bank and Janette said that she saw him at the train station on Monday."

"You don't think that he left town?" she asked incredulously.

"The stationmaster said he purchased a ticket for Portland. He didn't know if he was going any farther than that. In fact, he thought that he'd already come back."

"Portland?"

"Yes. I'm going to search for him there tomorrow. Janette stopped by with some food while I was over there. She said that the last time she saw Carlen he looked 'altered.' She's afraid he may have cracked."

"Cracked?" Hannah repeated, glancing around the corner of the doorway to make sure that none of the children had returned unawares.

"She's concerned that he's been in denial over Linda's death until now and, given the stress of the baby, has finally cracked under the pressure of it."

Hannah grimaced at the suggestion. "Surely not!"

Nathan looked across the room and then shrugged. "I don't know. I suppose anything is possible. You know him better than I do, love. Where do you suppose he might have gone?"

Hannah sank into a chair at the table. "I don't know. He doesn't have any living family besides the children, and I can't imagine that he would just leave them of his own will, not coming back when he was expected. He seemed to be dealing with everything so well."

"Well, there's no one to cover Sunday's sermon if he's not back by then. That's only three days away. In the meantime, Janette has suggested that we assume he's away on business."

Hannah shook her head and scoffed at the suggestion. "He would never leave his children for days at a time with no instructions and insufficient food just for business. Who do you think would believe such a story?"

"The station master for one," he answered. "We need to protect him from the speculation. No one but us knows the full extent of the situation. Even Callie was under the assumption that if he was away too long, she should bring the children over here. For all she knew, he left on some sort of business trip. No one else knows that the children were left behind the way that they were."

"Did you say anything about it to Janette?"

"No, but she knows they're at our house and that he's been gone for most of the week. She's far too wise to these types of things not to figure it out. She was the one who suggested the business alibi. She is anxious to protect him as well, especially with all the talk going around town."

"What talk?" Hannah was clearly confused.

Nathan heaved a sigh. "Agnes Dane was out on the road when I took Callie home and claims that you and Carlen are keeping time together. She's been busy spreading that gossip around."

"You know that's absurd! Carlen is our friend, Nathan; it's ridiculous of her to make such an accusation."

Nathan looked at her a little sadly before nodding. "I suppose we should give him every benefit of the doubt."

Hannah shrugged. "There could be a few legitimate things that might have kept him away. Maybe he became ill while doing business in Portland."

"Perhaps. Are you comfortable with all the extra children until we can find him?"

"I'll be fine," she answered; "though I'm concerned about the baby. She hasn't been awake all day. Callie has been using that abominable concoction in a bottle to make her sleep."

"Yes, she mentioned it on the drive home and I saw it on the counter while I was there. It was mostly gone. I can't imagine that Carlen would ever have such a thing in his home."

"He didn't," Hannah defended. "Christian said that a neighbor brought it over because Callie couldn't get Marianne to stop crying. You don't think that she would've used an entire bottle over the last five days do you?"

Nathan shook his head. "Possibly less time than that; it makes sense."

"What do you mean?"

"Callie had no idea what it was; only that it helped Marianne sleep. Mrs. Perkins told her it was colic medicine."

Hannah glanced back at the baby. "Poor Marianne; she'll be miserable once she wakes up. I've got the bottles out and several baby things ready, but we're going to need either the cradle or a crib set up for her. I have a feeling the next few days may be trying for us all."

Nathan pushed himself away from the table with a sober nod of agreement. "I'll get the cradle from the attic. You might want to check on the boys in the tub. You know how Chase gets with bubbles."

Listening a moment more, Hannah realized that the noise from the bathroom was starting to grow to raucous proportions.

Smiling, she shook her head.

"It will clean up just fine. Having a little fun may be a welcome diversion to the gloom those boys have been living under. For now, I think I'll get a bath ready for Marianne in the sink and see if I can manage some degree of wakefulness to her. If I'm guessing right, she'll be hungry as a bear when she wakes up. Well, better now than later, or in the middle of the night," she sighed. "Poor little thing!"

*

Marianne scarcely stirred during her bath, and only by using a damp cloth on her face had Hannah gotten her to consciousness enough to drink a very few ounces of milk. She then slept clear through the night and into the early morning.

Finally, concerned for her welfare, Hannah called Peter over to check her before he went to work for the day.

He could only shake his head in wonder as he finished the examination. "She's going to have a wallop of a hangover," he announced, "but you've done well getting what fluid you could into her."

"How do people justify using such tactics on a baby?" Hannah mourned.

"I don't know," Peter sighed, "but she should pull through it. Just keep trying to get fluids down her. She's very dehydrated."

"I know. I've only had to change her diaper once."

Peter nodded. "The fact that she's needed it at all is good news. Give me a call if you have any concerns. I should be at the office most of the day today. Where's Nathan?" he asked as he gathered his things back into his black bag.

"He's gone to Portland after Carlen."

"What? Doesn't he know they've got a raging case of the flu going on there? I hope he doesn't catch it or bring it home."

"We hadn't heard about any illnesses; what else was he to do? He has to find Carlen."

"I want my daddy," Hansel whimpered as he pulled at Hannah's skirt.

"I know you do, love," Hannah consoled, smoothing her hand over the little boy's head. "I'm sure he'll be back just as soon as he can."

"Where ith he?" Andy asked.

Hannah was about to say that she wasn't sure, when Peter announced: "I heard he was away on business."

Hannah was surprised at the announcement. Peter was in on it too.

"There you have it," she shrugged. "He must have unfinished business somewhere."

"Do what you can to wake her, maybe give her another bath and try to get more fluids into her. Have Nathan come see me as soon as he gets home." Peter finished his solemn instruction before closing the front door behind him.

"Can I hold her, Mommy, while you fix her bath?" Melanie asked.

"Of course you can."

Hannah wrapped the blanket a little more snuggly around the baby and handed her off, then went to the kitchen to start the water in the sink. It was only moments later that Marianne began to scream, making Hannah reach for the bottle of milk instead.

"Thank you, Mel," she soothed. "I'll take it from here."

"Grandma!" Chase shouted from the kitchen. "Grandma's here!"

Soon, all of the children gathered at the kitchen door, welcoming Sarah into the house.

Hannah had her hands full trying to coax Marianne to suckle the nipple between screams, so Sarah deposited a tray of food on the counter and followed her ears to the front room. Meanwhile, all the little Laynes and Sandersons surrounded the kitchen counter to peek into the covered tray of goodies.

"How is she doing?" Sarah asked, checking over the screaming bundle in Hannah's arms.

"Peter says she'll be okay, eventually. I suppose he knows what he's talking about, but I'm not as confident."

"Should I take the baby or the children?"

Hannah looked between them for a moment and closed her eyes.

"Honestly?" she sighed, "as concerned as I am over Marianne, I'd rather see you work your magic on the boys. Christian is especially blue. He doesn't say much, but I can tell it's weighing on him heavily."

Sarah turned back to the kitchen and got down to business. "Who would like a raspberry tart?"

As the children all climbed up to the table and began their feast, Sarah came back into the front room. Hannah relinquished the baby to her mother-in-law and was astonished at how quickly Marianne settled down in her arms. Within moments, she even started suckling from the bottle.

Hannah laughed. "How do you do that?"

Sarah only shrugged before venturing her thoughts. "I should probably take the Sanderson children home with me."

"Whatever for?" Hannah asked in surprise. "They are fine and happy here with their friends."

"It's just the rumors, Hannah. To have Carlen missing, and then you caring for his children would only seem to confirm it. Then with Hansel calling you his mother…"

"What?" Hannah interrupted. "Wait, what is that about?"

"Reverend Sanderson was in the store with the children last week and Hansel asked him to buy a gift for his mother. When he tried to remind the boy that Linda wasn't with them anymore, Hans told him it was for his other mother. I'm afraid it got everyone's attention and Reverend Sanderson was clearly confused, until Hansel mentioned your name. He tried to set him straight, but Hans claimed that you told him you would be his mother."

"Oh, Mother, surely…"

"There's more," she added, cutting Hannah off. "Agnes Dane was in the store. Oh, but that woman can gossip! As soon as the reverend left, she said it didn't surprise her one bit, since the two of you are keeping company alone together every time your husband isn't around."

Hannah dropped into the chair in complete shock. "It isn't true," she whispered. "I mean, Hansel did call me mother once; he had been so sad; I didn't think it would hurt anything, but I've not spent any time alone with Carlen. Surely, you don't believe her."

"I'd like not to, Hannah, but she said she sees him passing her house on the way to yours frequently and when she knows you are alone."

"And you believe her?" Hannah was stunned. "How could she

even know such a thing? We are old friends, Carlen and I, but you should know that I am never alone with him; at a minimum, the children are always here, if not Nathan as well, and Carlen visits our house the same as any other."

"It's not the same," Sarah hedged.

"What are you saying?"

"I saw a special something between you both when he first arrived, years ago. You might as well know, I asked Alannah about it and she said you had been in love with each other before."

"But it's not like that. Maybe once, in the past, we felt that way, but now we are only friends."

Sarah was quiet for a full minute, trying to ascertain the truth. "I'm sorry I even questioned it," she apologized. Though she was gracious enough to end the interrogation, Hannah could tell that she was still not convinced. "Either way, the gossip is out there and if Agnes finds out he's missing, then she'll declare it will be that he's left out of shame."

"It's ridiculous!" Hannah scoffed. "Surely, no one would believe it."

"The rumors are already flying from tongue to idle tongue, Hannah. I must say, I'm glad to hear you claim it isn't true. Unfortunately, Agnes is not going to let it rest."

"Hear me claim, or believe what I say?" Hannah was indignant. "Either way, while I'm completely stunned you would ever doubt me, we actually have a much larger problem on our hands. We must find out what happened to Carlen."

Sarah sighed deeply. It was true; for now, the reverend must be found and every effort to do so must be made.

Chapter Fifteen

Peter Gives a Warning

August 1918

"Listen to me, Nathan; you're not paying attention. You *must* follow my instructions or you'll be taking your life into your hands."

"I'm sorry; you're right. It's just that my mind is reeling with the task. It's such a huge city; how will I ever find him, Pete? My efforts so far have been completely futile."

"Are you sure no one knew anything about his business there?"

"No, not a thing; not Callie or the children. He just left, saying that he planned to be home that evening, or possibly the following morning if things took longer than he anticipated."

"Do you have a picture of him?"

"Yes; I have his wedding portrait from the house."

"That should work. I suppose all you can do is start at the train station and show it to every person you meet. Hopefully it will lead on a path toward him. Listen to me though, this is very important; you mustn't eat or drink anything from Portland. The plague is rampant there. Try not to touch anyone or anything that you don't have to; wash your hands whenever you can and here, wear this."

Nathan looked puzzled as his brother passed him a lump of gauze. "What is it?"

"It's a gauze mask; you'll need to wear it at all times once you've left Silver Falls. The street cars and most public places are requiring them. Remember, eyes, nose, and mouth; those are the places germs enter the body. If you find someone coughing, move away from them. If nothing else, the mask will help you remember not to eat or drink anything from the area, or to touch your nose and mouth. Are you clear on this?"

"I guess so. It seems an odd time of year for a flu outbreak, though."

"Yes, it's very odd; but this bug never slowed down for the

summer. Did Hannah pack a lunch for you?"

"Yes, yes." Nathan seemed downright distracted as he ran his hand through his hair. "I just can't imagine how I will ever find him. I'm certain he wouldn't leave his children like that. What if he met with foul play?"

"More likely he's met with illness. My question is whether or not he's still alive. At this point, the flu has less than a four percent death rate. That's still far too high, but Carlen, while he is strong and healthy, doesn't meet the typical criteria of this flu's victims. It is killing mostly young adults, with a high mortality rate among smokers."

Nathan's brows knit again. "So, say I do find him and he's ill. What then?"

"Well, seeing that he's gone missing, I doubt he'd be in any shape to travel. If you find him, just see that he's in a safe place with food and water, and then come straight home. I'll take it from there. For now, we'll all be relieved if you just find him alive."

Nathan nodded at his words.

"You must be careful though," Peter continued. "Don't touch anyone or anything that you don't have to. This flu strikes so dreadfully fast; there have been cases of people dying within a few hours of exposure. I can't emphasize how careful you need to be just to get there and back without catching it. Do you understand what I'm saying?"

This time, Nathan looked more sober as he nodded his agreement, and for the first time that morning, Peter felt that his brother finally understood the risks. With that, he walked to the back room and retrieved a few more masks.

"You may need extras; just put them with whatever else you're taking. Did you pack water?"

"No, but Hannah packed some milk in a jar. She was hopeful that I'd find Carlen and it would help him."

"If he has influenza, milk will be the last thing he needs. It might add to the phlegm and congestion. Water will be his most critical need." Peter looked around his office, as if hoping he would see some last item he could give his brother to assure him the safest journey possible. "I don't know, Nathan. I'd feel better if you were more prepared for this. Maybe you should go home and get that water, or wait another day to see if he comes back."

Nathan smiled and patted his knapsack. "I'll be fine, Pete; but thank you for the pointers." Listening another moment, he perked. "There's the train whistle now. I'm planning to be back by nightfall but if I get delayed, you'll check in on Hannah and the children won't you? Marianne still isn't well."

"I will," Peter promised.

*

It had been a long, jostling ride down the coast to his transfer point and then even longer through the winding mountain route alongside the river. Across Tualatin Valley he rode and into the Willamette basin where the City of Portland sprawled out in all directions.

Nathan looked around as he departed the train and stood in the vast, echoing space of Union Station. He hadn't noticed it before, but since Peter's warning he saw that the place was as vacant as the train had been. Apparently, people weren't risking any unnecessary exposure.

Seeing the ticket offices, he noted two people behind the windows and approached them.

"Excuse me," he began at the first window; "I'm looking for a friend of mine who is missing. Have you seen this man at all?"

The clerk shook his head, leaving Nathan to move to the next window, though having overheard the request, the second clerk shook his head as soon as the photo was presented.

Nathan turned around, methodically considering his course. "Where would he have gone from here?"

Leaving the building, he stood with his back to the river, facing the greater part of downtown and tried to think through each possible destination Carlen might have had. The seminary, the hospital, the courthouse? What business might have brought the reverend to this place? It was part of Carlen's job to register marriages, but he doubted that would extend to this county.

As he stood looking over the city, the clock tower began to chime loudly behind him. It was eleven o'clock and he had a very limited number of hours before the last train back. Peter had assumed the reverend was sick. If he had been too ill to get word of it back to his family, then where would he most likely be? Nathan determined that he would try the hospitals first, then the courthouse and, if time permitted, he would stop at the seminary. Hoping one of these places would offer a further lead in knowing where to go, he set off in a brisk walk toward town.

*

"Please, sir," a little voice called out. "Do you have any food? Me and my sister are very hungry."

Nathan had gone barely a mile when the child approached him. He was a young waif, not more than four, and carried a baby on his hip.

"Where are your parents?" Nathan asked, shocked that any adult would allow their children to wander the streets like this.

"They're gone, sir," the boy sadly confessed.

"Gone where?"

"To heaven."

Nathan suddenly understood the circumstance. "Who's taking care of you?"

The boy looked up into Nathan's eyes and asked again. "Please, do you have any food?"

"Yes, I do."

Sitting down on the curb, Nathan pulled his lunch from the knapsack and took the baby onto his knee. "Can you tell me your names?" he asked as he began dividing a portion of his food.

The boy only stared at the food and milk with large eyes of anticipation.

"You do have a name?" Nathan prodded again.

The boy nodded.

"Can you tell me what it is?"

"Oliver."

"What about your sister?"

"Nellie."

Nathan tried to garner as much information as he could while he had the boy's attention. "Where do you sleep at night?"

"Over there."

The little boy pointed to an area of homes as Nathan handed over part of his lunch. Breaking off a piece for his sister, they both began to devour what there was of the sandwich.

"Maybe, when you're done eating, you can show me your home."

Oliver scarcely slowed his ravenous attempts at quelling the pain in his stomach long enough to acknowledge the request. Gulping down the milk and the last of the bread, his eyes widened in disbelief when Nathan pulled out a strawberry tart and divided it between the two children. When they had at last finished, he let them drink the last of the milk.

Realizing he had given all of his and most of Carlen's food away, he stood with the little girl in his is arms, shouldered his knapsack and, taking the boy by the hand, announced. "Now you can show me where you live."

At first, the little boy looked up at him with apprehensive eyes, but seeing that Nathan was not to be dissuaded, he eventually led him down the road and up to a carriage house, next to a lovely home. This is where they stopped. One look at the pile of blankets in the shed and Nathan figured they had reached their destination.

"Who lives in the house?" he asked, nodding toward the larger building, though the little boy only shook his head.

"Please don't take Nellie in there."

"I'll just knock on the door then and we won't go inside. Will that be okay?"

"They won't come to the door," the boy stated sadly.

"Why not?"

"Because they went to heaven."

With that announcement, Nathan walked up the path and tried the door. It was completely unlocked.

"It's open. Why won't you sleep inside?"

Oliver shook his head. "It smells bad."

A little confused at the answer, Nathan leaned his head toward the opening, began to draw a breath through his nose and was immediately met with the pungent stench of death. Finally understanding the situation, he was still perplexed as to how no one had seen the plight of these children. How could they be left to wander the streets for food with no one to notice or help them?

Once again, taking Oliver by the hand, he led them back toward town and several blocks farther down the road toward the police station. It needed to be done and it would be a good place to ask about Carlen as well.

*

It was late at night when Nathan at last walked through the door of his home. Hannah was up in the front room, reading and waiting for his return. She was full of anxious questions as her husband dropped, exhausted, into the chair across from her.

"Did you find him?"

Nathan shook his head. "No; it is such a huge city, Hannah. I checked at the hospitals, the seminary, and courthouse. I even checked with the police and eventually out at the orphanage."

"The orphanage?"

"Yes; I had to take two children out there."

Hannah looked at him, confused. "Whatever for?"

"They were starving and approached me on the street for food, a young boy and his baby sister. Their names were Oliver and Nellie." Nathan smiled for only a moment before growing quite sober again. "Oliver was so good-natured, Hannah. I had them show me where they lived. Their parents were dead in the house, along with two other siblings."

"Oh, Nathan!" she gasped. "How horrible! Do you know what killed them?"

"The police said it was the flu. He said they've had orphans wandering the streets far too often from the same situation. He said if I find any more to bring them down to the station to collect their information, and then take them on out to the baby home."

"The baby home? I thought you said it was an orphanage."

"Yes, it is the orphanage; the locals just call it the baby home. They used to deal only with babies. When I signed the children in, the owner gave me the most pitiful look. I need to send them a hearty donation for their goodness. They are stretched beyond capacity now."

"I can't imagine how difficult it must be for them. Did they have many helpers?"

"No, not many at all, mostly just a husband and wife team, Mr. and Mrs. Blake; I think that was their name. Since the flu has struck they've been changed over from adoptive babies to a full-fledged orphanage, unwittingly so. Those poor children have no one to give them what they need beyond the very basics of gruel and water for sustaining life, maybe a little bread and milk for the babies. It was heart-wrenching. If it wasn't so dangerous and we weren't in this present predicament, I would take you there, Hannah, to see if you had it in your heart to bring one or two of them home with us."

Hannah looked at her husband with tender eyes. It was true that they had the means to support more children, and she had dreamed of a larger family during her younger days, but they weren't young anymore, and they dared not risk it with the plague out there as it was. Finally, Hannah sat up a little straighter in her chair.

"Did you find out anything about Carlen?"

"Oddly, yes. He was at the baby home last week. Mrs. Blake thought it was Monday, which would've been the day he left Silver Falls. Apparently, he goes out there on occasion to visit and help them however he can, as his own personal ministry. She mentioned that they'd had sick children that day and Carlen had prayed over and helped feed them. They hadn't seen him since, but it was nothing unusual since he only comes once a month at most."

"But they did see him. He was there," Hannah repeated hopefully.

"Yes, Hannah; he had been there."

"Did he tell them where he was going?"

"No; they only said that he looked very tired when he left. They hadn't heard about Linda's death and they had hoped he was thinking of adopting one of the children. They gave me another idea of where to look though, suggesting he might have gone to a hotel."

"Are you going back tomorrow?"

"Yes; I wanted to take a donation out to the orphanage, first thing; then I thought I'd go door to door through the hotels. They have guest registers I could check; it's worth a try. I don't know what else to do. If I can't find him, then maybe there will be another lead. I don't know what we'll do about church. The whole town will know he's missing by tomorrow."

Hannah shook her head. "Peter talked to Davy and they are spreading the word about the plague, encouraging people to stay home. By order of the mayor, all church services and large public gatherings have been canceled for tomorrow, at least until they can learn more about the threat. Judging from the phone activity, the town is pretty alarmed over it."

Nathan looked concerned. "People will want to talk to Carlen because of it. It will still draw attention to the problem."

"Not as much as if he were mysteriously absent from church. He doesn't have a phone; that will slow the questioning down. If someone actually goes to his house and no one is there, then how are they to know he's necessarily missing? We just need to find him, Nathan, and soon."

Weary to the bone, Nathan nodded his agreement. "That we do, Hannah. I will try again tomorrow."

Chapter Sixteen

Room 217

August 1918

Nathan stepped from the train, this time with purpose. The previous three days had been completely unsuccessful and this was his fourth attempt at trying to find the missing reverend. He had searched through most of the hotels and there were only a handful of places left. He had decided to make this day his last. Carlen could be in any of a thousand more buildings, if he was here at all, but Nathan was getting worn down from the effort. How long could he expect to escape the dreaded illness himself, especially if he continued giving his food away to wandering children and ill people each day?

He had systematically searched the churches, hospitals and boarding houses, even park benches, but with no luck. Today, he began in earnest to check the last few hotels, all the while asking anyone he could find on the streets if they had seen the man in the photo. If Carlen was to be found, then he would find him today. If not, then he would wait it out until the epidemic was over.

"I'm looking for a friend of mine, Carlen Sanderson. I wonder if you've seen him?" he asked the man at the front desk of the ninth hotel he had been to that day. It was the same question he'd asked hundreds of times, always with the same answer.

"What does he look like?"

Nathan had the photo ready to show. "Tall, thin, light hair."

"Why are you looking for him?"

"He's a friend of mine that's missing. I have his children at home; I'm just trying to find him, hopefully alive."

Nathan turned to leave; it was the same conversation he'd had a hundred times, with the same outcome. They always said no and his responses were becoming automatic, thus he had turned to start on his way to the next place.

"Is he in trouble?" the clerk called after him.

Nathan shook his head and continued toward the door.

"He might be here," the clerk called out.

When Nathan turned back, the young man shrugged his shoulders. "Or he might not. We don't have anyone by that name exactly, but we do have a tenant who sort of fits the description. How long has your friend been missing?"

"Nine days now."

The clerk nodded thoughtfully. "It's possible," he shrugged. "He's been here about that long. Won't answer the door though, and never comes out."

It was a long shot, but it was also the best lead Nathan had heard over the past four full days. The clerk pulled the guest register open and flipped back a few pages as Nathan came toward him.

"Here it is; says: 'C. Sanders,' I think; can't read it very well; room 217."

Nathan drew closer to check the register. It could have been Carlen's handwriting, under duress.

"Thank you. I'll check it out."

Climbing the stairs, he followed the numbers down the hallway until he came to room 217. There he paused. What if it wasn't Carlen at all, but a complete stranger? There was only one way to find out. Collecting his resolve, he knocked on the door and waited. After a full minute of silence, he knocked again - and again there was no answer.

Nathan stood outside the door and knocked several more times. He was about to leave when he heard a sound from inside, a glass or bottle falling to the floor, followed by a violent spasm of choking coughs.

"Carlen?" he called. "Carlen are you in there? It's Nathan. Are you all right?" Only the coughing met his questions, so Nathan knocked again, louder this time. "Carlen, if you're there, open the door; I need to talk to you." A small thud sounded from inside the room; then nothing more. Finally, Nathan returned to the lobby.

"Do you have a spare key?" he asked the clerk. "Someone is in there, but he's not answering. I think he might be sick and can't make it to the door."

"Possible," the clerk agreed. "We've had that awful flu going around."

"Can you give me a key?" he asked again.

"Nope; it's against hotel policy."

"Could you go with me and unlock it so I can check on him?"

"Nope; can't leave the desk."

Frustrated, Nathan began pacing the lobby before finally heading back upstairs. He followed the same pattern as before, but this time without any result. It was obvious someone was in the room. Unfortunately, this time there was no noise, no response at all. This had been going on for four long days and Nathan was beyond weary, hungry, and discouraged. Not only had he scarcely eaten during the day, but with Marianne still crying much of the night, he'd hardly slept either. In his exhaustion, he became filled with doubt as to the identity of who might be on the other side of that door.

Finally, checking his watch, he saw that he was out of time. There were only minutes left before the train home was due to leave, barely enough time to make it back to the station at a run. Tomorrow was another day; perhaps he could try just one more time.

*

It was late by the time he reached home, and the children were asleep. Only Marianne was still awake and fussing, as Hannah tried to work the bubbles out from her last feeding.

"Any luck?" she asked as her husband came through the door.

"Maybe," Nathan shrugged.

Hannah looked at him in confusion. "What do you mean by maybe?"

Nathan rehearsed the happenings of his day and his experience at the hotel. To his surprise, his wife was completely irritated by what he had to say.

"Do you mean to say that you just left him there?" she asked incredulously. "Nathan, he was probably too sick to come to the door!"

"We don't even know that it was Carlen, remember? What else was I supposed to do? I couldn't just break the door down."

Hannah just shook her head, clearly annoyed over the whole situation. "I would have! Oh, I'll go there myself," she announced.

"I don't think that's a good idea, Hannah."

"Why not?" she asked impatiently.

"Because we don't know who may be in that room. There's nothing that says it's Carlen."

"No, nothing except that there is a man who matches his description, who has been in that room for just the same amount of time that he's been missing, and who isn't coming out. I have to go, Nathan. You can come with me if you like, but I am going."

*

"Carlen!" Nathan called as he knocked on the door again. "Carlen, open the door."

"Let's get a key," Hannah suggested.

"They won't give us one; I asked the clerk yesterday. He said it was against hotel policy."

"Try again, Nathan. Would they rather give you the key, open the door, or have you kick it in?"

"Hannah, I'm not going to kick in the door. We don't even know it's Carlen in there."

"Then *I* will kick it in," she insisted.

Despite the circumstances, Nathan looked at her with a crooked smile on his face. "You can't kick in the door, love. You're not that strong."

"I can try…"

"Alright, I'll go ask again."

With that, Nathan left down the hallway toward the stairs while Hannah continued her attempts at knocking.

"Carlen, it's Hannah; I know you're in there. Can you make it to the door?"

Hannah heard some movement in the room shortly before something bumped the door… then, another sound. Was it a thud? Did something fall? She waited another minute before deciding to try the handle. To her great surprise, it gave way against the lock. Slowly, she opened the door as far as it would go and stepped into the darkness.

"Carlen?"

The room was very dark and she fumbled her way past the threshold before hearing a moan close by. It was then that she saw him collapsed behind the door. Hannah dropped to the floor in alarm.

"Carlen!"

"Please... leave." The whisper was so quietly that she could scarce make out his words.

"I'm not going to leave; we're here to help you."

"Hannah," he whispered again, "leave; I…" his rasping voice trailed off to silence.

"Carlen!" Quickly examining his person, she tried to ascertain what was wrong with him. "Carlen, stay with me," she urged, though the man did nothing more to respond.

Just then, Nathan appeared in the frame of the door.

"Oh, thank goodness you're back. Help me get him onto the bed."

"How did you get in?"

"The door was unlocked; he must have unlocked it at some point, who knows when, but he's too weak to get up."

As Nathan settled the minister back onto the mattress, Hannah went to the window and opened the curtains, then pulled up the shade. Looking back at their friend with the advantage of a little light, she saw the sunken eyes and hollow cheeks of a very sick and dehydrated man. Reaching into her bag, she pulled out a cloth and began to look around the room.

"I need some water, Nathan."

"There's a bathroom down the hall. I'll be right back."

"Carlen," she tried again, though he didn't stir.

Nathan soon returned and as Hannah began wiping the damp cloth against his face, his eyes began to flutter. Slowly, he opened them, briefly trying to adjust his vision to the daylight before closing them again.

"Hannah," he rasped once more, "leave… don't want… spread," he managed, with great effort.

"Is that what this is all about?" she asked. "Carlen, you're not contagious; can you still hear me?"

Small slits opened again and shifted toward her face. "Please... leave…" he asked once again.

"We're not leaving you; I brought some soup, though I'm afraid it's not warm anymore," she announced as she dug through her bag for the jar. When that was retrieved, she searched for the cup and a spoon. Just then the minister doubled over in another wracking spasm of suffocating croup. It continued for more than a minute before he could clear his lungs enough to breathe. The effort left him barely conscious.

"Carlen, when was the last time you ate or drank anything?"

He tried to move his head. "...don't know..." he whispered at last.

"You need nourishment. Here," she encouraged.

The man was too weak to protest as Hannah poured the soup, a spoonful at a time, over his parched lips. She noted that he was cool to the touch and surely not contagious as he had feared. All the while she offered quiet conversation to put him at ease.

"Your children are fine."

"Callie..." Carlen tried to speak.

"No, they're at our house. Nathan's mother is watching them as we speak. Christian is understandably worried about you. Not knowing where you were, a few people put out the word that you were away on business."

The hint of a smile labored to tug at one corner of his mouth. It wasn't much, but it was enough to show that he understood her words.

"You didn't tell anyone where you were going. Janette just happened to see you at the station when you left. The station master said you bought a ticket for Portland. Janette said you didn't look well."

"Flu..." Carlen whispered. "Is it..."

"Silver Falls has been spared, at least so far. Peter has us all diligently washing our hands every hour, it seems. The railway won't let anyone ride without a mask and the restaurant has all but closed from the lack of business; most people aren't traveling anymore. George is keeping the bank open, but most of the employees have refused to come in. The streets are so quiet, even at home. Peter feels that if people stay away from the gathering places then we'll be able to keep the cases down."

Hannah chatted on in friendly fashion, and after slowly draining tiny spoonfuls of soup for some twenty minutes, Carlen began to look as though he might just live through another hour.

"The church?"

This time it was Nathan who answered the question.

"David Harrison has asked all the congregations not to meet for now. He said it was for the flu, but he knew you were missing." Nathan looked out the window and shrugged.

"Honestly, so many people are afraid to leave their homes; many places outside of Silver Falls even have laws against public gatherings right now.

Hannah nodded. "Peter thinks the salt air might be helping us on the coast; he thinks it might be weakening the plague. Either way, it hasn't hit us yet."

An hour later, the entire jar of soup was empty and Carlen was in a profound sleep; the effort to open the door and speak had drained him of what little strength he had. Hannah began to look around the room, noticing for the first time the markers of his ordeal from the past ten days, including a trail of his efforts to make it to the door from the day before. How had he even survived?

"We have to get him home, Nathan," she whispered. "How are we going to do it?"

Nathan pulled out his watch and shook his head. "I don't know. We have a couple of hours yet before the train leaves. He can't walk, Hannah; he can't even sit up. I don't know how to get him home before he's stronger."

"Doesn't Peter have a wheel chair in his office?"

"Yes, I think so. Originally, Pete told me he wanted to bring Carlen home if we found him."

Hannah nodded. "You and Peter can do it tomorrow. It's little wonder he has no strength, between the illness and no food for days on end. I'm surprised he's still alive."

"Barely at that," Nathan whispered.

"Let's get him home tomorrow; we can fix up a sick room for him at the back of the house. There's no fever; I'm certain it'll be safe. Peter said it isn't contagious once the fever breaks."

Nathan nodded his agreement. "We can check with Pete to be certain, but you're probably right."

*

Peter joined Nathan early the following morning in transporting Carlen home, while Hannah busied herself getting everything in the back room ready for his arrival. At first he refused to go, not that he could've resisted two strong men with any efficacy at all, but when the doctor assured him that he was no longer contagious, he ceased to struggle against their efforts.

To say his children were relieved to have him back was an

understatement. The boys glommed onto him, refusing to leave his side as though afraid they might lose him for good. Thankfully, Marianne had begun to recover from her own ordeal as well.

In four short days, though he was still fighting the cough, Carlen announced that he was well enough and should be back on his own.

"What about Marianne?" Hannah asked. "Maybe I should keep her, at least a few more days, so you can rest at night."

"I can't put you out any longer, Hannah. She is my responsibility. I know she doesn't sleep well, and you are an angel for tending her as long as you have. Thank you, but I'll take her home with me."

Hannah shook her head, trying to come up with another approach. It was true, Marianne was not the easiest baby she had known, but not only was Carlen still weak, he was also unaware of her bout with the alcohol, and no one wanted to burden him with those details just yet. Ultimately, though the baby was improving, she felt Marianne needed more care than what the reverend could reasonably offer.

Looking down at the sleeping infant in her arms, she hedged, searching for the right words. "Please, Carlen," she began. "I want to take care of her. She's still so tiny and I'm not entirely sure that you're up to giving her the attention she needs right now. Will you trust me with her just a few more days? She's been through a lot while you were gone. She could use a mother's touch a little longer."

A mother's touch. Those words cut through him like a flaming sword. Looking tenderly down into Hannah's earnest eyes, he sighed in defeat. He was certain he knew exactly what she was doing, trying to shift the conversation in a fashion that would release him of further responsibility. Had it been anyone else, he would have refused. In his grieving heart, a part of him wished she could raise all three; surely, she would do a better job than he had managed.

Quietly nodding his consent, he ran his fingers over his daughter's sleepy face.

"Thank you, Hannah," he whispered at last. "You are right, she is sure to fare better under your hand than mine."

Chapter Seventeen

The Mayor Calls a Meeting

August 1918

Despite the numerous ceiling fans circling at full power, the temperatures in the auditorium were too warm to begin with, but adding more than a hundred bodies into the mix made it unbearable. Women fanned themselves to no avail, while men used their hankies to wipe the trickling perspiration from their faces and necks.

The Silver Falls Auditorium was mostly used in the evenings for performances and plays, all of which happened before spring planting or after the fall harvest. At those times, the challenge was found in sufficiently heating the building, not cooling it down. Unfortunately, today's venue was not entertainment.

As mayor of Silver Falls, David Harrison had been pressed upon by the town's doctor to call a meeting of imperative importance. It had taken some work to convince the community that it was safe to gather, but ultimately their curiosity overtook their caution and the people turned out in droves. Taking the stage, he briefly tested the microphone and then stepped to the front and center.

"I'm sure many of you are wondering why we're here today. I know that it's hot and uncomfortable and we've discouraged public gatherings, but please bear with us. You all know our good doctor, Pete Layne. There is critically important information he feels we need to hear, after which, we'll need to make a few decisions that may affect the well-being of our citizens. First we'll hear from Dr. Layne and then we'll open it up to questions from the audience. Pete."

Peter stepped from the side curtains and into the spot light at the microphone. A very few people applauded out of nothing more than habit, but the majority of gathered citizens simply continued fanning themselves with whatever they could get their hands on to create a little more movement to the stifling air.

"I'd like to thank all of you for coming today. I know it's never convenient to do something like this, especially under the present circumstances, but there is news that must be shared which many of you may find alarming. I also have information that will hopefully diffuse any panic."

While there had been some chatter among the group as he took the stage, Peter had so much of their full attention now that he thought he could hear his own heart beating over the sound system. He was sure they were all wondering the same thing, what could he possibly say that might cause panic?

"As many of you know, there has been a virulent new disease going around. It is worldwide, what we call a pandemic, and it has claimed very many lives. The influenza generally strikes each fall or winter and is most serious with the very young or very old. Typically, it fades out and disappears in early spring. This sickness, however, has been thriving through the spring and summer months as well. Oddly, it is also most deadly among those who would normally not be so affected, young adults and those in their prime, the strong and healthy. In a typical year, the influenza may claim one percent of the population. By contrast, this year's flu has claimed closer to twenty percent, which is shocking enough, but it has recently mutated into an even deadlier strain."

"How deadly?" a voice called out from the back.

"I received one cable from the east claiming a seventy percent mortality."

The gasps and mumbling chatter from the audience grew louder and louder, threatening to drown out the doctor altogether.

Peter looked off at David Harrison and shook his head. He had been concerned all along that the townspeople would panic at the information, but David felt that knowledge would equate to power for them all and insisted that the message be delivered. Now, he nodded back, encouraging the doctor to continue. Peter waited a few more seconds for the din to quiet down.

"So far, we've been very lucky in our little community; it has already hit Portland en masse. The symptoms of the lighter strain are typically a high fever for three days often followed by lingering pneumonia for many. This latest version, however, has been hitting with extreme haste and proving very deadly. Our own Reverend Sanderson was struck down only hours after any possible exposure and nearly died. Reports from the east have claimed cases of death within a mere ten hours of exposure."

Again the nervous voices began rising in volume and Peter could clearly sense a growing anxiety among the group. He had carefully prepared his remarks to both disseminate the necessary information while quelling as much of the naturally resulting fear as he could.

"There is some good news," he called out above the growing roar. "Ocean air appears to help. Fresh air hospitals, and especially those along the coast, have had the highest survival rates. Also, if you don't smoke, you're in luck. The highest death rates have been among heavy smokers."

"What can be done?" a woman called out, followed by several other murmurs of agreement.

"I'm glad you asked. Wash your hands often! Avoid traveling outside of Silver Falls and, if you absolutely must leave, try not to touch any common surfaces, railings, doorknobs and such. Wash your hands immediately if you can't avoid them. Gloves may help. Don't eat anything that you haven't brought with you, or don't eat at all while you're gone if you can avoid it. Always wash your hands before you do and keep a mask on at all other times when out of your home. If your travel can be put off, then wait on it. If you do become ill, isolate yourself as much as possible. Look, people, it's inevitable that it will reach us eventually, but if we can delay that moment until it has a chance to weaken into a less deadly strain, then we will be all the better off."

"What about a quarantine?"

The question had come from Grant Andrews and was met with stunned silence. Actually, the situation had been planned out in advance. David Harrison was in favor of a quarantine all along, but knew it would bring hardship to some. If he were to have suggested it, there could be heavy backlash. However, if someone else brought it up then it could be discussed more openly.

Peter nodded. "A quarantine would, of course, slow the likelihood of the influenza reaching us. I must warn you though, it *will* reach us eventually. All we can hope is that it will have weakened by then."

At this, David walked back onto the stage and toward the microphone as Peter stepped a short distance away.

"Under these extenuating circumstances, if we were to consider an official quarantine of the town, by a show of hands, how many of you would be in favor of it?"

Most of the citizens in Silver Falls had little business to do outside of their community anyway and could see very little problem with the proposition; these raised their hands in assent.

"By contrast, how many of you would be unwilling to honor such an action?"

Several people scattered throughout the hall raised their hands, most of them being involved with commerce in the town. Oddly, Janette, clad in her trademark classic fashion, wasn't one of them.

Carefully, she approached the steps to the raised area. "I have a proposal that we all might consider. May I take the stage?"

David nodded. "Yes, certainly. What did you have in mind?"

Walking to the microphone, Janette looked out over the crowded auditorium. Every seat was taken and others were standing in the aisles; even the balconies held those willing to brave the added heat. She had never seen so many people in this place before.

"I know that many of you are wondering what you will do for employment if a quarantine is imposed. Remember that it would only be from the outside and would not be endless. We would still be free to associate within the town as long as we are healthy, and it would only be considered until this germ has weakened; possibly a month or two?" she asked, looking over to Peter for confirmation.

Peter shrugged and then nodded his agreement.

"I would be willing to keep my employees on, doing whatever could be done to serve only our local clientèle; but I was thinking, what if we had a grace period before the quarantine was put into effect? We've been lucky so far. What if we had another week before something like this began, to prepare ourselves and stock supplies for things that we couldn't obtain locally? Would you, the good people of Silver Falls, be more willing to abide it then?"

At her words, David stepped back to the microphone. "What

do you say?" he asked the crowd. "We already know who is in favor of such an action, but what about the rest of you? Would you be willing to cooperate under these circumstances?"

David could see most of the previous dissidents nodding their heads and only a very few to the contrary.

"There are a few things we cannot control. Mail will still come in, and it may carry the illness with it. Also, while the trains have become mostly vacant of natural consequence, all we can do is put a sign out at the station notifying visitors that the town is under quarantine." David gave a little chuckle. "Under the circumstances, it should be enough to scare them off. As for the general populace, however, this will have to be upheld by your honor."

There were no more objections from the crowd. With so many people in favor of the quarantine, there were few willing to make a huge protest against it, at least openly so.

"Let's give it one week then," David continued, "and let the quarantine begin next Sunday. Be sure to spread the word to anyone not here and I will be available to take your concerns as soon as we conclude." David looked over the assemblage a last time. "Are there any last questions for the doctor before we dismiss?"

"Yes," the comment came from Janette at the side of the stage. "What else did that cable say, the one that you received from the east?"

Peter looked at her ominously and shook his head. But the murmurs of curiosity from the crowd had started up anew.

"Maybe it don't say it's as serious as we think," a man called out from the crowd.

Peter was surprised that anyone might consider his motives as being anything less than benevolent. Finally, pulling a paper from his pocket, he held it up for all to see, cleared his throat and spoke once again into the microphone.

"It reads: 'In our city, there are not enough coffins for the dead, and especially no doctors for the sick, as they are dying alongside their patients. My advice is to prepare yourselves; gather your carpenters and have them make coffins now; set your laborers to digging graves before the illness hits. You will need it. God have mercy.' And that's the end of it," he finished, holding the paper forward, inviting all who might disbelieve him to examine it for themselves.

A portentous silence once again settled over the auditorium before the crowd quietly turned and began to shuffle toward the doors. There was nothing more to say. From here on out, the only thing left to do was prepare.

Chapter Eighteen

Legal Notice

September 1918

The house was quiet and mostly dark as young Robert Channing sat at the kitchen table, eyes red-rimmed and wondering what he should do. To one side of the room, a meager fire in the hearth struggled to change cold to warmth and at the table, an oil lamp flickered its scant light across the walls.

Not two weeks prior, this place had been a home filled with joyful noise, security, and love, but his entire family had succumbed to the plague - all except for him. The last to go had been his oldest sister, just a few days prior to this. The proprietor of the business where he worked had died as well, shutting down all operations for the unforeseeable future. There was no money coming in and very little food left in the house.

It seemed the entire city was in chaos, not only from the dead and dying, but the disruption of so many services. Most of the remaining population was afraid to go anywhere, venturing outside only when their hunger or need compelled them beyond their fear. Robby wondered how long it would last. How long would such a previously grand city have to wallow in the mire of death? Was it this way everywhere? Was there any way to escape?

As he sat, head in his hands, pensively contemplating the dreary details, a knock sounded at the front door. Cautiously, he got up to answer it, not having a clue who it might be - friend or foe.

"Mr. Channing?"

"Yes."

"Mr. Robert Channing?"

"Yes; what is it?"

"My name is Edward Thurman, attorney at law. I'm afraid we have a situation."

Robby tensed at the words. What further "situation" could

have happened that would require an attorney at his doorstep?

"What is this about?" He had forced the words out only to see the man square his shoulders, as if to deliver a heavy message.

"According to my client's will, you are next of kin to Clara Blake."

"Yes, she is my sister; or, was."

"In her will, you are designated to inherit her business, should anything happen to her."

"The baby home?" Robby visibly shuddered at the pronouncement. "I can't take the home! There's no way I could take care of all those children. How would I feed them? I don't have any money; I barely have any food. I wouldn't know the first thing to do."

"Not that it should be a consolation, but there are far fewer children than there used to be. This last strain of influenza claimed the majority of orphans in the home."

"How many are left?"

"Not many; twelve to fifteen, I believe. Either way, with both the Blakes having passed, and you listed as survivorship, you will need to take charge of the establishment. I have documents here that need to be signed and there is a file of records your sister wanted to be sure you received."

"Sir, I just buried my entire family; it took the last of what I had. Isn't there someone else who can take charge of this? I'm barely eighteen. I can't possibly take care of those children."

"I understand your concern. Unfortunately, legally, there is nothing else to be done. These are extraordinary times, young man. We are all desperate and living beyond what we might feel we can endure; we have all lost loved ones."

In another few minutes, Mr. Thurman had gone, leaving Robby alone and wondering what to do next. The children would be there in a matter of hours.

Leafing through the files, Robby came across one for donors and another of admissions. "Why don't these people just keep the children themselves instead of abandoning them to the home?"

Shuffling further from page to page, he happened upon an envelope filled with cash, enough cash for maybe two or three months of food. Looking over the record of donations, one name kept coming up over and over again.

"This guy must be rich," he whispered as he looked over the record. "Surely, he can afford to feed a few, at least better than I."

Being young and inexperienced, Robby closed the files and sat back in his chair, settling on a course of action.

Amiss though the path may have been, in his youthfulness, he could see no other way; and so, he began to plan.

Chapter Nineteen

The Larssen Bakery

September 1918

"Reverend Sanderson! Come in, come in; it's so good to see you out and about again. Are you getting your strength back?"

"Yes, it is coming, slow but sure."

Elise Larssen welcomed the minister into the house and grabbed a chair to include him in a group gathered around the large, wood-plank table.

"I say," David Larssen began, "you couldn't have picked a better day to show. Maria, fix him a sample plate as well; we could use his good opinion."

Carlen settled into the chair. "Just what are you all up to here?"

Elise smiled warmly as she received the plate from her daughter and placed it before their visitor.

"With the restaurant mostly closed, we've decided to open a bakery. This is today's sampling of products."

Carlen laughed. "Well then, I did choose the right day to visit, didn't I?"

"I'll say so!" Mr. Larssen agreed.

"Will you open a shop in town?" Carlen asked.

"No, not at all," Elise answered. "We have so many of us to bake the goods here, after which David will take them door to door on a delivery wagon. Apparently, it's common enough elsewhere. Lauren and Emma are joining us as well."

Carlen nodded his head at the idea of Emma getting involved in anything, especially something so productive. "Do you think there will be enough demand to make it work?"

Elise pushed the plate a little closer. "Try the samples, and you tell us."

With that, Carlen began to taste the several items on his plate. There were bits of sweetbreads, and lemon bars, tarts, cakes, donuts and pies. After each one, he raised his brows and nodded his approval.

"They are indeed delicious!"

"David has been adding onto the wagon all week long. Would you like to see?"

"I would very much."

As they all filed outside, Carlen had to smile at the prospects. It was obvious that the Larssen family was near to bursting with enthusiasm for their new venture. In all the time he had known them, they had struggled to make ends meet even in the best of years. It would be especially good to see them succeed in something like this now.

Turning the corner into the barn, the reverend was met by the sight of a splendid delivery wagon, with drawers, shelves, and counters. From the faint scent of fumes, he guessed they had recently finished the yellow coat of paint covering all that fresh wood.

David Larssen climbed aboard to demonstrate its many features. A full door opened up at the back with steps that folded down from the inside. Another opened on the front to the driver's seat, and a rolling retractable canopy adorned the side where a window opened to a counter inside. It was then that Carlen noticed the numbers.

"You're getting a phone?" he asked in surprise.

David beamed with pride. "Already gotten. We wanted to give our customers the convenience of being able to call in their orders."

"Well, that is wonderful! It looks as if you've thought of everything."

"We're trying," Elise replied.

"I didn't see Emma in the house. Is she here?"

The group went a little quiet before Elise spoke up. "She's still a bit too downtrodden to be fully involved just yet, but we're hoping she'll perk up a little more soon. Work can be a great distraction from worry, I always say, especially since there's nothing we can do about Hayden in the meantime."

Carlen nodded. "Yes, that's so true."

Elise thought another minute. "If you'd like to visit her, I believe she's at her mother's house. She could use some cheering up, I'm sure."

"Thank you, yes, but I just stopped in there before I came here and they said she was with you."

"Oh, dear me," Elise muttered. "Have you tried Nathan and Hannah's; or her own house? I know she doesn't like to be alone much, but she might be out at either of those places."

Carlen smiled his appreciation. "Thank you so much. I guess I'll just have to check over on that side of town. Good luck with your new business!"

*

After a lengthy walk from one side of town back to the other, Carlen knocked at the door of Nathan Layne's home and was soon welcomed inside where, as always, the conversation freely flowed.

"You say the Larssen's are starting a bakery wagon?" Hannah asked.

Nathan nodded thoughtfully. "It's an excellent idea. I think they may have finally set their hand to something that could flourish. I'm sure we'd support the cause if they came around here."

"It does seem to be an idea with potential." Carlen obviously had other things on his mind. "Emma wasn't there when I went to visit. Have you seen her lately?"

Hannah shook her head. "I thought she was staying at her mother's house. Did you try there?"

"It's the first place I went, but they hadn't seen her since yesterday. They thought she was at the Larssen's."

Nathan began to put the pieces together. "Why the mission to find Emma?"

"Just wondering how she's holding up and thought I'd check on her."

Hannah shook her head. "Until they find Hayden, I'm afraid that she won't be up to her chipper old self. It's been nearly a year since she lost contact with him and she's never really come to terms with it."

"I understand," Carlen said quietly. "The Larssens seem to be handling it well enough."

"Yes, but they are convinced that he will come home eventually. Emma doesn't share their hope or confidence. She was just beginning to get back on her feet with singing engagements at The Falls when the quarantine went into effect.

It's a pity it didn't last longer; singing for others brought her at least some joy."

"We can try to keep closer tabs on her," Nathan offered.

"Thank you, but I still feel compelled to find her today," Carlen added. "Do you think she's at her house?"

"By process of elimination, I would think so," Nathan mused. "It's a short walk up the hill to find out."

The walk was made, though Emma was not there. Finally, Carlen bid his goodbyes and headed off toward home. Grace had been watching his children for several hours and he was certain she was ready to be relieved.

*

As Carlen passed through the last of the heavy trees, beyond the school house and church and toward the open area near his little home, a small voice, almost undetectable, called out from the forest.

"Hello, Reverend Sanderson."

"Who's there?"

At first his question was met with silence, but eventually the same quiet voice answered back.

"It's me; Emma."

Looking farther into the darkness of the woods, his eyes finally landed on the small figure of Emma Larssen, sitting on a rock among the trees, as if secured in a fortress of solitude.

"Emma!" he greeted, making his way over to her. "I've been looking for you the better part of the day. Have you been here all along?"

"No. I was at the church and cemetery earlier, and out at the waterfall before that. Why were you trying to find me?"

"Just checking up. How are you doing?"

"I'm okay."

The words were right enough, but Carlen heard something quite different in the tones. As his eyes began to adjust more to the dim light within the refuge of trees, he could see traces of prior tears on her cheeks. Spotting a log nearby, he took a seat and made himself more comfortable.

"Do you want to talk about it?"

"Maybe." She shrugged.

"Can you tell me, Emma, what the problem is exactly? Can you put it into words?"

"I'm very frightened."

"Of?"

Emma tried to stem her grief long enough to speak. "I'm afraid Hayden is dead and I will never see him again. I'm afraid I will be left hurting and abandoned, heartbroken and lonely for the rest of my life. It is a very frightening thought and there's no one to talk to, no one that understands. All I get is lectures about courage and being childish."

"How old are you now?"

"Nineteen."

"That isn't very old, is it?"

Emma actually managed a smile. "I used to think it was plenty old enough, but it doesn't feel that way anymore. It was easy to be grown up when Hayden was here."

"I understand."

"Listen to me, Reverend Sanderson; here I am feeling so sorry for myself, being frightened over the what-ifs, and there you are, looking my very fears straight in the face, but for real. I should ask how you are doing."

"Well now, Emma that would be a very grown up thing indeed. In fact, there are many adults that wouldn't make it to that point at all."

"How are you doing?" she asked.

"Managing, barely at times, but making it somehow. Thank you for asking."

"I feel so ashamed. My burden can't be half of what yours is."

"Don't be so hard on yourself; your situation is very difficult. At least the outcome for mine has already happened."

"You are so sure of yourself. Isn't there anything you wonder about?"

"Of course; I wonder how my children and I will make it through this next year. Chris is so sad and tries too hard to fill the gaps left by his mother's passing."

"That is very sad."

Carlen looked up at the flickers of light filtering down through the canopy of trees. "It is. I probably worry more for him than anyone."

"Then you do worry. Are you afraid for him?"

Carlen smiled at her quick observations. "I'm concerned for him, but to be frightened…" he shrugged as his voice trailed off.

Emma looked into his eyes. "It's not having faith to be frightened; is it?"

"Maybe not exactly."

"That's one of the very many lectures I've been given. I could probably preach a full sermon on it myself."

"Well, that's tempting," he laughed. "Then I could take a vacation."

Emma laughed at that too. "The thing is, hearing something isn't the same as believing it. And trying to deny that I feel the way I do, doesn't change the way I truly feel."

"You're right about that."

"I fear so often for Hayden that sometimes I think I convince myself he is dead, just so I don't have to wonder."

Carlen nodded. "The unknown can feel tortuous at times, can't it? But what other roads are before you?"

"What do you mean?"

"Well, are there other choices you can make, honestly, feeling as you do?"

"Stop worrying, I suppose," she shrugged.

"It sounds like you're repeating sermons again."

Emma smiled sheepishly. "I suppose I am."

"Look into your heart, Emma. Do you really want to believe that Hayden is dead?"

"Oh, no, of course not! I want to believe that he is alive and well; but if he is, then why hasn't he written to me? Why has he disappeared as if from off the face of the entire living earth?"

"Is there any part of you that can believe he is still alive, but maybe in a situation that might keep him from writing?"

Emma shrugged and looked down at her feet hanging from the front of the rock. "The Larssens think he has been taken prisoner. Actually, they are convinced of it."

"Why do you suppose they feel that way?"

"Maybe to keep from worrying about him; I don't know. It doesn't seem very convincing to me. I've read about people getting letters and post cards from their husbands and sons in the prison camps. Surely, if he was alive, he would have managed to write."

Carlen smiled. "I highly doubt that many prison camps are that generous. Do you suppose it's possible he might be in a camp that didn't feel quite as kindly toward their captives?"

"Are there camps like that?"

"Oh," he laughed, "a very many, I'm afraid. I've read that some prisoners are able to sneak letters out, but Emma, most of them aren't going to be so considerate as to distribute paper and pencils to the prisoners and then pay for postage to send their letters home. I'm sure such circumstances would be rare indeed."

"I didn't know that."

"Does it give you any inkling of hope?"

Emma smiled and held her thumb and forefinger together with just the slightest bit of space between them.

Carlen smiled too. "Well then, that is an improvement; isn't it? Of course, you are free to believe whatever you will; but tell me, would you be happier clinging to that sliver of hope or resigning to a despairing outcome?"

"I think I'm afraid to hope. Maybe if I face the despair now, then when it is confirmed it won't be so painful to accept."

"When it is confirmed?"

"Well, if it is confirmed."

"And what about if it is never confirmed. The greater chances are that he is alive but not in a position to let you know."

Emma nodded. "I wish I could believe that."

"You can practice believing it. There is, after all, far more reason to believe he is alive than not. Think about it."

Emma was quiet after that, considering what the reverend had said before shaking her head. "It's just too frightening to let my heart hope," she admitted at last.

Carlen nodded his understanding. "I suppose that's why faith and hope are so closely tied. Do you still pray for him to come home?"

"I do, but not with much hope."

"Or faith?"

Emma lowered her eyes. "Yes, or faith." Suddenly, the young girl looked up, her face full of question. "Reverend Sanderson, do *you* think he is alive?"

Carlen was quiet for a moment and Emma suspected that he

was searching the feelings of his soul to discern the truth.

Nodding, he smiled at last. "I think I do."

"What if you are wrong?"

"What if I am right?" he countered. "If I am, then you have spent an awful lot of tears and despair on something that isn't true. You do realize that he is much safer as a prisoner than a soldier, don't you?"

Emma shook her head. "I hadn't thought of it that way."

"Then I guess you have a decision to make."

"What do you mean?"

"Well, do you want to continuing fearing the worst and grieving for something that probably hasn't happened? Or would you rather hope for something that is more realistic and which might bring you peace. Fear and faith do not keep a very harmonious company with each other."

Emma nodded. "Thank you, Reverend Sanderson. I will try a little harder to be brave, at least enough to hope."

"That's my Emma. Now, tell me what you think of the bakery. I was at the Larssen's earlier and the goods were incredibly delicious."

"Oh my goodness!" Emma cried out. "I forgot about the bakery and I was supposed to help cook today. Reverend Sanderson, they're going to think I don't care about it at all."

"I'm sure they understand."

Emma had climbed down from the rock and was brushing the wrinkles from her dress. "Maybe so, but I must go right now. They're probably wondering where I am."

"That they are."

"I'm sorry, Reverend, but thank you for finding me. I have to go." She waved as she started off down the road, walking with haste to the north.

"You'll think about our conversation?" he called out after her.

Emma, who had broken into a jog, stopped and turned around. "Yes, I will practice having faith. Thank you, Reverend Sanderson. Goodbye."

With that she waved and turned again on her way toward the other side of town, while Carlen started back toward his home.

"The Larssen Bakery," he whispered to himself. "Surely, it will be a gift to us all."

Chapter Twenty

Carroll's General Store

October 1918

A bell rang out above the door as the young man stepped from the misty rain outside and through the portal to a dry oasis. This was truly an old-fashioned place. Glancing up at the neatly braided garlic hanging from the ceiling by their stems, he nearly ran into a pickle barrel and then into an empty candy rack. Robby cringed at the disturbance. So much for going unnoticed.

Glancing further around the premises, he debated who best to approach in order to put his plan into action. Behind the counter stood an older woman with a black band around her arm, the all too commonly seen symbol of mourning. In front of the counter, a middle-aged lady quietly purchased black material. Was the entire town in mourning?

The shelves were mostly empty of canned foods and other long-term food items, however the glass-sided bakery cabinet was filled to bursting with delectable looking treats. Robby's mouth watered at the mere sight, but he had no cash to spare. Since being forced to assume responsibility for the orphanage, he had tried his best not to spend a cent on anything not essential.

Soon, a man stepped from the back room, also with a black band on his arm.

"May I help you?"

Taken aback by the question, Robby was unsure of what to say. He had only hoped to linger near people and gather information, not speak to anyone directly. Consequently, he hadn't formulated an alibi for his presence. He was young and very new at this.

"I… I got off at the wrong stop. I was only trying to escape the rain while waiting for the next train to come through. Do you mind if I loiter for a while and just look around?"

Sarah looked up from her cutting and smiled. "You're not from around here. How did you miss the quarantine sign? Aren't you afraid of the plague?"

Robby smiled too. Something about the old woman was inviting and effused kindness.

"I've already had it. I don't suppose you can catch it twice."

"What stop were you aiming for?" Dan Carroll asked.

"Amber Glen."

It was a lie, and Robby knew it, but how else would he find out what he wanted to know?

"There you go, Kelly," Sarah said, folding up the black silk and trimmings, wrapping them in brown paper and taping it all closed. "Why don't you pick out a pie for your family?"

"I couldn't, Mother; not with the quarantine and things so tight in the store."

"Please, take one," Dan insisted. "It's on the house. It's the least we could do to spread a little cheer."

"Yes," Sarah agreed. "Please, Kelly; take it home to John and the girls."

"All right," she finally conceded; "if you insist."

"That we do!" Dan declared.

When she turned to the pastry cupboard, Robby saw that she was also wearing a black armband.

Kelly looked through the cupboard, chose a cherry pie and brought it back to the counter, where Sarah wrapped it in brown paper and tape as well. Then she was off, out the door and putting her goods into the covered carriage.

Robby watched quietly through the store windows as she drove off down the road to the edge of town, beyond the brick pavers and onto the muddy road headed out to the country.

"Can I interest you in a piece of cake," Sarah asked the stranger.

"Thank you, but I don't have any extra money just now."

"It's on the house," Dan called out as he turned and disappeared once again to the back room.

"Free?" Robby asked. "Are you sure?"

"That's what the boss said." Sarah smiled, nodding toward the shelves.

"It's very generous of you. Thank you, very much."

As he stood before the pastries, pies and cakes, Robby was drawn to a flaky treat, drizzled with lines of white frosting.

"Is it all right to choose one of these instead?"

Sarah smiled again. "My raspberry tarts? Of course, but I'll have to warn you, you'll be back for more."

"Did you make everything here?"

"No, most of them are from the bakery. I only made the tarts."

"They look delicious!"

"People tell me they are. Go ahead and try it; I'll bet you can't eat just one."

What was it about this woman that seemed so pleasant and inviting? She could easily have been the resident grandmother of Silver Falls.

"You're in mourning?" Robby asked as he took a bite of the pastry.

"Yes, for Jimmy Layne. That was his mother who just left."

Robby perked at the name of Layne. "I'm so sorry to hear it," he offered. "Did he die from the plague?"

Sarah shook her head. "He was a soldier in the war. We just received word last week, though it's been a long time since we've heard from him. They buried him in France, months ago. He was only eighteen, you know, and such a good boy. We trust that he has gone to a far better place."

"I'm sorry; it's very tragic."

Robby finished off the last of the tart and began trying to subtly suck the frosting from his fingertips before he spoke again.

"Is he related to Nathan Layne?"

"Yes," Sarah answered carefully, "his nephew. How do you know Nathan?"

"Oh, no; I don't know him at all. I only heard his name mentioned on the train," the boy lied again. "I guess he is a man of some importance to the area, at least it seemed so, listening to the people talk."

"Pashaw," Sarah laughed. "He is president of the bank, when he's not wrestling horses or tending to his farm, that's all. He would never consider himself of any importance."

Robby looked skeptical. "Bank president and farmer?"

"Yes. Now, what did you think of that tart?"

"It was wonderful; truly the most delicious thing I've ever

eaten."

Robby had answered correctly. Many things gave Sarah Carroll pleasure, and seeing people enjoy her tarts was right up there at the top.

"Then you must have another and a fresh glass of milk; you look rather hungry."

Robby tried to resist, but it was useless. Sarah had another tart out and was calling to her husband to bring out a glass of milk for their guest.

Sitting down at the counter, the boy began to eat up. "Have you lost many men to the war?" he asked between bites.

"Jimmy is our only confirmed death, but others are missing."

"What about the plague? Has it hit here particularly hard?"

"No," Sarah replied. She didn't especially want to reveal that they hadn't actually contracted it yet, so she tried to think of a diplomatic answer. "We haven't lost many at all. Apparently, the ocean air is good for such things."

"Lucky for you," he stated. "It has ravaged Portland."

"Is that where you're from?"

Robby tried not to cringe at the fact that he had just slipped up and given more information than planned. "Yes, I am. I recently lost my family to it."

"Your whole family? Oh, I'm so sorry to hear that," Sarah offered. Stepping to the cabinet, she grabbed two more tarts just as Dan rounded the corner with a glass of milk. "Eat up," she encouraged the boy. "There's no sense facing grief and hunger both."

"Thank you very much; I appreciate your kindness. Is the quarantine affecting your store much?"

"Yes, very much, I'm afraid. Most people around here are barely hanging on to their livelihoods. As you can see, most of our shelves are empty. It's been difficult getting supplies since the quarantine began."

"I can understand their fears. Is the bank open? I'd love to get a peek at this Nathan fellow."

"You'd have to head south of town for that. The bank closed at three o'clock."

"How far from town?"

"Three miles south."

The young man shrugged. "A little far to walk in the rain, I guess. With the quarantine going on, what do you do for entertainment?"

Sarah smiled gently as she glanced out the window and across the road. "Emma Larssen occasionally sings at the restaurant, when there are customers. Other than that, the only excitement around here anymore are the prayer vigils. We meet once a month and share letters from anyone who has written. Harrisons probably have the biggest news. Their boys, Jason and Jonathan, recently became ace pilots."

"Ace? Don't they have to shoot down ten planes or something for that?"

"I think it's only five," Sarah corrected. "But they'd shot down eight last we heard."

"Have they seen the Red Baron?"

"Thank heavens, no! I guess he's met his maker at last, but it's been nerve-wracking in the meantime. Those boys will have enough stories to write a book when they get home. Their letters are entirely gripping."

"Did you know, he landed his plane in a field before he died?" Dan called out from the back.

Robby shook his head. "Enemy or not, that is an amazing pilot."

Sarah took a cloth to the counter and wiped off the strings from Kelly's most recent purchase. "Maybe so, but this town is all a little happier that our boys are safe from him now. We've shed no tears over his demise. Now then, what did you say your name was?"

"I didn't," he smiled, "but you can call me Mike."

With that, Dan rounded the corner from the back and began to untie his work apron. "Well, Mike, we're about to close up for the day here. I'm sorry to say it, but you'll need to wait for your train either at the station or the restaurant."

Robbie looked out the shop window at the sky. It was still drizzling gray and very wet outside.

"Fair enough," he nodded. "Thank you for the refreshments; you've been more than kind and I'll not soon forget it."

Sarah waved as Dan walked the young man to the door, letting him out, then closing and locking it tight behind him.

"What do you suppose that lad was looking for?" Dan asked as he watched him step onto the brick pavers of Main Street and then sprint for cover at the station.

"I don't know," Sarah answered. "But his name wasn't Mike; that much is certain. Well, 'cast your bread upon the waters,' as the Good Book says. Hopefully the kindness will return."

Chapter Twenty-one

The Inevitable Happens

November 1918

"Really? That's wonderful news! Thank you for letting us know!"

Nathan was all smiles as he replaced the ear piece to the phone and turned to see six questioning faces, all waiting to hear what could be so "wonderful" as to elicit his enthusiastic response.

"That was Janette," he began. "She just got word that the war is over!"

"Oh!" Hannah clasped her hands to her heart. "That is beyond wonderful! Now everyone will be coming home."

"Well, mostly everyone," Nathan added quietly.

Hannah nodded. "Yes, mostly."

There was quite a bit of happy chatter after that, as the children began to barrage their parents with questions.

"Does that mean Uncle Caleb will be home soon?" Meredith wanted to know.

"It will probably be a little longer," Nathan answered. "The war just barely ended. I'm sure it will take some time to get everyone back."

"How much longer?" Meredith persisted.

Clearly, she was concerned over the possibility of her short-lived medical career. Seeing through his daughter's transparent desires, Nathan smiled.

"You're probably safe for another month at least."

Meredith heaved a sigh of relief and only Melanie remained quiet, looking sallow and sad.

Noticing her daughter's somber mood, Hannah sought after her opinion on the matter. "What's wrong, my love? Aren't you happy about the war being over?"

"I don't feel so good," Melanie complained as she rested her head on the table.

All of the family stopped their chatter in unison and suddenly stared as though nothing else existed. Meredith, who was sitting next over, felt her sister's forehead and shouted in alarm.

"She has a fever!"

At her words, Hannah jumped to her feet, feeling her daughter's face. "She's burning up, Nathan. You don't suppose..."

Hannah didn't finish her sentence. No one wanted to say the actual words acknowledging that the deadly plague may have struck their home.

"It can't be possible," Nathan refuted. "She hasn't been anywhere that she would be exposed."

"Maybe it's just a fever from something else." Hannah was hopeful, though something in the pit of her stomach told her otherwise.

"Do you have a headache, Mellie?" Meredith asked.

"Yes," she answered quietly. "I'm just so tired. Mother, do you mind if I go back to bed?"

Standing from her chair, the young girl fought to steady herself, before collapsing into a heap at the side of the table.

"Mellie!" Hannah shouted, quickly gathering her daughter up into her arms.

Melanie briefly opened her eyes. "I'm so sorry, Mother. I didn't mean to catch it."

"Oh, Mellie, my love, it isn't your fault at all. Nathan, can you carry her to the front room?"

Nathan took the girl from Hannah's arms and hurried to settle her on the couch near the fire just as Meredith appeared with a glass of water for her sister.

"She needs fluids," Merrie announced. "Mel, can you drink this?"

"I... I think so," she whispered. As she attempted to lift her hand, it dropped back onto the surface of the couch.

"Just take a sip," Merrie encouraged, holding the cup near her sister's lips.

"Merrie, do you think this is necessary right now?" Nathan asked.

Meredith only shrugged. "It can't hurt. Uncle Peter said that when it struck, it was critical to get liquids down. She's already been through the night without any food or water."

"Drink, yes, but what good is water going to do to replace the food?"

"I put sugar in it," she answered. "It should help her, at least a little."

Hannah raised her brows and nodded, then began to encourage the girl to drink more. "Merrie's right, love; it can't hurt. Mellie, can you manage another drink?"

"I think so," she answered quietly, sipping on the beverage as she could.

Soon, Nathan was at her side with another cup. "Here's some grape juice from the pantry. It will certainly help more than sugar water."

"I'm sure you're right," Hannah answered. "Someone call Uncle Peter and let him know what's happened."

Nathan fidgeted nervously before leaving to see to the phone call, all while Melanie attempted to finish off the cup of juice before succumbing to sleep.

Hannah looked around the room, trying to decide how and where to set up a sick room. Melanie was going to need constant and close supervision and, unfortunately, she surely wouldn't be the only one to catch this dreaded illness. Soon, Nathan returned to the front room.

"Merrie was right. Peter said to have her drink whatever juice we could get into her. He said that even if we got lucky and it was only a three day fever, it would spread and we need to be prepared. He also suggested we start a pot of chicken soup right away; it's likely to hit quickly." Nathan started for the door and the chicken house. "Oh, and our house is officially under quarantine, so there won't be any help."

"We'll be fine," Hannah soothed, as the younger children looked up at her in fright. "We'll manage." Considering how the three girls always slept in the same bed, she began to assess the others. "Annie, how are you feeling? Does your head hurt or is your throat sore?"

"No," the little girl shook her head. "I feel fine."

"Merrie, what about you?"

"I'm fine too."

"Andy?"

"I have a headache, but only a little one," he tried to reassure her.

"Can you finish your breakfast? All of you try to finish your breakfast. Like Meredith said, we'll all be better off if we're not hungry from the night."

As the children started back to the kitchen, Hannah tried to get Melanie more settled and comfortable, plumping up the pillows of the couch around her. The sick room would need to be here in the front, where there was a fire. Should they all fall ill, they would be better off where one of them could maintain the fire.

In the next hour, a pot of soup was bubbling on the stove and Nathan began hauling Melanie's bedding to the main floor. Chase and Andy had their own mattresses, which were easy enough to move, but the girls all slept in one large bed. With great difficulty, he squished and pushed and folded and struggled until he finally had it down the narrow, curving staircase. Once he reached the bottom, he assessed Hannah's plans.

"Don't you think we should set her up in the back room and at least try to keep the illness isolated from the others?"

"What if we all get it at once?" Hannah asked.

Nathan shrugged. "We can only hope for the best."

Hannah looked worriedly around the house, lowering her voice to a whisper. "Oh, Nathan, what if one of us dies, or both, like those poor orphans you found in Portland?"

"Shh now, Hannah; we'll just have to do what we can and hope for the best. I'm sure it will all work out."

"But so many people have died from this."

"Yes," he soothed, "but so many more have lived. We have the ocean air, remember? Peter said it would be an advantage."

"But it's winter. It's not like we can spend the time outdoors to take advantage of it."

Nathan only looked at his wife with soft eyes and tried to smile. "We'll do our best," he shrugged. "It's all we can do."

"Mother, I'm afraid I'm getting it," Andy announced, coming to Hannah's side. "I feel so cold."

"But you're very warm with a fever. Here, lie down on the rug. Your dad will get your bed all set up just as soon as he can."

"I'm starting to feel sick too," Annie announced, holding her hand to her head.

"You might as well bring the rest," Hannah called out as Nathan headed back upstairs.

They soon had the mattresses lined up in the back room, complete with pillows, blankets and extra quilts.

"How are you feeling, Hannah?" he asked.

"I'm all right, so far. What about you?"

"Tired; getting the beds down seems to have taken most of my strength. I'd better get more wood brought in while I still can."

"Be careful, Nathan; don't push yourself too much."

"Well, someone has to bring it in. If we all get sick, we won't feel like traipsing outdoors clear to the woodpile for it."

"Then let's all go get it, those of us who are still well. You need to not push yourself any further."

*

Hannah forced her bleary eyes open long enough to look across the room, wondering who was moving through the house. Nathan was either asleep or unconscious on the rug near the fireplace and she could hear faint crying from the back room.

Closing her eyes again, she tried to remember what happened?! The last thing she knew, she was fighting exhaustion and a blinding headache.

"Soup..." she whispered, recalling that she had left the soup simmering on the stove. She remembered struggling to get to it and turn it off before it burned. Had she made it that far before all had gone black? She simply couldn't remember; everything had happened so fast. She tried to force her eyes open once again, but couldn't muster enough strength even for that.

Hannah heard the footsteps come near. Maybe it was Sarah, dear Sarah, coming to their aid. She felt arms go under her, lifting her from the floor and carrying her to the other room. She briefly wondered how Sarah could be so strong, but she could not summon her eyes to open. She felt those arms settle her onto the bed and cover her with quilts. She was so cold.

"Stove..." she managed in a small whisper.

"Yes, Hannah; don't worry. I turned off the stove."

"Sarah?" she called out. She tried to say it loudly, as loudly as she could manage, but the sound barely escaped her lips.

"No, Hannah, it's Carlen. I need to help Chase; he's crying. Are you all right for now?"

There was no answer to his question. She tried to acknowledge it, but the blackness was closing in around her mind again. Carlen and Sarah, she thought to herself in those final few seconds before her mind closed completely. They would take care of Chase; they would turn off the stove. In her misery, she sank back into the relief of unconsciousness, while choking coughs sounded from the front room and the footsteps walked quickly away.

It was three more days before she recovered enough to make sense of her surroundings. The first thing she heard was Melanie's voice, clear and sweet, conversing in the other room, then the boys, Andy and Chase, began jabbering as well. She was glad for that; the plague had confined itself to a three-day fever for them. However, she could still hear the heavy, wracking coughs from the front of the house. Weak and dizzy, she did her best to leave her bed and check on the others.

Walking to the doorway, she paused to observe the scene. Carlen was bent over Nathan, a cup of steamy broth in his hands, urging him to drink, though Nathan did not respond.

"Try a spoon," she strained at the words to speak. "It's slow... but it works."

Carlen was surprised to see her up and so coherent. "You shouldn't be up," he censured. "Go back to bed, Hannah; I'll bring some broth right in."

"No," she shook her head, managing to take a seat nearby. "I think I can get it myself. Are the children all right?"

"Yes. Merrie and Chase are still weak, but they're all eating lunch in the kitchen."

"How is Nathan?"

"Very weak; it's gone into pneumonia for him. He should pull through though." Shaking his head, Carlen continued. "Every time I look at him, I remember how it felt. He seems to have taken it hardest of all."

At that point, Nathan erupted into another spasm of choking coughs.

"Are you sure he's okay?"

Carlen nodded. "Peter has been coaching me over the phone,

as he has with everyone else. Either way, we should know soon."

Hannah would like to have gone to her husband's side right then, to smooth the hair from his forehead and tend to him herself, but she had barely made it to the chair and was incredibly weak.

"How long have you been here?" she managed.

"Four days, off and on."

"Four days? What about your family?"

Carlen smiled. "They are fine. Your mother-in-law is taking care of them for me and, despite the chaos in town, I dare say they are happier than they've been in a long time. I'm afraid I haven't been the most doting parent of late. From what I hear, Sarah's cooking is food for the soul. With the store closed, she said she has plenty of time to spend on the children."

"Sarah." Hannah smiled. It was true; Sarah could cook like no other and her meals were solace to both body and heart. "How did those arrangements come about?"

"Peter came over to check on you and saw half the family lying on the floor. He remembered that I'd already had it and would be immune, so he asked if I would come help out. He arranged for Sarah to take my children. It was the least I could do. I would have died had you both not found me. Anyway, people are pretty much afraid to leave their homes now, though it is spreading quickly despite that."

Hannah shook her head. "I don't understand how we caught it."

"George's family. Apparently, Melanie was visiting with Grace just before she fell ill. They think George brought it home from the bank. One of their customers broke the quarantine, traveling to Tillamook. He came into the bank to make a deposit when he came home and fell ill that night."

"Has anyone died?" Hannah wanted to know.

"Not that I've heard, but it's spreading fast. Since doctors have some of the highest mortality rates, Peter has been very cautious, but it's only a matter of time. He estimates that nearly half the town has it now. He's hoping it has weakened though, being that the death rate has been so low."

"Who took care of George and his family?"

"I have; I've been making the rounds under Peter's direction. I suppose I'll continue as long as I can; but enough about me. I'll get some broth and we'll see if we can't get you back on your feet."

Hannah tried to stand, thinking she would walk to the kitchen, but sank back into the chair and decided to let Carlen do as he'd suggested. Though she was beginning to feel a little better, she still greatly lacked the basics of strength.

As he brought her a cup of steaming soup, she watched her husband's breaths come and go. The children were steadily recovering, but Nathan wasn't faring well at all. His breathing was so heavily labored.

"I'm worried about Nathan; are you sure he's okay? He sounds terrible."

Carlen nodded. "He definitely has the worst of it. Even with Peter's updates, this illness is just so new; no one really knows what to expect. We've never had anything like it to compare."

"You have to wonder why it strikes the strong so much harder than the weak."

"It's a mystery at this point, but drink up," he smiled again. "I'm sure you'll be right as rain in no time."

Carlen was correct about one thing; within an hour of finishing the soup, she began to feel a hint of energy seep back into her system. As soon as she could, she began tending to the children, though Carlen insisted on caring for Nathan himself. It took Hannah a while to convince him otherwise.

"Let me give it a go," she said that afternoon, as the reverend relinquished his place and let her attempt to coax her husband into taking some nourishment.

Taking a spoon, she filled it half-full and let it drip from its side in between his lips. Bit by tiny little bit, she ladled the clear soup, merely drops at a time. It reminded her so much of another era and time when she had done the same for Laurel.

At one point, Nathan opened his eyes, no more than narrow slits, but he met her gaze before closing them again. When he did, she knew that he would do his best to recover, if nothing else than for her.

Soon, the phone began to ring, one short ring and two long; it was their line.

"I'll get it," Carlen offered. "I'm sure it's Peter, checking in on

Nathan again."

Hannah watched him go to the kitchen and then listened for details as he answered. There was some little conversation on Carlen's part, and then it was quiet for a while after that. Finally, the minister said goodbye, hung up the ear piece and returned to the front room.

"Was it Pete?" Hannah asked.

"It was Alannah; the flu has finally reached them. Peter is down with the fever and she thinks the children are getting it as well. Let's hope it has weakened."

"Are you going over there now?"

"Soon. Are you feeling well enough, Hannah, if I leave Nathan in your care? I can still check in, and you can call for me if there is a problem."

"Did you get a phone?"

Carlen smiled. "No, but you can call around for me."

"Thank you, Carlen." Looking over at him, she noticed for the first time the deep weariness in the reverend's eyes. "I don't know that we would've made it without you."

"It was my pleasure," he smiled. "I'll be at Peter's tonight and elsewhere before then, but call me if you need help."

"Where else besides Peter's?"

"I need to check in with John and George, then out to see Agnes Dane. She's down with a serious case of it as well."

"Agnes Dane?" Hannah gasped.

For a moment she sat speechless, wondering at the audacity of the woman, to slander the minister's good name as she had and then expect him to tend to her illness.

"There is no one else who will care for her," Carlen smiled and then shrugged. "It is a sweet irony, I suppose."

"Or a bitter one," Hannah ruminated. "How dare she ask you for help after all she has done to sully your reputation? And not yours alone." Hannah shook her head again, still in wonder over the way things had turned out.

Carlen shrugged as he headed for the door. "She is sure to survive it."

"Why do you say that?"

Carlen shook his head. "I'm certain she's too ornery to die."

Hannah laughed. "That has to be the least charitable thing

I've ever heard you say."

"It's not the least charitable of my thoughts," he confessed. "Oh well, cast your bread upon the waters, right?" he finished.

With that, he opened the door, waved goodbye to the family and started on his way through the misty rains and waning light to Parish Road.

Chapter Twenty-two

News from the Front

December 1918

Frigid ocean mists gathered on the tree branches, threating to freeze into icicles before dripping down to the ground. These were the drops that landed upon the windshield as Marian drove slowly down the lane alongside Silver Brook, carefully avoiding the potholes and extra muddy places. It was all fine enough for a horse and buggy, or a harvest wagon, but her little coupe motor car hadn't been serviced since before Caleb left for the war. Even worse, it had been in need of attention before that and had, of late, become frequently temperamental, dying on her at the most inopportune times. The last thing she wanted was to be stranded on Nathan's driveway, either in a mud hole or some other murky place in between.

Slowly closing in on the house, she breathed a sigh of relief to see a brick-paved area ahead. Here, she stopped the car and turned off the engine, not even completing the distance to the hitching post. It blocked the driveway a little, yes, but she seriously doubted that anyone would be leaving before her.

Silver Falls was so different from her beloved mountain home, and while Colorado had its fair share of pot holes and mud, it at least froze over solid during the winter months, giving a reprieve to such things from December through February.

Marian had contemplated going home for the time that Caleb was away. Ben, Paul, and Alice were all overseas as well; if she could only talk Emma into leaving with her, they could have spent that lonely time among family with which they were both a little more familiar. However, Emma would hear nothing of it; she wanted to be in the very place Hayden had left her, should he ever return... or news of his demise reach home. Not feeling she could leave her youngest alone in such circumstances, Marian had stayed.

Leafing through the letters in her purse now, she selected the one she wanted to share, a post from Caleb that had information for Nathan and Hannah. Then she disembarked the coupe and hurried against the heavy mists, up the stairs and onto the porch of the little stone house across the brook to knock on the front door.

"Marian! Come in."

Hannah greeted her sister-in-law with a friendly embrace and ushered her into the house. Nathan, wrapped in a quilt before the fire, made an attempt to stand, though Marian quickly waved him off.

"Don't stand on my account, Nathan. I'd rather you spent your energies getting well."

"I'm working on it; I really feel much better," he answered, shortly before erupting into a fit of violent coughing.

Marian smiled. "You need to work on it harder; you don't sound at all convincing."

Nathan only nodded and pulled the quilt tighter around himself as he sat in his chair before the fire. At that point, Marian turned to Hannah.

"Where are the children?"

"Upstairs. Meredith was reading a book to them last I checked. I'm sure they'll be down as soon as they realize there is company on which to eavesdrop."

"Well, before they do, I have a letter from Caleb to share with you."

"Wonderful! By all means, let's hear it while there is still some peace in the house."

Marian settled onto the couch, and retrieved the letter from the envelope. "I'll skip all the introductory parts..."

"Don't skip too much," Nathan interrupted. "We're all very interested in what's happening over there."

"Alright, well, let's see." She perused the beginning and then started to speak.

I am still in the hospital at Reims. While many of our patients have gone home, many others here are in no condition to travel as yet. Additionally, the hospital has been opened up to service the local population. There is so much starvation and attendant disease, not to mention we are still seeing new cases of the pandemic; I'm afraid my duties will be required for some time more. It goes without saying that we're also still in dire need of nurses, so Alice will be staying on a while longer as well. I saw Paul just yesterday and he thought he might be able to leave for home soon. There are no more casualties coming in on the trains, but the army has kept him remarkably busy in the meantime doing all sorts of odd jobs.

It is amazing to consider all the work that goes into the business of war. While there is much relief on everyone's part for an end to the fighting, there is still so much work that continues, providing civil authority, staying the famine, reestablishing local governments and dismantling the unnecessary parts of the old supply lines. Consequently, many of the soldiers were transitioned into civil forces, who attempt to distribute food to the starving citizens on both sides of the line. Those left behind constitute a moderate city, requiring meals and services; it all takes many people continuing to work almost as though there has been no change. As one area is stabilized, the rest merely go on to their work in the next place. It will be at least another month or two, possibly even three, before I will be able to leave.

At least there is peace to greet us and no more shelling in the distance. I use that word, peace, loosely. The city streets are often a riotous place at night with crime and chaos. It is strange to see how low people sink when left without the order of government. Additionally, many soldiers occupy their evenings with copious amounts of liquor, which occasionally lands them into our care. I suppose they are trying to escape the horrors of war that still haunt them, but I wish they would stay sober long enough to get home and occupy their own local physicians with the business.

I was glad to hear about Emma working with the Larssen's bakery, and also that she has been singing at The Falls. I believe her voice has a gift of bringing joy not just to others, but to herself as well.

I was sorry to hear that Nathan is still so ill. Tell Hannah to give him lots of fluids, especially hot mullein tea and honey; it will help to clear his lungs. We've had a lot of success with it over here.

While on the subject of Hannah and Nathan, and their little Meredith... I hear that my job at home might be in jeopardy, at least according to our little niece. She wrote to me last month to ask if I could stay in France a little longer so that she could "continue her medical practice with Uncle Peter."

I'm not really sure what that's all about, but if you could let Meredith know that I am complying with her wishes and staying a while more.

"Oh dear!" Hannah exclaimed. "I had no idea she had written to him. Please let Caleb know that we're sorry! There is no threat to his job at all."

Marian only laughed. "I'm sure he understands. She is such a precocious child though; I don't know how you manage her."

"Obviously we don't," Nathan piped in.

"Please continue on with the letter," Hannah urged.

Marian turned the pages back and forth. "That's mostly it. Just a few personal notes and mild complaints over the cold."

"I wonder how much longer they'll have to stay."

Marian shook her head. "I don't know, but at least there is no more war to worry about. Once he is relieved of his duties, Caleb plans to stay only long enough to try and secure some kind of information about Hayden."

Hannah lowered her voice, just in case any children might be within earshot. "Now that the fighting has ended, you would think all the prisoners would have been released."

"Caleb said the Germans held more than two million prisoners of war. I imagine their release would take a while. So many people!"

Nathan agreed. "I suppose they can't just turn them all loose on the neighboring towns and villages. Some might want revenge and take it out on German citizens."

Hannah thought about that. "You would think they'd just be happy to get home as fast as they could."

"Auntie Marian!" Melanie called out. "Hey guys, we have company!"

With that, a herd of little feet scrambled down the stairs and into the front room. The quiet of the moment was effectively over.

"All right, children," Nathan called out, "give your aunt some room to breathe."

"I hear you've all been reading stories."

"Grimm's Fairy Tales," Annie announced.

"How do you like them?"

"The boys like them," Meredith answered. "I think they're quite morbid."

"Well put," Marian agreed. "I guess you're enjoying your medical training?"

Meredith looked suddenly sober. "Um... yes."

Seeing the letter in her aunt's hand, she didn't dare to pursue the matter, though her father wasn't about to let it pass.

"What's this about you telling Uncle Caleb to stay in France?"

Meredith's sobriety took on ashen proportions.

"Um..."

"It's a bit rude, don't you think?"

"I wasn't trying to be rude; I just thought Uncle Caleb might appreciate another letter from family."

Nathan shook his head. "A letter telling him not to come home?"

Meredith dropped her eyes, while the rest of the children sat in classic silence. It was the predictable pattern, that if one was in trouble, perhaps the others wouldn't be noticed if they were silent and still enough.

"I'm sorry," she whispered. "Auntie Marian, will you tell him I'm sorry?"

Marian was about to agree to Merrie's terms of penance, when Nathan shook his head.

"Not good enough, little Miss. You will write an apology letter yourself, and I want to read it to make sure it's sufficient before it's sent."

"Yes, sir." Merrie fully moped while acknowledging the verdict.

"I suggest you get to it right now," her father continued.

"Yes, sir."

With that, the girl rose and started for the stairs with all the other children in tow. Grimm's fairy tales were fine entertainment, but a penance letter from Merrie to their Uncle Caleb was sure to be even better. As the last child's footsteps rounded the corner on the stairs, Marian smiled.

"I see you haven't lost your authority around here. It's good to know you are well enough for that."

"I'm fine," Nathan assured her. "I'll be back on my feet in no time."

Hannah smiled and nodded. "Yes, and tell Caleb I will be sure to make lots of mullein tea and honey until he is."

"That I'll be happy to do."

With her visit done, Marian bid her in-laws goodbye and then made her way through the misty rain back out to her car. While there was still a quarter mile of mud and potholes out to the main road, and another three miles of the same before safely reaching the brick pavers of town, it did not presage the future of her life. She could see that the end was clearly in sight. A few more months and Caleb would be home, hopefully with better news than they'd been able to garner to date.

Life would soon return to normal, pot holes and mud or not, and she would hold on with the promise of that hope for the future

Chapter Twenty-three

Surprise Delivery

January 1919

The early evening train pulled into Amber Glen station allowing the few residents belonging to this stop to depart. Though a majority of the area had already suffered the influenza, the trains were still largely empty, with only an occasional civilian or returning soldiers here and there. Robby wondered if the lack of civilians was from lingering fear, or if there were just so few people left.

He had monitored the situation in Silver Falls as closely as he could, but it was difficult at best. The children left to him were those who had survived the prior outbreak, and despite the bone-weary exhaustion that such a load had caused, he didn't want them left to a situation that might be worse than where they'd been.

Checking his parcel, he waited until the last person had left before stepping from the passenger car himself; the last thing he needed was to be noticed. Unlike Silver Falls, Amber Glen offered a livery near the station where he could secure a horse and buggy. Luckily, it was still in business. Gathering his bundle, he quickly walked the short distance, paid his fee and was soon ready to go. Everything was set and he had planned this out to the finest detail.

Now, as the sun sank over the frosty horizon, he started his horse on its way. Under cover of darkness, he would make the first delivery. It was several miles to his destination, and in the quiet of the night he couldn't help but consider the circumstances.

The delay of his plan due to the plague had made life much more difficult than he had dreamed. He was nearly out of money for everything - food, train fare, and livery fees. Any future means while he cared for the orphans would come to him only through the humiliation of street begging. This was to be the first of a very few visits, simply because he could not afford to do it any other way.

He had done his research, subtly asking around, and felt assured that the Laynes were not only good people, but that they had all survived the illness and were now well on the mend. This particular package had been hand-picked to test out the reputation of their kindness, as it was the most irresistible of the lot.

Soon, the darkness closed completely around them, as horse and driver struggled to make out their course through the faint lamplight attached to the rigging of the carriage. Quiet and deserted, the road offered only metal horse shoes and carriage springs to break the silence of his quest. The air was bitter cold, with the wind blowing off the ocean while the horse trotted along. All the while, the young man shielded the bundle with his narrow frame, occasionally adjusting the basket closer to his side and away from the elements.

Eventually, he crossed the bridge over Silver Brook, rounded the corner, and stopped a few hundred feet from the drive. Here, Robby tied the horse to a tree and retrieved the covered basket from the buggy seat. Looking, first one way and then the other to make sure he was alone, his stomach knotted and gnarled from the apprehension of what he had to do.

Keeping to the shadowy edges, he crept silently down the lane, set the basket on the porch, gave it a jiggle, and then retreated back to his predetermined hiding place where he would wait to see what happened next.

*

"What was that?" Melanie asked.

"What was what?" her mother replied.

"Listen. Can you hear it?"

All activity in the household came to a halt as everyone tried to hear the sound. Meanwhile, Melanie followed her ears to the front door.

"I heard it again; I think it's outside."

"I heard it too," Merrie agreed.

Opening the large wooden portal, Mellie let out an awestruck gasp. "There's a baby on our porch!"

Hannah was immediately on her feet and at the door. Lifting the basket, she brought it inside and set it on the couch before the fire. Here she proceeded to unfold the layers of cloth in an attempt to inspect the child inside.

"There's a note," Melanie announced, handing the paper to her mother.

Please accept Annabelle into your home. Her parents are deceased and she has no other known relatives. I can't feed her anymore and relinquish all custody. She is three months old, or thereabouts. God bless you for your kindness.

Hannah turned the paper over, looking for more information on the back, but there was nothing. Lifting the infant from the basket, she was awestruck in wonder as she cradled the babe in her arms.

"Can we keep her?" Andy asked.

"Yes, can we?" the girls chorused.

"I don't know what to say," Hannah whispered. "I hardly know what to think. Who would leave a baby on someone's porch, not knowing who they were or if the child would be safe?"

Walking to her chair near the fire, she gazed at the pink cheeks and rosebud lips, all while the child gazed back with large blue eyes. Little tufts of strawberry-blond hair peeked out from the sides of her bonnet.

"She looks healthy," Hannah mused further. "Andy, run out to the barn and get your father. He needs to see this."

The boy quickly heeded the request while the rest of the children gathered closely around the new baby, completely entranced at the sight. In the next minute, Nathan entered the kitchen door and came quickly to his wife's side.

"What's going on?"

"Someone left her on our doorstep; her name is Annabelle." Hannah looked up at him with shining eyes. "She's beautiful, Nathan."

Nathan took the child from Hannah's arms and inspected her closely, as if hoping to find some hidden letter telling them more about her.

"It's hardly shocking," he said at last. "What with that plague killing so many young parents and orphans wandering the streets; but why did they choose us?"

"I don't know. I've never heard of anything like this in Silver Falls before."

Finally Nathan handed the babe back to his wife. "We've talked about adopting a child from the orphanage, Hannah, it's not a new thought; but it appears one has found us instead. I suppose it is the least we can do to help out where we can. Surely, we can find room for one more in our home."

"Do you mean we can keep her?" Melanie gasped the question which all the others were thinking. She was so excited now that she could scarcely stand still.

"Unless someone comes looking for her, then I think we'd better," her father answered. "Who would take care of her otherwise?"

Hannah nodded in agreement as she stood before the window, happiness flooding through her heart while she lifted the baby to her shoulder. "We'd better dig out those bottles again. We're going to need clothes and diapers too. Girls, go upstairs and find the baby things that are packed away in the attic. Nathan, what will we do for her bed?"

Nathan, still trying to absorb the information of what had just happened, merely shrugged his shoulders. "She's pretty small; the cradle we used for Marianne is just upstairs as well. It won't even be dusty."

Hannah thought back for a moment over the days she had cared for Carlen's little daughter. How long ago had that been? Four months?

"I suppose Marianne was a blessing for this child. We are all still quite in practice from her."

Deep in thought, Nathan glanced out the window, wondering who would leave a baby this way and again, why they had chosen his home. Looking back at the wistfully happy expression on his wife's face, he smiled and headed for the attic.

Outside the house, from his hiding place in the brambles, Robby strained to view the last of the commotion. It had worked; Annabelle was safely placed.

Stealthily feeling his way in the darkness back out to the waiting carriage, he hurried away in the direction he had come, silent and unnoticed.

Heaving a sigh, he whispered. "One child down; twelve to go."

Chapter Twenty-four

Overflowing

January 1919

Annabelle flourished under the doting attention of so many adoring caregivers. Melanie was especially quick to her aid at the first hint of a whimper. Since she had been the one to discover the beautiful baby with her fair, peach colored curls, she felt especially bound to her and very much obliged to attend her every need.

Though she was not yet twelve, Melanie helped her mother with the laundry, cooking, and cleaning without so much as being asked and requiring minimal direction. Her favorite task of all was feeding that little bundle of cooing smiles. With the exception of their brief time in caring for Marianne Sanderson, the Laynes had never even owned a baby bottle. Feeding Annabelle now was, for Mellie, the closest thing to heaven that her young, maternal heart could absorb.

Hannah was relieved at the ready help, which made caring for this baby easier than any she'd known in the past, allowing life to quickly settle into a very comfortable routine. After a thorough examination, Peter happily pronounced her as healthy and whole. Though she was a little thin at the beginning, she always ate well and inside of two weeks, she had gained as many pounds and was sleeping through most of the nights.

Nathan also quickly adjusted to the idea of adding another child to their clan. He was enjoying that novelty one cold, rainy night as they were all gathered in the front room near the fire. Suddenly, the sound of a child's cry came from the area of the front door. He and Hannah both looked at each other with widened eyes while the older children rushed to open the door and see to the distress outside.

Hannah was gathering Annabelle in her arms in preparation to follow when she stopped cold in her steps at the sight. Nathan also stood still, stunned at what he saw. There, on the porch, were not only three more baskets, each holding babies of differing sizes, but four other children, not one of them older than five! Each had a note pinned to their blankets or clothing and two of the toddlers sat on the porch, crying after whomever had ventured to leave them.

"Please accept this child into your home," each note began, explaining as with the last, that they were orphans with no living kin and that the original caregiver could no longer provide for them. The notes were all in the same careful handwriting as Annabelle's had been.

The entire family stood spellbound for some time before coming to their senses enough to gather the children into the house and out of the frigid cold of the blackened and stormy night.

"They can't be far off," Nathan announced. "Should I go after them? They can't just abandon seven children on our doorstep."

"No, don't leave us," Hannah pleaded. "We need you right now to help with these children. They are chilled and wet, every one of them. Andy, fill up the tub with warm water; we need to get them warmed up quickly."

Hannah passed Annabelle to Melanie and lifted an inconsolable toddler to her shoulder as she directed the rest of the family in what needed to be done.

"Meredith, warm up the stew on the stove and mash a part of it for the littler ones. They look half-starved. Annie, run up and try to find any pajamas you can that might fit them. Oh, dear; Nathan, what are we going to do?"

"I don't know Hannah; bathe them, dress and feed them, I suppose. I'm sure the scoundrel has gotten away by now."

It took more than two hours and the whole family working together to get so many children bathed and warmed up, then dressed and fed. Hannah was right in her assessment; they were beyond hungry. However, given a good meal, it became obvious that they were also wearied and worn from the ordeal of their abandonment. As they began to nod off to sleep in the front room, she could only shake her head at the situation.

"Where will they sleep? How will we ever take care of so very many children? Oh, the poor little things."

Nathan, who was still ruminating over the nerve of whomever had abandoned them, hadn't even made it that far in his thoughts. "I don't know, love. I suppose we can make up beds for them in the back room, but I don't know what we'll use tonight."

"What about the rug?" Hannah mused. "We could spread that out on the floor in the corner and put a quilt over the top. That will take care of the toddlers, but what about the babies?"

"I suppose we'll just have to bed them down in their baskets for now," Nathan shrugged. "There really isn't much more we can do tonight. I'll call around in the morning and see what we can gather up among the family."

Hannah shook her head in wonder. "We're going to need more food as well. We don't have near enough put up for the winter to feed such a crowd. Maybe we can call the Larssens and have the wagon come by first thing."

Nathan nodded absently. "Yes, bread will help. Maybe we should call them tonight."

The words had barely left his lips when the clock began to chime the half-hour. It was eleven-thirty and both Hannah and Nathan could scarce but stare at the numbers. The last four hours had fled faster than could be noticed.

"Tomorrow, first thing," he noted to himself. "Come, children; it's very late. Let's have prayer and try to get some rest."

*

It was a long night and an early morning that greeted the bleary eyes of the Laynes. Annabelle had not been a difficult adjustment, but three more babies, crying in the night to be fed and burped and changed was another story altogether. Added to that, four other toddlers, confused and frightened by their new surroundings, wandered through the house in the night, calling for the mothers who could not come to them.

By the time the rooster began to crow, anyone of age enough to help was walking around in a daze, trying to quiet the crowd while tending to their needs. The orphans were all very timid, which was actually more help than not, since wandering through the night had exhausted them as well, making their supervision the tiniest bit more manageable.

Hannah put in the call for baked goods at the crack of dawn, while Nathan took Clyde and Clementine around with the wagon, gathering up what beds and blankets any of their family or neighbors could spare. There was still sickness in the area and, remembering his own hard weeks of recovery, Nathan chose carefully.

By early afternoon, he had the sleeping arrangements set up, all while Hannah busied herself in the kitchen, trying to organize the family into ranks enough to see that each child was fed and clean. Meredith fed one of the babies, while Melanie cared for another. Annie and Andy helped with the toddlers, leaving Hannah with Annabelle, Chase and the final infant. It was impossibly chaotic.

When lunch was finally over and the children settled down in their new beds for naps, Hannah nearly collapsed into her chair in the front room. Slowly, the rest of the family gathered near the fire as well. All seemed to heave a collective sigh of relief at the sudden quiet of eight new children under the age of five, sleeping soundly in their naps.

"Oh dear," Hannah whispered to herself. "I don't even know what to call them; how will we ever figure out their names? Andy, will you bring me the notes that came with them, please?"

The papers were retrieved and Hannah read through the stack. "Albert, Bessie, Eliza Mae, Henry, Joseph, James, and William. Which belongs to whom?" she asked as she shook her head.

"Bessie is the older girl," Melanie piped up. "I remember that; and I'm pretty sure Albert was one of the babies."

"Yes, Albert was a baby," Meredith agreed.

"Okay, so Albert is one of the babies; but there are two other infants as well."

"We can ask the older children when they've woken from their naps," Nathan put in. "By process of elimination we should be able to figure out the rest."

"Yes, I suppose you're right," Hannah agreed as she rested her head against the back of the chair and closed her eyes, "but we can't possibly keep so many children, Nathan. We'll need to find homes for them."

"Even Annabelle?" Melanie asked sadly.

"No, my love; we will keep Annabelle, at the very least."

"How many others can stay?" It was Annie, coming in from the other room who asked this last question.

"We'll see, Annie. First we need to find out if there are other families who would like more children."

Suddenly, Nathan let out a tired chuckle. "A family of fifteen? I think you are right, Hannah. We need to see who else would like to share in the blessings."

"Oh, there's the bakery wagon now," Hannah announced. "I'll take care of that if the rest of you want to catch a nap with the babies."

"No naps for me," Nathan replied in a very weary way. "I've got far too much wood to chop just to keep the hearth burning and the house warm. Andrew, do you want to nap, or help me? You're one of the older men around here now."

Andy brightened at that proclamation and quickly followed his father out the kitchen door as Hannah answered a knock at the front of the house.

"Where are they?" Elise asked. "I simply must see this to believe it."

Hannah smiled and then whispered. "Follow me."

"Oh, but they're precious!" Elise smiled over the scene of so many tiny, sleeping children. "Emma needs to see this; it would surely cheer her up."

"How is our dear Emma?" Hannah asked.

"Still not herself; but she has begun working more regularly, which keeps her mind busy at least. She's hoping that busy hands will help heal her heart; it can't hurt. Either way, I'm sure she'll come around eventually. We're all greatly saddened over Hayden's disappearance, but she has taken it so hard, even harder than I, if that is possible."

Hannah nodded. "It is a horribly bitter pill to swallow."

"Well, let's see to those loaves you ordered."

Walking outside to the waiting wagon, Hannah waved to David Larssen and then followed Elise to the back. "Do you have anything extra?" she asked. "I can't help but think that a sweet morsel or two might help cheer the little ones up as well."

"Well then, let's see what isn't spoken for. It looks like we have plenty of Jelly rolls, three cream puffs, applesauce donuts and..." Elise was combing through her inventory, "... three more cream puffs and a couple of cherry pies."

Hannah rubbed her hands together in exaggerated

excitement. "I'll take it all! It will save me having to bake for the rest of the week."

Elise smiled as she looked back toward the house. "Well, maybe half a week, if you are lucky."

Tallying the items into the Layne's account, she eventually gathered the goods into baskets. Handing two to Hannah, she carried three more, filled with the several loaves of bread and pies, into the kitchen to be put away.

As she left the house, back out for the wagon, Elise shook her head. "It's going to be a challenge feeding a crew of such numbers."

Hannah nodded and sighed. "Yes, but having the Larssen Bakery come around will surely help."

"We thank you most kindly for your business," David added as he tipped his hat to Hannah.

"Oh, thank you both so much. You can't imagine how it has helped already."

With another wave, the wagon was off and Hannah nearly danced into the house to gather her children into the kitchen for all the merry refreshments. One entire chore was done for the week, or at least half of a week, as Elise had said. Either way, for now, she would treat her children to jelly rolls and milk and enjoy the moment of quiet that they had.

Soon, the babies would be awake, but that was at least an hour and a jelly roll of joy away.

Chapter Twenty-five

Emma Comes for a Visit

January 1919

It wasn't three days before Hannah was on the phone to the Larssens again, begging another delivery of bread and whatever else they could spare. This time when the wagon arrived, it was not only David and Elise, but Emma along with them. Hannah, waiting anxiously for the goods to arrive, saw them as soon as they had turned into the drive and met them at the bottom of the porch.

"Emma!" she called out with a wave as she walked out to greet them.

"Hello, Auntie Hannah."

Emma managed a rare smile as she returned the wave and climbed down from the wagon. Soon, she was welcomed into Hannah's arms for a warm hug.

"We've missed you," Hannah whispered.

"I've missed you too," Emma answered back. "Do you mind if I see the children?"

"They're all in the house; go on in."

Emma soon disappeared while Hannah approached the back of the wagon hopefully. "What do you have for us today?"

"I brought a sampling of sweet butter," Elise answered. "We're considering the possibility of adding that to our fare, if there is enough demand anyway."

"Oh, definitely sign us up!" Hannah laughed. "We barely have enough milk for the babies and certainly not enough cream for butter; we're completely out."

"I have some on the wagon now; do you want it?"

"I don't want to take all your samples."

"No, it's fine," Elise insisted. Loading up the first basket, she placed the crocks of butter on the bottom and the bread on top. "We're also fully stocked with donuts, jelly rolls, cakes, and pies." Elise nearly burst into laughter at the look on Hannah's face. "We decided to come here first this time. I think you have more need than most of our other customers."

"Oh, yes; thank you very much."

Once again, Elise helped Hannah carry all the many goods into the house and settle them on the kitchen counters.

"I have your other baskets to return there by the icebox," Hannah remembered. "I'm sure you can't have many extras."

Elise laughed as they both gathered up the growing pile. "Lauren will be happy to see these. Making baskets has become almost a constant pastime for her; we are always running low."

When they came out of the kitchen, Emma was standing at the doorway to the back room, looking in on the youngest children, still sleeping in their morning naps. Hannah handed the baskets off to Elise and approached Emma's side.

"You must be terribly busy," Emma mused.

Hannah nodded. "Very busy, but I have five good helpers, so it's not as bad as it might otherwise seem."

"How will you manage with thirteen children?"

"We're hoping to find homes for most of them. We're still trying to decide how many we might be able to keep with us. We've been through extraordinary times, Emma. I suppose we all need to do our part to help each other through."

Emma looked at her aunt rather timidly, as though she might have something on her mind but wasn't sure if she should voice it. Finally, she collected her courage and spoke.

"Do you mind if I help you with them today?"

Hannah smiled and gathered her niece's face into her hands, kissing her on both cheeks. "I would love nothing better, my dear Emma, as long as the Larssens can manage without you."

"I'm sure we'll be fine," Elise nodded.

Truthfully, Elise was rather relieved to see Emma take an honest interest in something, anything. She hoped that seeing the children would have the power to cheer the girl up, somehow, even if for nothing more than comparing her own plight to theirs.

At a call from David Larssen outside, urging her along, Elise bid her farewells and closed the door behind her.

"Are you enjoying the bakery?" Hannah asked.

"I suppose," Emma shrugged. "It is at least earning my keep; but tell me about the orphans. I really don't want to talk about the bakery today. How will you find families for them?"

"John and Kelly are considering one of the older boys, and your cousin, Frederick, in Colorado, said he knows a good family who might take two. There are a few other couples we haven't spoken to yet, but we're hopeful of finding good homes for most of them. Annabelle will stay with us, and possibly one or two more. I guess it will just depend on how many good homes we can locate for them. We may need to keep more if we can't find a better situation than here."

Emma looked around the house and breathed a deep sigh. "I've missed being here, Auntie Hannah. Sometimes, I wish I could go back in time and change the way that things have turned out."

"We all do, Em. It's often a challenge to accept things as they are."

"Milk's in," Nathan called from the kitchen door. "Well, hello, Emma!"

"Hi, Uncle Nathan."

Hannah walked to the counter. "Would you like to help me strain the milk and fill bottles, Emma? We'll have four hungry babies to feed very soon, as soon as they're awake." Looking at the clock, she finished her thoughts. "In fact, they've overslept already."

"Don't you want them to sleep?"

Hannah laughed at the thought. "While it would be nice, if they sleep too long now, then they'll be off schedule for their afternoon naps. That's when all the orphans go down and we rather need that time for our own work and sanity."

Emma giggled. "I guess I can understand that."

The milk was strained, the bottles filled and the remainder of it chilled for the rest of the family. Finally, Hannah headed into the "nursery," as they had come to call the back room, to wake whatever babies hadn't yet stirred.

Standing at the cradles, she turned back toward Emma. "Do you want to feed Henry or Eliza Mae?"

Emma smiled and wrinkled her nose. "Henry," she declared.

Hannah, Emma, Melanie and Meredith all settled down with one baby apiece, leaving Andy, Annie and Chase to handily entertain the toddlers.

"How will you decide which children go and which stay?" Emma wanted to know.

Hannah shook her head as she tucked a burp rag under Eliza's chin. "Ideally, we'd like to keep the siblings together, but it will depend on who is willing to give them a good home. For instance, John and Kelly are interested in James, but don't feel they can take on two children at their age."

Emma's head came up at the mention of James. "Is that because Jimmy was killed in the war?"

"It might be. We haven't really discussed it with them. Whatever the motivation, they are kind people and will be excellent parents to whatever child is lucky enough to have them."

"Who's this one?" Emma nodded toward one of the toddlers.

"That's Bessie."

"Is she related to anyone?"

"Yes, Bessie is the younger sister of William."

"It would be sad to split them up."

"I agree. I know how I felt, having my brother with me throughout my life. It was a huge comfort and helped establish a certain identity as I grew older, one I'm sure I wouldn't have had otherwise."

"What about Henry here? Does he have any siblings?"

"Henry is Eliza's twin," Melanie piped up. "Momma's feeding Eliza Mae."

"So, Mellie has Annabelle, whom you are keeping. Does she have anyone else in the group?"

"No, she is alone."

"Who are the rest?"

"Just Joseph and William."

"I'm William," a little boy announced, turning and putting a forefinger to his chest, "and Joseph likes to be called Jojo."

"And there you go," Hannah smiled. "Will is our resident information file. He set us all straight as to whom everyone was right from the beginning. We had a stack of names and couldn't get it straight which tag belonged to which child. He's been very helpful that way."

"Are any of them troublesome?"

Hannah smiled. "The babies are a lot of work but, no, they've all been very sweet. I think at this point, everyone's just happy to have a warm home and food to eat."

"It's so sad. Did someone really just leave them on the doorstep?"

"Robby did," William piped in.

"Well, see now; there's something new. Apparently, Robby is the person we'd all like to meet."

"Would you make him take them back?"

"No," Hannah shook her head. "I can't imagine giving a child back to anyone so irresponsible as to leave them on the doorstep of a perfect stranger, in the middle of a winter night no less. Nathan would very much like to have a word with the fellow though. We would also like to know if there are records for the children. We've only had notes with their names, but surely they have some sort of extended family."

"Auntie Hannah?" Emma began, before dropping her eyes and losing her courage to speak.

"What is it, Emma? You know you can speak freely here."

"I'm afraid you'll say no."

Hannah smiled. "Try me."

"I was wondering if… honestly… well, I would love to stay here and help."

"Oh, Emma," Hannah smiled, "I would love that! It's a little crowded right now, but you could have your old room upstairs. Though I'll have to warn you up front, there won't be much privacy."

Looking off in the direction of the crest of the hill, Emma became rather somber. "I know where to go if I need privacy, and it is much closer to here than it was from the other side of town."

"As long as you feel you're ready for that."

Emma nodded. "I haven't been in that house for months. The memory of Hayden haunts me there, but I'd love to be here."

"Very well then," Hannah smiled. "We'll talk to Nathan and get it arranged."

Lifting Henry to her shoulder, Emma snuggled her nose into the child's hair and breathed deeply. "I think I will be happier here than anywhere. It's something I haven't felt in a very long time."

Chapter Twenty-six

A Question for Carlen

February 1919

Exhausted, hungry, and feeling completely overwhelmed at his circumstances, Carlen Sanderson gave little Marianne a kiss to her sleepy forehead and snuggly tucked the blankets around her for a morning nap. She was nine months old and there hadn't been a day since her mother's passing that wasn't a struggle for them all. His sons were still frequently depressed, and his own life was reaching yet another crisis point, as if sinking further could even be possible.

Closing the bedroom door, he quietly called the boys into the front room. The house was beyond visible redemption for clutter, but he had greater concerns. They were out of wood for the fire, or would be within the next hour. There were a few logs outside, but they needed to be split, and Carlen had not been able to find or create enough spare time to get that job done. Between caring for the children, trying to prepare sermons, and tending to the flu stricken victims of his parish, his life had been consumed in "doing" for everyone but himself.

At least the influenza was abating; that was one large relief. It had been a terrible illness, but the mayor's plan had worked in that they'd been able to stave it off long enough for the plague to weaken and a less lethal strain to come through. Still, since he had been the first to suffer and was subsequently immune, it seemed he was the only one that people thought to call on for help. As a result of his going from one sick house to the next, his children soon fell victim as well. Thankfully, it was only three fever-ridden days for them and they had recovered quickly.

"Chris and Hans, I need your help outside; you need to bundle up for the cold. Chris, can I leave you in charge of getting ready while I start splitting the wood?"

"What do you need us for?" Hansel wanted to know.

"I need your help stacking the wood after I've split it. See the stove over there?"

"Yes," both boys answered, looking at the range surrounded by stones.

"We're all out of wood. I just loaded the last pieces in a few minutes ago and Marianne is down for a nap. If we will be quiet so she can sleep, then we can all go out and get enough wood split to last us a few more days. Can you get dressed quietly, so you don't wake Marianne?"

The boys nodded and began to search for their mittens and scarves while their father left the house and slowly made his way to the woodshed nearby.

Outside, a frozen fog had gathered on the green boughs of the surrounding trees. It was beautiful, though it hardly eased the burden of his heart as he collected the last of the logs and stacked them near the chopping block. Spring was still a full month off and they were nearing a point of desperation to their food and fuel supply.

He wondered how Linda had done it. How had she managed to make everything stretch and last for as long as they always needed? How had she found the energy to care for the children, clean the house, and cook the meals, to quietly fill everyone's needs, and remain so pleasant? He had not appreciated her goodness as much as he should have. Trying to do her job now, along with his own, left him feeling crushed, defeated by the demand.

Church attendance had been down as well, long beyond the epidemic's mandatory bans. He wondered how much of it was due to fear of further illness, or possibly the local gossip that had yet to abate. More likely, it was the disintegration of his hope, which he was certain showed in his sermons, as they sank from thoughtful and inspired messages, to the last minute allegories of his own life struggles, disguised as best he could. Either way, the pews had remained mostly vacant for the late fall and winter, and the church coffers correspondingly empty.

Carlen set a log on the block and brought the axe down for a square hit on its end, causing the wood to fly apart.

"Have I not been faithful enough?" he whispered under his breath. "Have I not done the best I could do while managing my little family? Dear God, why are we struggling so desperately? Why are my children not conquering their grief? Why are we on the edge of destitution for our most basic needs?"

At that moment, the front door swung open with a bang against the wall that shook the entire house.

"Dad!" Hansel screamed from the porch in a fit of tears. "Christian won't let me wear the red mittens; he said I have to wear the black ones instead!"

In the background, Carlen could hear Marianne burst into frightened screams at the unruly disruption of her nap. He stood for a few seconds more to see if she might calm down and go back to sleep; there would be no splitting wood with her awake and they desperately needed the warmth. Unfortunately, her distressed cries only increased.

As Hansel quietly retreated back inside and closed the door behind him, Carlen dropped the axe and sank under his heavy burdens onto the surface of the chopping block, burying his head in his fingerless gloves.

In utter spiritual agony, he cried out. "Dear God, what do you want from me?"

"Dear Carlen, what do you want from me?"

With scarcely a moment to draw his breath, the thought formed so clearly in his mind that it took him by surprise. In all his prayers, he had never conceived of such a response.

"Food for my family to start with," he whispered in return; "wood for warmth, comfort for my children, and help for us all." He could have gone on for quite some time, but he was soul-weary and, quite frankly, the basics were what he longed for the most.

"Go out and serve," that inner Messenger commanded him. "Your children are not orphans."

The word 'orphans' reminded him that there was yet a great blessing in his life that he had not acknowledged and he knew, in that moment, exactly where the Lord wanted him to be. He'd heard quite a lot about the orphans left with the Laynes, but he had not managed to visit them himself. Nathan's family had been missing from the pews of church as well. He should have checked on them long ago.

*

"Carlen; what a pleasant surprise! Chris and Hansel, how are you boys? Please, come in."

Hannah welcomed the reverend and his children into the house as Carlen passed Marianne to Melanie and mustered his best ministerial smile, shaking the children's hands one by one.

"Hello, Reverend Sanderson," little James greeted.

"James! So this is where you've been." Looking over the rest of the toddlers, he saw another that he recognized as well. "Hello there, William… and Jojo. Fancy meeting you boys in Silver Falls," he smiled as he lifted each one for a hug.

"You know these children?" Hannah asked in astonishment.

"Yes, I saw them last at the baby home before I got sick. I tried to visit them not a month ago, but the entire place was closed down. I wondered where they had gone."

"Well, here, for the last several weeks." Hannah was still visibly taken aback at this new development.

"Oh, I'm glad to find you." Turning to Hannah, he asked, "What happened to the Blakes? I was mystified to find that they'd closed the place down."

"I don't even know who the Blakes are," Hannah declared, "but if they are the ones who have been leaving orphaned children on our doorstep en masse, then I think I'd like a word or two with them."

"No, no," Carlen shook his head. "They would never do such a thing. They are the kindest, most considerate people you could know. They have always been very devoted to the children in their care." Looking over the group, he shook his head again. "James, where are the Blakes?"

"Robby said they went to heaven."

"Robby? Do you mean Mrs. Blake's brother?"

James only shrugged and turned back to the game he was playing with the other children.

"Robby is the only name we've heard, and that wasn't until after James was dropped off, James, William, Bessie, Joseph, and four other babies."

"Four babies?" Carlen asked. "Oh, Hannah, you have had your hands full!"

"It's been a challenge to be sure, but Emma and the older children are a tremendous help."

"How are you even feeding them all? I can't imagine trying to care for four babies. How old are they?"

"As best we can tell, they are all under six months. With my energies being taken up so much in their care, I'm afraid we've been making heavy use of the Larssen's Bakery. Thank heavens for their deliveries, or I'm certain we'd all be living on gruel."

Carlen looked around. "I feel so out of touch lately; how has that been working out for them?"

Hannah laughed. "Judging from our monthly bill, I'd say they are prospering quite nicely!" Ushering him into the kitchen, she pulled out a chair and collected a large slice of pie. This, she set in front of him, along with a slice of sweet bread.

"See for yourself," she smiled. Retrieving milk from the icebox, she set a full glass near his plate.

Carlen merely stared at the food while Hannah took a seat at the table to the other side. As the color rose in the reverend's cheeks, she was startled to see tears form in his eyes. It had been two days since he'd eaten more than a scrap of stale bread, though no one would ever know.

"Carlen, are you all right?"

The minister nodded and did his best to collect his senses. "You don't mind if I share this with my children, do you? I'm afraid they haven't had anything so fine to eat for a while."

"No, no," Hannah nearly jumped to her feet. "You eat up! We have plenty for the children."

Gathering a bowl full of cookies, she left for the front room while Carlen bowed his head in prayer. His clasped hands were still pressed against his brow when she returned, so she quietly waited at the doorway until it was clear that he was finished.

"I'm wondering if this is an entirely proper meal," she offered, dishing up a bowl of stew from the stove. "I suppose you know the rules;" Hannah smiled as she set the bowl before him, "supper first and then dessert."

Carlen dared not to speak as he returned a grateful smile. In fact, it wasn't until he'd taken several bites that the lump in his throat at last gave way and receded to where it belonged.

"Eat up," she encouraged, as she spread butter across a slice of bread. "We may be busy and overwhelmed with children at the moment, but we are far from lacking good things to eat, thanks to the Larssens."

"Thank you, Hannah," he finally managed. "Where is Nathan

today?"

"He's at the bank. I imagine he'll be back before long if you want to wait around."

Glancing at the clock in the other room, she looked back at Carlen and tried to guess what would stir such emotion from him over a simple plate of food. She wondered if they needed to make arrangements for the Larssens to stop by the reverend's home with some complimentary fare. She would make sure that Nathan was apprised. None of them had any idea that Carlen's family might be suffering from hunger!

In another minute, the kitchen door swung open and Emma entered from the outdoors.

"Emma! Hello!" the reverend exclaimed, standing from the table to greet her. "I didn't expect to see you here today."

"Hello, Reverend Sanderson; it's good to see you too," she smiled.

Then, setting the sparse basket of eggs on the counter, she removed her gloves and took a seat at the table.

"You have another hen setting, Auntie Hannah. That makes four. I think we should mark the eggs so we can limit their stash. The setters are surely taking eggs from the other hens and there's no dearth of need with all the children."

Hannah rose from the table to collect two more slices of pie. "We'll be fine, Emma. It's nothing that they don't do each year. Eggs now or chicken later," she laughed, causing Emma to smile as well.

"I think I'll pass on the pie for now. Where is Marianne?" the girl inquired, sensing that she had, perhaps, interrupted a private conversation.

"In the front room, with the other children," Hannah said.

"I haven't seen her in months! I think I'll just go see how she's doing." She then followed her ears to the ruckus coming from another part of the house.

"It's so good to see her happy again," Carlen whispered, as soon as she was out of the room. "Is she staying with you now?"

"Yes. It seems to be helping. She still cries herself to sleep too many nights, but the children keep her occupied during the day." Hannah looked once again at her dear friend. "Are you all right, Carlen? You don't seem your chipper old self at all."

Carlen raised his chin and tried to muster a brave smile. "We've seen better times, but I'm sure we'll get through it well enough eventually."

Sensing that he was not going to divulge more, she changed the subject. "How has church been? We've hardly left the house since the bulk of the orphans arrived. I've missed your sermons. Maybe you should preach one to us all today while you're here. We could certainly use it."

The reverend only shook his head. "I'm afraid I don't have even that to give, Hannah. I've been trying to decide if I've failed the congregation completely or whether it is time for Silver Falls to welcome a different minister."

Hannah was startled through to her core. "You wouldn't leave, would you? You mustn't leave! What would we ever do without you? Oh, Carlen, please tell me this is only a jest."

He merely shrugged. "It would appear I've lost favor here."

"Surely not!"

"If it's not the flu that's keeping people away, then maybe it's the gossip."

Hannah lowered her eyes. "Yes, I've heard my fair share of it;" she shrugged, "at least until the children came."

"Either way, popularity has turned against me; the church has been mostly empty for months. There's no sense punishing the good people of Silver Falls." Carlen fell quiet again.

"You can't leave under such a cloud. Being the victims of that gossip, we both know it isn't true."

Hannah struggled to think of more to say, before determining then and there that she would personally call all of the family and encourage them to church if she had to. They would also find some way to go themselves, it was a must! They couldn't lose Carlen.

"You're discouraged," she continued. "I'm sorry we haven't been to church; we haven't been able to think of how to transport so many children, let alone keep them quiet once we got there, but we are working on their adoptions. It won't be much longer. Nathan thinks he's found a home for two of them in Colorado. It will take us down to four babies and only two toddlers. Surely we could manage a Sunday excursion to church then. I suppose there is the quiet room… we could go and stay with the children in the quiet room."

"Oh, Hannah, it's not you, really," he confessed. "It's all me; I haven't had time. Between Marianne and the boys," he shrugged, "it's impossible to accomplish my ministerial duties. I've not visited our parishioners or mustered a proper sermon for months."

"Dear Carlen!" Hannah laughed, putting her hand over his and giving it a gentle squeeze. "Don't expect too much of yourself and you mustn't ever say such a thing again. We are indebted to you. How would we have survived that plague had you not come to help us? How would half the members of the congregation have survived had you not gone to help them? It will pick up again soon. It is nearly spring..."

This was the scene that met Nathan's gaze through the row of kitchen windows just before he reached the door. He watched a few moments more, until Hannah had taken her hand off of Carlen's, before twisting the handle and coming in.

"Nathan," she rose to greet him; "Reverend Sanderson is here."

"So I see."

Directing him to the table, she dished up a bowl of stew and then set Emma's abandoned piece of pie at his place.

Carlen smiled. "How are you doing, Nathan? Is everything in order at the bank?"

"Fair enough, I suppose."

Hannah was buttering some bread for her husband while she contemplated the earlier conversation, wondering how much she should share with him now and how much would be better saved for later. One way or another, it was going to happen and these problems resolved.

"Carlen knows our orphans," she announced.

"Well, some of them," he smiled. "They were at the baby home in Portland."

At his words, Nathan looked at him oddly. "I wonder if they would mind taking a few of them back. Do you suppose this is their retaliation for my bringing children in off the street?"

"No, oh no," the reverend disagreed. "The Blakes were splendid people with the highest standards for adoption; but apparently they are gone now. It sounds as if they didn't survive the epidemic. Mrs. Blake had a younger brother, Robby. I'd only met him once."

"Yes, one of the older boys said that Robby had brought them. I have a thing or two I'd like to mention to him."

"He's only a boy, Nathan, maybe seventeen or so. You've done a good thing by taking the children that you have; though I wonder where the others have gone."

"James said most of them had died," Hannah added.

Nathan went suddenly quiet. "I wonder what happened to Oliver and Nell. I had no idea that's where the children were coming from. I hope they survived. Do you think he would at least have records? It would be good to know their full names and exact ages as we try to find proper homes for them."

"I can't imagine there wouldn't still be records. If I knew his last name, we could look him up in the Portland directory. I'll do some looking around as soon as I can make arrangements for my children and go to the city."

"Just bring them here," Hannah offered. "Honestly, they can spend the day playing. A few more won't make any difference at all."

"I thank you," Carlen managed.

He had tried to get the words out before his voice betrayed him. Quickly standing and turning away, he hoped he could keep his emotions in check before they could be seen.

Clearing his throat, he announced. "I suppose we should be on our way. Chris, Hansel," he called as he walked to the next room and gathered Marianne from Emma's arms. Turning back to his hosts, he shook Nathan's hand and gave Hannah his usual smile before starting for the door.

"I'll walk you to the road," Nathan offered.

Outside, the frost had abated as the sun struggled to warm the area through a layer of thick ocean haze. The maples stood bereft of leaves and the brook hardly made a sound as it ran over the icy stones. Almost immediately, Christian and Hansel took off in a quarter mile race to the road.

"The visit has lifted their spirits immensely," Carlen observed.

Nathan nodded, figuring that now was as good a time as any to say what was on his mind. "I have to know what happened between you and my wife," he stated at last.

Carlen stopped and turned to Nathan, clearly confused and concerned. "Hannah? I'm afraid I don't understand; you do know that the rumors aren't true, Nathan. Nothing has ever happened between us. I would never..."

"I know you would never," Nathan cut him off, "but something happened between the two of you, back in Mapleton. It haunts me. There is a part of her heart that I will never be able to claim. What happened between you? Hannah won't speak of it at all and I want to know; I must know what you did that made her love you as she does."

This time the reverend smiled. "Nothing," he shrugged. "It was nothing, really. I was standing at the door of the church, greeting parishioners on my first day when I looked out to the cemetery and saw her there." Carlen's eyes looked soft as they ventured far away to the past. "She was running her fingers over the top of a headstone and looked so sad. I knew I needed to talk to her. I went out with the intent of helping her, perhaps giving her some message of hope, but when I looked down into her eyes... I don't know," he shrugged. "She seemed so familiar, as if we had known each other for a thousand years and I had found her once again. From that moment on, I was certain I needed her, just to live, just to be able to breathe, to exist." Carlen smiled as he looked back to Nathan. "And then she left, and I found that my breath still came and my heart continued to beat, despite itself."

Nathan slowly nodded his understanding. He had felt it as well, though perhaps not as dramatically at first.

"I'd never felt that way about anyone," Carlen continued, "shamefully, not even about God."

This was not helping Nathan feel reassured at all. "Was there anything you didn't like about her?"

Carlen laughed at the question. "Come now, Nathan. Is there anything that *you* don't like about her?"

Nathan was not as mirthful as his friend. "Yes; that she obviously still cares for you."

Carlen smiled, his eyes soft and pleasant. "Only as friends. It isn't like that, and you know it. I will always love Hannah in a special way, but more than anything else, I love that she adores you just the way that she does. It really isn't a marriage sort of thing, our friendship; it's just old souls, old friends who have somehow found each other again after a long absence. Does that answer your question?"

Nathan nodded and gave the reverend a friendly smile as they continued their walk to the end of the lane. There, he waved goodbye, watching him walk away to the west with his little family, before turning and heading back to the house.

Hannah was still sitting at the table when he came through the side door. Looking up to greet him, she smiled.

"Did you have a good chat with Carlen on the way out?"

"It was an interesting one at least."

There was something in the tone of his voice that piqued her interest.

"What about?"

"You. We talked about you, Hannah and he told me what you were to him in Mapleton."

Hannah looked at her husband in confusion. "Nathan, why would you even ask him?"

"Who says I did?"

"Because Carlen would never bring up something that might cause you pain."

At this, Nathan took a hasty seat at the table near his wife and clasped her hands into his.

"I had to know, Hannah. You will never speak of it."

Hannah looked at him and slowly shook her head. "Because *I* would never want to say something that might cause you pain either."

"Because you loved him?"

"It isn't like that now..."

"Not now," Nathan cut her off. "What was it for you then?"

Hannah looked away from him, out the windows beyond, and was very quiet.

"I just want to understand," he persisted. "I feel like there's a part of you I will never know, a part of you that will never belong to me."

Looking back at her husband, she shrugged. "Yes, I loved him; of course I loved him. I thought we were going to be married, but then I had to leave. I was certain he would come for me; for years I couldn't consider anything else. But he never came."

"So you settled for me." Nathan sat back in his chair, defeated, and looked off across the room.

"No," Hannah shook her head. "I fell in love with you."

"But you have so much history with him."

"No," Hannah grabbed his hands, "*we* have history, you and I. We've known each other for most of our lives; we have children together, we've been through the thick and thin of life together, and I have loved you for the greatness of your soul through all of it. But there's more than that, Nathan." Hannah looked deep into his eyes. "*You* would have come for me. As long as you knew that I loved you and I was still alive, you wouldn't have married anyone else. For that one thing, if nothing more, I wouldn't trade what we have for a thousand Reverend Sandersons. Can you understand that? Carlen is a friend. He's a wonderful person and a wonderful friend, and I will always love him in a special way, but he will never compare to you."

A smile tugged at the corner of Nathan's mouth as he considered her words. It was true. Given that circumstance of long ago, he would have searched the earth to find her.

Looking over at his wife now, he smiled and breathed out a contented sigh.

Finally, he understood it all.

Chapter Twenty-seven

Helen Daley

March 1919

Helen Daley sat poised at the end of the large conference table, quietly tapping her pencil against a pad of paper, trying to speak the words that were on her mind. The meeting had officially ended and the brothers were mingling among themselves, as they usually did before parting to their separate ways.

Normally, once the meeting was over, Helen hurried to her office to type up the minutes while the information was all still fresh in her mind. However, today was different; she had something to say, an important issue that needed answers.

Nathan noticed the change in routine, but didn't give it much thought, figuring she had something she needed to cover with one of his brothers. It wasn't like he or Helen ever had much to say to each other. Since George had management of the bank, Nathan's exposure and interaction with her were mostly limited to these once a month occasions.

Finally, George took notice of the pencil tapping. "Was there something more you needed to discuss, Miss Daley?"

"Not about the bank," she answered.

"What about then?"

"I need to talk to Nathan, privately."

Silence fell over the group at her statement, as each of the brothers stared at her in surprise, each wondering the same thing. What could Helen Daley ever have to say to Nathan that would require a private setting?

Fortunately, Nathan was quick to his feet, ushering her out of the room and into his office before either of the other Laynes could verbalize their musings.

"What can I do for you, Miss Daley?"

Helen, a normally forthright person, now languished in sudden shyness before finally summoning the gumption to say what was on her mind.

"I was wondering about the orphans."

"What about them?" Nathan was clearly at a loss over what she could possibly want to discuss.

"Have you found homes for all the children yet?"

"No," Nathan hedged at the question, hoping that she wasn't going to suggest what he thought she might.

"As you know, I've never been married, Mr. Layne, and I've pretty much abandoned the hope of ever being a mother, until now."

"Miss Daley, before you go any further; I appreciate your concern, but we are trying to find proper homes, with a mother and father both. It wouldn't be reasonable to carry on with your job at the bank and raise a child on your own, especially not a baby."

Helen looked down at her hands as she wrung them around each other in her lap. She was obviously nervous about the entire interview.

"What if I could get married? Or what if I could secure a job that would allow me to stay with the child?"

"Do you have any marital prospects?"

"Not yet, but what if I could find someone?"

"What did you have in mind?"

"Your minister; I happen to know that he needs help at home."

"Reverend Sanderson?" Nathan asked incredulously. Helen could have knocked him over with a feather.

"Yes, and I'm also aware that you often pay on the sly for that help to happen."

Nathan laughed at the announcement. "Just how would you know something like that?"

"You pay Grace to help. I've heard George talk about it over the phone."

Nathan only shrugged. "So, what's your point?"

"I want to adopt one of those babies. I may never have another chance at this. Anyway," she shrugged, "your minister needs a wife and I need a husband."

Nathan smiled broadly. Helen had never been one to mince words, but this was a little too out there for bizarre ideas, even from her. Trying hard to contain his mirth at her obviously serious request, he merely shrugged his shoulders.

"What do you want from me? It's not like I can tell the reverend where to put his heart."

"No, but you could help."

"Do I dare ask how?"

"You could arrange for us to meet, for one, and you could assign me to work for him in place of Grace, for another."

"What about your job here? Mark and George won't be at all pleased to lose your expertise at the bank. Besides, if you want to meet him so badly, why not just come to church?"

"I do attend church; just not that one. Though I'd be willing to convert."

That was it. Nathan could hold his laughter no longer.

"I'm sorry, Miss Daley," he chortled, "I realize that you've gone out on a limb over this, but if you're so interested in him, why haven't you attended church there in the past? It would've given you plenty of opportunity to meet him. Besides, he has three children already, you know; you wouldn't need to adopt an orphan. You may not even like him, once you get to know him."

"Reverend Sanderson?" she asked, a look of incredulity sweeping across her face. "He is a legend here. Who wouldn't want to be with him?"

"Then come to church. I won't play the matchmaker, but I'd be happy to introduce you to him."

"What time? Doesn't your other minister hold meetings as well?"

"No; Pastor Stephens won't arrive back until next month at the earliest. They're only holding the ten o'clock meeting for now."

"Then I'll be there," Helen answered. Standing to leave the office, she paused at the door and turned back. "Thank you, Mr. Layne."

*

Hannah had been washing the dinner dishes, but at Nathan's words, she took a seat at the table and stared at him, wondering if she had heard him correctly.

"She really asked you to play cupid and match them up? Helen Daley? Wasn't she leader of the suffragettes for Silver Falls?"

"Yes." Nathan was still chuckling every time he thought about it. "She's a very strong-willed, determined woman, and capable! She could probably run the entire bank single-handedly if need be."

Hannah paused in thought. "She's very different from Linda, isn't she? She doesn't seem at all his type. I mean, she doesn't even go to church and she wants to marry a minister?"

"Apparently, she does attend elsewhere," Nathan corrected.

"Really?" Hannah looked doubtful. "I've never thought Helen had any sort of religious inclinations."

"That's what she said." Nathan was presently snacking on a sweet roll as he discussed the situation with his wife. "What do you think I should do?"

Hannah thought a long moment. "Carlen would say to follow the golden rule. What would you want him to do if the roles were reversed?"

"I'd want to know what was going on before someone just tried to match me up with a stranger."

Hannah nodded. "I would too; but wouldn't that be a betrayal of her trust?"

Nathan shook his head and shrugged. "I don't know. Sunday is only a few days away; let's see if she shows up to church at all."

Those days went by very quickly for Nathan, who was rather dreading the idea of having anything to do with such a crazy plot. Carlen and Helen? Who could even imagine it?

As a result, he got everyone up earlier than normal on Sunday morning so they could arrive ahead of the crowds. Unfortunately, it wasn't early enough. When they pulled into the churchyard, Helen was already there in her car and waiting for them.

"Good morning, Helen," Hannah offered. "How nice it is to see you here. How are you doing today?"

"Oh, I'm fine, Hannah," she smiled; "and don't think you can feign your way into making me believe that your husband hasn't told you all about this. If it's all the same to you, while I am here, I'd like to help with the children. You obviously have your hands full."

"Did I miss something important?" Emma wanted to know. "Why is she here?"

Nathan raised his brows at Helen and smiled. "See there, you've spilled the beans yourself."

"I came to help with the children," she answered simply.

"Well, we can certainly use it," Emma replied. "Thank you for your kindness."

Helen looked back at Nathan with a smirky smile as they entered the building, leaving Nathan and Hannah to wonder at just how interesting the day could get. Nathan was suddenly regretting having arrived as early as they had. He had hoped to warn his friend ahead of time, but now would be forced to endure an awkward half-hour of trying to keep thirteen children confined and entertained, while Helen was full witness to the events.

Hearing a commotion in the chapel, Carlen came out to see who was there.

"Nathan, Hannah! Good Sabbath to you. Emma, how are you this fine morning?"

"I'm doing well, Reverend Sanderson; thank you. This is our friend, Miss Daley, from the bank," Emma volunteered. "She has come to help with the children in church."

"Miss Daley, it's so nice to meet you. Welcome to our services. Please, make yourself comfortable."

As Helen extended her hand to the minister, Hannah noticed that they were nearly the same height. True, Helen wore heels, but Carlen was a tall man, nearly as tall as Nathan, even if rather thin. Helen's build was the same – long, thin and graceful. It was odd to say, but something about them almost matched.

As Hannah and the children filed into their places on the longest bench available, Helen turned to give Nathan another smirky smile. Each of them had their hands full, those that were old enough to manage, with either a baby, a toddler, or both, as they settled in and waited those long and painful minutes for the other families to arrive.

Silver Falls was a small town, and many in the congregation knew Helen from the bank, though few could understand why she would be here, in their church. She was older, single, and had a reputation for being independent and outspoken over whatever cause she happened to be taking up at the time. There was a hint of whispering and lot of curiosity sparked by her presence, at least until the reverend stepped to the pulpit.

"All rise," Carlen announced. "We'll begin this morning's service with 'No Greater Love,' page thirty-eight in your hymnals."

At the sound of the organ's first strains, they began to sing.

There is no greater love,
No greater gift than Calvary ...

While the congregation sang a hymn unfamiliar to her, Helen began to look around the building. The windows were tall and arching; the ceiling was very tall as well, at least twenty feet to the peak. Off in a corner, the wood stove blazoned a gentle heat through the room, and on the front pew of the church, over to the opposite side from where she stood, two little boys and a baby girl sat unattended. The older boy had his hands quite full, holding the wiggly baby, while the younger boy tried to pinch his sister without being caught.

Leaning over to Hannah, Helen ventured a question. "Who are the children, alone on the front row?"

"That's Christian and Hansel," Hannah answered. "The babe is Marianne; they're Reverend Sanderson's children."

At the mention of the reverend, Helen's interest perked while she continued to watch them. Christian had successfully avoided several rounds of pinch attempts from Hans already, and the meeting had barely begun.

"The boys are cute and the baby is adorable. Do they always sit alone?" she asked.

"Not usually; Grace often sits with them, but I don't see her here today."

Hannah looked back at the hymnbook and tried to find her place, while Helen continued to watch the antics of the children sitting so alone, out of anyone's reach.

As the music finally faded away and the minister seated the group, he stepped back to his pulpit and began to read:

"In Saint John, chapter fifteen, verse ten, we read: "

If ye keep my commandments, ye shall abide in my love... This is my commandment, that ye love one another, as I have loved you.

"Turning next to Saint Mark, chapter twelve, verse twenty-nine, the words of our Lord declare:"

The first of all the commandments is, Hear, O

Israel; The Lord our God is one Lord: And thou shalt love the Lord thy God with all thy heart, and with all thy soul, and with all thy mind, and with all thy strength: this is the first commandment. And the second is like, namely this, Thou shalt love thy neighbor as thyself. There is none other commandment greater than these.

"Can we draw anything more from these words than that it is our duty, our sacred obligation to love? And how shall we love? Love, like faith, should compel us to good action..."

Hannah noticed a movement off to her left and saw the ongoing tussle between Chris and Hans, as the older boy struggled to protect Marianne from those taunting, little pinchy fingers. A moment later, Hansel looked to see if he had been caught and met Hannah's gaze. She raised a finger and shook her head, bringing instant soberness to the boy.

Several more times over the next hour, Hansel glanced back over his shoulder to see if he remained the object of scrutiny, only to find that, indeed, he was! Each time, he turned back around and sat quietly in his pew.

Meanwhile, Helen was completely caught up in the sermon. When the meeting finally came to a close and they began to file out of the building, her eyes glistened with joy.

*

A cool, moist breeze washed past them as they exited the building and gathered the children together in preparation to leave. Standing at the bottom of the steps to the church, Helen could contain her comments no longer.

"Are all his sermons like that?"

"Pretty much," Nathan replied.

"Nathan, did you see Hansel trying to pinch his poor baby sister through most of the meeting?" Hannah asked.

"No, I didn't notice."

Helen suddenly laughed. "Well I did! Leave it to a man not to notice such things. I dare say, the good reverend himself never saw it. I was impressed with Christian and how he kept her safe from those spiteful, little fingers."

"He doesn't mean anything by it," Hannah put in. "Hansel is a good boy; he just needs an extra dose of love and attention right now. He's a little like a raft at sea, floating without direction. The boy needs a mother and there isn't much else that will fill the need until he has one."

Helen looked across the yard and then back inside the building, where she could see the reverend speaking to a few of his parishioners near the door.

"Yes," she nodded; "I'd have to admit I agree."

Nathan glanced at Helen and broke into a smile as she turned and parted from them to her car. He'd seen that look before, resolute and determined. If she was anything, it was iron-willed. When Helen Daley set her mind to something, he'd never known her not to achieve it.

He noticed David Harrison watch with keen interest as Helen reached her car. Looking back to Nathan, their eyes met and David raised his brows in silent but intense question.

Nathan could only shake his head at the idea of it all as he smiled and whispered to himself.

"Heaven help us all."

Chapter Twenty-eight

Penance and Atonement

March 1919

"Hello, sir," the little boy began before breaking into a smile of recognition. "Hey, it's you!"

Nathan answered the door that evening after a tiny knock had stirred him from his chair. On his porch stood two more orphans; however, these were two that he at least knew. Oliver stood tall, holding his baby sister, Nellie, by the hand.

"Come in, quickly. Did Robby bring you?"

"Yes, sir." Oliver was clearly apprehensive at the question.

"Hannah, we have two more children here. Can you get them something to eat?"

Oliver's eyes grew large at the mention of food and even Nellie, though scarcely over a year in age, clearly understood the meaning of those words.

"I'll be back in just a moment, lad," Nathan said, giving the little boy a squeeze to the shoulder as Hannah appeared at the door and ushered them both to the kitchen.

They were barefooted in the cold, scantily dressed, and she was half-tempted to shoo them to the bathtub first, if for nothing more than to warm them up. Checking the children's customary name tags, she smiled warmly.

"Tell me, Oliver, do you like hot chocolate?"

"Oh, yes, ma'am!" he replied.

Stepping back out onto the porch, Nathan quietly closed the door behind him. "Robert Channing!" he called out.

Though, of course, there was no immediate response, Nathan knew better. If what Carlen had told him was correct, then Robby would be hiding someplace nearby to make sure the children had gotten safely into the house.

"Robby, I know who you are, where you live, and what you have done. So help me, if you don't come out here and face me like a man, you will answer to the law for this."

Nathan waited a few moments more before the skinniest

teenager he'd ever seen emerged from behind a group of trees toward the end of the lane. Slowly, he walked toward the house, filled with obvious apprehension, until he came to within twenty feet of where Nathan stood on the front porch.

"This has got to stop!" Nathan declared.

"I'm sorry, Mr. Layne. I have no food for them, nothing to give them besides water and the roof over my head. We have been begging our living now for weeks. I knew you had money enough to care for them. I had to borrow fare from a neighbor just to get here. I can't hold a job down with the children, and I can't feed them without a job."

"Are there more?"

"No," Robby replied. "I found families for the others. These are the last two. If I take them back home with me, they will starve and die. I, myself, haven't eaten for two days."

Nathan heaved a sigh at the complete retraction of his resolve to be firm, while his dominating sense of compassion overtook his senses. Shaking his head in defeat, he waved the boy over to him.

"Come inside with me. We need to talk."

Robby's dread was palpable as he took a few hesitant steps closer to the house.

"I'm not going to hurt you," Nathan assured him.

"Will you turn me over to the law?"

"Not if you'll help us. Now come on into the house. There is leftover roast and potatoes on the stove. We're trying to find homes for the children, but we're going to need your help. We need proper records for them if we're to find adoptive families."

At the mention of food and homes for the orphans, Robby picked up his pace for the final distance to the porch, stopping just out of the reach of Nathan's arm.

"I do have records; I can send them."

Opening the door, Nathan beckoned him further before taking his arm and ushering him into the house.

"Robby!" the children chorused.

"Where are Nellie and Oliver?" Nathan asked.

"They're in the kitchen eating," Hannah replied. "They seem half-starved."

"That's probably a fair assessment. Can you dish up some

food for Robby as well?"

Hannah looked at her husband in surprise; after all, this was the miscreant who had unloaded so much burden on them as to turn their lives upside down. Taking another look, however, she could see that he was skin and bones himself and she suddenly wondered at what trials he had endured in caring for the children as long as he had?

Dishing up a hearty portion, she and Nathan also took a seat at the table and waited patiently until his hunger had been satisfied. At length, the boy began to speak.

"I'm sorry," he offered. "Honestly, I didn't know what else to do. We were all slowly starving to death. I'm not a fit guardian. I saw your name and address with the donation information. I made inquiries enough to know you were good people. I figured you could at least keep the children alive. I knew I couldn't."

"Eat up," Hannah consoled, placing some bread before him.

Had it been anyone else, she would have buttered the bread and offered a tall glass of milk, served up pie or cake as dessert, just for his pleasure; but this was no welcomed guest. She was still very much struggling between compassion for his need and anger for what he had done.

Sensing the strained tension, Robby said little more until the bread and water was completely gone.

"Thank you for your kindness," he finally offered, and with such sincerity that even Hannah couldn't help but soften.

"We were very sorry to hear about your sister," she said at last, summoning what sympathy she could.

It was true, they were very sorry about his circumstances, just very put out at his approach in trying to solve the problem.

Robby dropped his head. "It wasn't just my sister; it was my entire family, my brothers and little sister, my parents. I've done what I could for the children. I'm sorry."

"Hannah love, Robby said there are no more children and he's promised not to do this again. Oliver and Nellie were the last ones. Do you suppose we could send him on his way with a bit of food to see him through?"

The gentleness of Nathan's words softened her heart even further as Hannah rose from the table and gathered a loaf of bread, a few donuts and an apple. The bakery wagon would be there in the morning; surely they could make do with what they had until then. They were obviously far better off than this skeleton of a boy.

Nathan reached over to tousle young Oliver's long hair. "Thank you for bringing Nellie and Oliver; I've been worried for them; but no more!" he added firmly. "Do you understand?"

"Yes, sir!" Robby had taken to his feet and was ready to bolt, with or without the food, when Hannah approached him with a basket.

"Goodbye, children," he said to those around the table, "and God bless you both," he offered to the adults as he turned to leave.

When he exited the house, Emma approached the door and stood astounded. "Was that him?" she asked incredulously. "And you just let him go?"

"I think he has suffered enough," Nathan announced, putting an arm around his niece. "There really isn't more that should be done. It is the end of it," he concluded, "and the children are all safe at last."

Chapter Twenty-nine

Foundling Histories

April 1919

The knock at the door startled both women from their places of repose as they scurried to answer it before the untimely transgression could repeat itself. They had just gotten the last baby down for an afternoon nap and were relishing a rare moment of quiet when the affronting sound came.

"Carlen," Hannah greeted in a very quiet whisper. "Please, come in."

"Why are we whispering?" he asked.

Emma put a finger to her lips and spoke in almost imperceptible tones. "Because we have eleven children all finally taking naps at the same time."

"Where are they?"

Hannah pointed to the back room.

"May I see them?"

"Of course," she smiled. "Just be very quiet, if you would, please."

The reverend shook his head. "I know a few of them, but how do you keep them all straight?"

Hannah smiled at that. "It was easier when Annabelle was the only one. She is the strawberry blonde and was the first to come to us. She has the sweetest disposition and has been a pure joy. She is six months old now, or thereabouts. Albert is the next over, the little boy with all that mass of brown hair. We think he is about five months old."

"Henry and Eliza Mae are after that," Emma quietly put in. "They are the twins, and my personal favorites. I love their black hair and soft, white skin. They are completely irresistible."

Hannah smiled. "They must be somewhere around seven months now. Next over is Oliver and Nellie; they are siblings, four and two years old. Bessie, the little blonde lying at the edge of the mattress, is two. She's so quiet; I sometimes forget she's even here. Her brother is William."

"Yes, I know William and the rest."

Motioning the way to the kitchen, they welcomed the reverend to a place in the house where they could close the door on their visiting and hopefully maintain the napping peace a little longer.

"Where are your children today?" Emma asked the minister, while Hannah quickly gathered the plates and portioned out three helpings of the most recently delivered bakery treats.

"They are at home. Helen Daley has very kindly volunteered to watch them so I could run a few errands."

Standing behind the minister, plates in hand, Hannah looked at Emma with raised brows, making Emma nearly laugh.

As Hannah set the plates on the table, Carlen smiled.

"You'll appreciate what I have today."

"What could that be?" Hannah asked as she grabbed the pitcher of milk and poured glasses full for them all.

"The orphanage records; I just picked them up at the post office this morning."

"Why did Robby send them to you instead of us?"

Carlen smiled. "His note said that he was too frightened of Nathan and asked me to deliver them."

Hannah laughed at that. "I suppose he may have seemed a little forbidding when they met."

Carlen smiled as well. "I'm sure it was well-deserved. His note said he has a job now and that he bought the postage with his first pay check. Anyway, here they are."

Carlen set the large envelope on the table and settled back in his chair to enjoy the sweet bread drizzled in raspberry sauce and icing.

"Thank you," Hannah offered. "Hopefully they'll answer a few questions for us."

"You're welcome and where is Nathan today? It's Saturday; I expected him to be home."

"He took Meredith to see Peter. Apparently, she's suffering from an ailment that only she and a doctor would understand."

Carlen burst out in laughter. "Isn't that about the fourth 'illness' she's had this month?"

"More like within the last two weeks," Emma corrected.

Hannah shrugged. "Peter keeps assuring her she isn't sick at all, but now that she knows all that can go wrong, she's convinced that she's suffering from one thing or another nearly all the time. You know, her knowledge has been very valuable though. She's properly diagnosed and treated a few of the children, saving Peter a good bit of time."

"Which he then spends on her," Emma put in.

Hannah smiled and nodded. "He said she's very handy to take on calls though, since she notices things that he doesn't. All in all, I suppose a few hypochondriacal trips to town are a small price to pay."

Carlen shook his head, smiling broadly. "She is the funniest child I think I've ever known."

Emma nodded her agreement. "And you don't know the half of it. Try living with her sometime."

"I'm sure you're right. Well, I suppose I should get back to relieve Helen of her duties. Thank you so much for the refreshments. I'll just let myself out the side door, so as not to risk waking your little orphanage in the other room."

Hannah rose to see him out, while Emma pulled the papers from the envelope.

"Thank you again for bringing those by," she waved, as he quickly walked away from the house and down the lane.

Hannah turned back to the table. "Well, that was a bit of luck, getting the records today."

Emma nodded, though she had gone from cheery to silent.

"What do you see that has your interest so riveted, Emma, my love?"

"Eliza and Henry's admission papers; they have a next of kin not very far away. It says right here that Oscar and Gladys Smith of Seaside are next of kin to the twins. I was really hoping..."

Emma let her voice trail off. She didn't need to say more; Hannah was well aware of her secret dreams. While Nathan had established the rule that the children would go only to solid homes with both parents, Emma's deep attachment to the twins was more than obvious, along with a hope that Nathan might, somehow, bend the rule. While she was still convinced that Hayden would not return to her, she held out on the dream that somehow it would all work out, that Henry and Eliza would one day become hers and she would know the joy of having a family of her own.

In the meantime, any mention of actively seeking adoptive families for them had been put on the back burner. There was always the possibility of Hayden being found. If he was found alive, then all the better. If he were to be found dead, then there was the chance of Emma moving on with her life, meeting someone else, and having her wishes realized.

Of course, those weren't Emma's thoughts; she couldn't imagine ever loving again. It was only Hannah who hoped for such a thing, meanwhile allowing the twins to stay with her in their home.

Hannah put a hand over Emma's own. "We'll have to check it out; but don't fret yet, Em. In the end, I'm sure that whatever happens will be for the best."

Scanning down the paper farther, Hannah pointed to some numbers. "Look, it gives us their actual birth dates, day and all. That's an improvement."

Emma shuffled through the papers. "Several of these have the children's birthdays listed. I wonder why Robby didn't include that in the first place."

Hannah shook her head. "I don't know, but look at this; it's Nathan's admission for Oliver and Nellie. It has their address and approximate ages, with a follow up from the police on their deceased parents' and siblings' names. They'll surely want that information someday. Their next of kin is listed only as a guess from the neighbors as being possible grandparents from Ireland."

"How would you ever track something like that down?" Emma wanted to know.

Hannah only shrugged. "I doubt we ever could, unless the relatives came looking for them. There is plenty of documentation regarding their whereabouts with the police if that were to be the case. Otherwise, I guess they will need to stay here. Who knows if they are even still alive?"

Emma sat back in her chair, holding the papers for the twins, Henry and Eliza Mae McCullough. She thought back to their last feeding, the dark hair and bright blue eyes of each as they had looked up at her, holding onto her fingers and gazing so trustingly into her eyes.

She loved those babies and could hardly stand the thought that they might ever be taken from her. In the partial reconciling of her grief, she had settled all her hopes on the welfare of those two beautiful infants.

Now, her heart fully ached at the knowledge that what Hannah had said was true. They would have to do what they could to locate their next of kin before any adoption might be final. Bitter as the thought may be, it was a truth that must be faced.

Chapter Thirty

Prospects of Promise

April 1919

Hannah read the contents of Jonathan Harrison's hastily scrawled letter a second time and shook her head in wonder as she looked up toward her niece's room. Feeling anew the surprise from his request, along with the rest of what he'd had to say, it seemed a bold leap to assume what he had, an assumption she didn't dare to mention at this time.

Many of the soldiers had returned from Europe, including those from their own families, but Jason and Jonathan had work yet to finish overseas before they could be released of their duties. Jon was more anxious than his brother to return, hoping there might be a future to his hopes, afraid that someone else might claim it before he could reach home. He, apparently, didn't fully understand the situation as it stood. Hayden was still missing and Emma could not be declared a widow – yet.

Hearing the sound of footsteps nearing the kitchen, Hannah quickly refolded the letter and shoved it into the pocket of her apron. Opening the oven door, she bent over to check on the bread just as Emma entered the kitchen holding little Henry on her hip.

"I can't find his pacifier, Auntie Hannah, and he won't settle down and go to bed without it."

"Have the twins already been fed?"

"Yes, Henry was the last."

"Well, it isn't like we don't have a dozen more of them lying around all over the house. It probably fell between the mattress and railing of his crib. Check the drawer over there. Maybe there is one left from the last time we washed them."

Emma walked to the drawer and searched until she had found what she was looking for. Retrieving the rubber nipple, she held it up as Hannah brought the loaves of bread from the oven.

"Why are you making bread? With such a crowd coming, I would think you'd order from the bakery and be done with it."

"I did order desserts, but the wagon won't be here again until Thursday and we'll need more bread before then. Besides," Hannah smiled. "I don't want to forget how; I can't be losing my touch, you know."

Beyond Hannah's smile, Emma could see something else in her eyes.

"Are you all right?" her niece asked. "You look…" the girl shrugged, trying to think of the right words. "You look worried or… you're not ill, are you?"

"No, Emma dear, I just have a lot on my mind. The dinner needs to be finished and on the table in less than two hours and I'm already falling behind."

"Well, let me get Henry down and I will help. What would you like me to do?"

Hannah looked around the kitchen and considered the space around the table, wondering how comfortably it would hold twelve grown people. They were hosting a dinner for several potential adoptive families, though few of them knew the real reason they'd been invited. Unfortunately, between the large table and four high chairs, the kitchen was quite cluttered.

"Maybe if we cleared out the high chairs it would give our guests a little more space to breathe," Hannah mused. "I do want this to be a pleasant occasion."

Emma nodded. "Where should I put them?"

"I don't know; maybe in my bedroom? It will be a tight fit, but it's only for the dinner."

"Where's Uncle Nathan?"

"He's gone to the train station to see if the Smiths are going to show. He figured they would need help getting here."

"Oh."

It was all that Emma had to say as she held Henry a little tighter and quickly left the kitchen.

The Smiths were aunt and uncle to her beloved twins. Nathan had written to them but had never heard back and Emma hoped beyond hope that they wouldn't show, or at least not be interested.

As she left the kitchen, Hannah fingered the letter from her nephew once again. The information weighed on her and she hardly knew how to approach such a sensitive, and ultimately mistimed issue. Either way, she could not speak to Emma about it at all, not yet, nor could she spend her energies worrying about it this night. Drawing her hand back out, she walked to the stove, gave the soup another stir and then left to gather twelve potatoes from the cellar.

*

The savory smell of roast, gravy, and fresh bread filled the home as Hannah stood back from the door, showing the couple into the house. Meanwhile, Nathan tied the horses off at the hitching post.

"Welcome, please come in. It's good to finally meet you; I'm Hannah Layne," she said as she took their coats and hung them near the door. "This is my niece, Lillie, and her husband, Mike Baker."

"Hello," the Smiths answered.

Gesturing to another young woman and a man in a wheelchair, Hannah continued. "This is another of my nieces, Janice and her husband, Ray Gibson. Next over is Nathan's brother, John and his wife, Kelly Layne. Last, but not least, is our nephew Ben Layne and his wife Lauren. Everyone, this is Oscar and Gladys Smith, aunt and uncle to the twins."

At the completion of introductions, Nathan walked in through the front door and with a happy clap of his hands began to rub them together.

"I say, let's get this dinner going; I'm hungry as a bear. Hannah, are you ready for us?"

"Yes, it's all on the table."

"Then, right this way." Nathan ushered the Smiths into the kitchen and the others followed.

"Might we see the children first?" Gladys asked.

"Emma is still settling some of them down for the night. It would be better if we waited; if that's all right with you."

"Yes," Gladys nodded. "I suppose that will be fine."

It didn't take long for everyone to find their seats and the food to be passed around. Hannah had done her best to make it a nice meal. They had a large roast and gravy, with potatoes and carrots aplenty, cream soup, fresh rolls, sweet breads, and a choice of several fruit pies for dessert. Not long after the eating began, Ray brought up the inevitable.

"I'm sure you'll get around to telling us why we're here eventually, but just to appease our curiosity, why don't we make it part of the dinner conversation."

Hannah smiled at the forthrightness. "It's about the children," she confessed.

At this, Nathan took charge. "We're hoping to find good homes for several of the children; they need more attention and love than what we can possibly give to all of them in order to grow up in as normal a circumstance as possible. You are the first couples from a very short list that we were hoping might be willing to consider adoption. John and Kelly have mentioned their interest in James, and the Smiths, here, are actual relatives of the twins, Henry and Eliza Mae."

Noticing their rather advanced ages, Lillie wondered at the tie. "How are you related to the twins?"

"They are the children of my niece, Nan; God rest her soul." Gladys answered.

"Then you are their great aunt," Lauren observed.

"Yes."

Ben thought that odd. "And they have no other surviving kin?"

"No, I'm afraid not," turning to Nathan, she continued, "nor are we in any position to take them on, Mr. Layne. I'm sorry if you had counted on that being the case."

A small gasp sounded from the next room, causing Hannah to smile when she heard it. Emma was obviously within earshot of the kitchen.

"Really, it's fine," Nathan nodded. "But we will need you to sign a release, so they might be considered by another family."

"I do want to know where they end up," Gladys continued. "It's important to me that they are given a good home. I just don't see how we can manage raising a child at our age, let alone two infants. We are both well into our sixties and couldn't reasonably expect to see them into adulthood."

"Yes, I understand," Nathan agreed. "We'll do what we can to find the best possible situation for them, hopefully together."

"Oh, yes; they mustn't be separated," Gladys insisted.

"What about the rest of you?" he continued. "Do you think it possible to consider adopting any of the others?"

"We definitely want James," John answered. "I know we're a

little old for this as well, but Grace is seventeen and Mary is twelve. They're both anxious to welcome another child into the family and have agreed to help. We still need to get a room set for him," John added, "but we can be ready by next week."

"Excellent!" Nathan smiled.

"What about the couple in Colorado?" Kelly asked. "Didn't you say they wanted to adopt?"

Nathan nodded his head. "Yes, we just heard from them today. They were hoping for siblings, so we thought Will and Bessie would be happier there than anywhere."

"Who does that leave?" Lillie asked.

"We have Jojo, who will be three in July, and Albert, who is the youngest child, still just a babe. We plan to keep Annabelle, Oliver and Nellie with us; and I dare say that Emma rather has her heart set on the twins."

"But what about Hayden?" Janice asked quietly.

"He may yet come home to us," Hannah offered. "God willing, we hope it will be so."

"We've not heard a word from him," Lauren added, "but my parents feel certain he's still alive."

Nathan nodded. "We can still hope, and I'm sure we can make room for the twins with us until we know."

At this, Lauren took hold of Ben's hand and voiced another bit of news. "I'm sorry to say, I don't think we would be good candidates for this. You see, we just discovered that we are expecting a baby of our own."

"That's wonderful; congratulations!" Hannah offered.

"We would like to consider Baby Albert," Ray finally stated. "It was doubtful before the war that we would have any children, but after my injuries… well, I'm afraid our chances are even more remote. We'd take both the remaining boys if I was able to be more help with it, but we'll be happy to at least give Albert the best home that we can."

Janice's eyes glistened at the announcement and Hannah smiled at the thought of her niece finally becoming a mother. It had been a long six years for them and Hannah was certain they would give Albert all the love he could possibly stand.

"Can you give us a couple of weeks to get everything set?" Ray continued.

"Yes, of course," Nathan agreed. "It's not like they'll be going anywhere in the meantime."

Ray nodded and smiled. Taking Jan's hand into his own, he gave it a gentle squeeze.

"That leaves us with Jojo," Nathan concluded. "Lillie, Mike? What do you think?"

"How old is he again?" Lillie asked.

"Just past two and a half," Hannah answered.

"The same age as Jane," she mused.

"Yes, almost," Hannah confirmed. "I think they're a month apart."

Lillie laughed at that. "Two two-year-olds under the same roof? I don't know, Auntie Hannah. Can we think about it?"

"Of course; this is only the first attempt we've made at finding families for them."

With that, Nathan joined in. "We don't want to pressure any one of you. In fact, we only want you to consider an adoption if it is what you'd truly like to do. There are still a few others we can ask. Please, don't feel pressured or obligated in any way."

Lillie smiled at those words. "Well, don't count us out just yet; we'll think about it and let you know."

In time, dinner began winding down and Gladys was getting anxious to see that for which they had come. "Do you have the release papers to sign," she asked. "Then we'd really like to see those babies."

Nathan retrieved the documents and showed them where to sign, after which, as if in one single motion, the group stood and quietly made their way to the nursery at the back of the house.

Hannah opened the door and directed the couples, one at a time, to see the children. The happy smiles which came after each viewing gave Hannah a heartfelt assurance that what they were doing was right; the children would be well cared for in each case.

Only the Smiths seemed to be in any hurry to leave. Checking his watch, Oscar finally announced.

"If we are to catch the next train and make it home at any sort of reasonable hour, then we should probably bid our goodbyes to you now. Thank you for letting us see the children. Would it be possible to get a ride back to town?"

"Yes, of course."

Nathan gathered his coat and soon escorted the older couple back out to the buggy, taking them back to catch the evening train home.

Lillie, Jan, and Lauren all lingered a while longer, joining with Hannah in discussing parenting plans and tactics before eventually calling it a night and leaving with their respective husbands as well.

Finally, only Emma and Hannah were left to clean up from the evening and discuss the outcome of the night.

"I do so want to keep those babies, Auntie Hannah! You can't imagine my relief when the Smiths declined to take them."

Hannah laughed as she washed another glass and slid it into the rinse water. "I think your gasp at the announcement was pretty well a confirmation to everyone of that."

"Really? You could hear me?"

"Loud and clear, Emma."

"Well, that's embarrassing; but what if Hayden never comes home? So many of the soldiers have already returned. Do you think Uncle Nathan would ever relent and let me have the twins anyway?"

Now, more than ever, that letter in Hannah's apron felt as if it would burn a hole into her clothes unless she retrieved it. Pressing it between herself and the sink, safely within the folds of her pocket, she shook her head and washed another dish.

"It's too early to give up on Hayden; but if he wasn't to return, I'm certain there would be hope for your future yet. You are still so young and there are plenty of fine, young men who would be happy to join you in the endeavor of raising those babies. In the meantime, let's keep our prayers alive for Hayden's safety. You mustn't give up yet."

"I know," Emma lowered her eyes as she retrieved the next item from the rinse water to dry. "I haven't given up. It's just that, for the first time since he left, I feel loved again and free to pour my heart into another human being, into two of them - those beautiful, little babies. I don't want to lose that feeling, Auntie Hannah. If there was only some guarantee, some way to assure that my heart won't be completely broken again. I need those babies as much as they need me."

Hannah smiled. "Have faith, Emma. If it's right, then it will be. Surely, in the end, something will work out."

Away, across the house, in a dimly lit back room, ten little children slept peacefully in the night, unaware of the changes soon to take place that would ultimately bless their lives.

Chapter Thirty-one

David Harrison Tells a Story

May 1919

It had been three weeks since the adoption dinner and two since Nathan had left - more than enough time to make it to Colorado and back - yet he had not returned. Hannah was getting concerned. It was enough to wonder where he was, but with five extra children still to care for, the burden and worry had worn her clear through. Added to that, the stove had stopped working and now the icebox was blinking off and on in its function.

Feeling beyond her limit in stress, she sent Andrew to fetch his uncle, hoping that Davy might have a suggestion or be able to help. Hearing his jolly voice at the front door now, she left the kitchen to greet him.

"What seems to be the problem here?" he asked, giving Hannah a quick hug and a kiss to the cheek. "Have you heard from Nathan yet?"

"Not a word," she whispered, adding a small shake of her head.

It was enough; David understood that it was not to be discussed in front of the children. Waiting until they could be alone in the kitchen, he inquired further.

"Have you contacted Adam?"

"Yes; I wired him yesterday and he answered right back, but he said that Nathan left over a week ago. I've expected him home for the past three nights; yet each time I've gone to the train he's not there."

The creases deepened on David Harrison's forehead. "That can't be good. What do you suppose might have kept him between here and there?"

Hannah shook her head. "I have no idea. To make matters worse, the stove isn't working, so I can't use it to make dinner, and then this afternoon the icebox began getting warm. The children have been living on jam sandwiches and bakery goods, but I'm almost out of bread even at that." Hannah sat at the table and put her head into her hands. "What will I do if he doesn't come home? What if something has happened?"

"There now," David consoled, giving her shoulder a gentle squeeze, "he'll be home soon, I'm sure." Hoping to divert her attentions, he began poking around the kitchen appliances. "What seems to be the problem with your stove?"

Hannah gave a weary shrug as she looked up from the table. "It just isn't working. I don't know why."

"And you say that the icebox isn't working either?"

"Sometimes it does, and then other times it just stops."

David rubbed his chin thoughtfully as he mentally assessed the situation. Going to the wall, he checked behind the stove, eventually following the wires to the power outlet.

"Ah, here's your problem."

"Is it serious?" She was bracing herself for the worst and the exhaustion, worry and stress were clear to be heard.

"Oh, very serious!" he smiled. "The stove has come unplugged and the icebox is teetering by the prongs, barely in the outlet."

A look of recognition crossed Hannah's face. "Chase was back there getting a toy for one of the babies the other day."

"Well, he must've bumped the plugs, that's all. Anyway, it's as good as new now."

"Thank you, Davy. I don't know what I'd do if you weren't here to help."

Taking another look at Hannah, he summoned his compassion. "How long until the evening train is due in?"

"Another hour; maybe a little less... if he comes."

"Sure he will! Why don't you go on ahead and leave a little early; take some time for yourself, Sis. A little peace and quiet are sure to help your nerves. I'll hold down the fort here until you can get back."

Looking at him with grateful eyes, Hannah nodded and left through the kitchen door.

*

"Alright, children, gather 'round. Who would like to hear a story?"

"Oh, yes, please!" Melanie answered. With a baby on each hip, she called to the others. "Oliver, Chase, Nellie; Uncle Davy is going to tell a story."

Slowly, they gathered all the children, babies included, into the front room and onto the rug, where anticipation and wonder continued to build over what sort of story David Harrison might share. The Layne children had been privileged to hear many of his stories over the years, but the newcomers had no idea what they might expect.

"Well now, if you aren't a passel of sorry lookin' young'uns," he laughed. "There's fewer of you though. Where did everyone go?"

"Daddy took Bessie and Will to live with a nice family in Colorado," Melanie answered.

"James lives with Uncle John now," Meredith added, "and Jojo here will soon be adopted by Cousin Lillie."

"Ah yes! He and baby Albert are to be my newest grandsons!" David agreed. "So why the long faces? There are worse things in life than being an orphan, you know."

"Like what?" Oliver asked doubtfully.

"Well, like living alone, with no food or home, or even worse, with someone who is very, very mean."

"How would you know?" he asked again.

"Because I was an orphan too. So was Hannah. Our mother died when Hannah was only two weeks old, just a tiny babe, much smaller than anyone here."

"Who took care of you?" Oliver wanted to know.

"No one; at least not for a very long time."

"How long?" Andy asked.

"For a whole year. I was ten years old and I had to take care of Hannah all by myself. During the day, I had to go out into the forest to find whatever food I could, and when there was nothing else, well, then we had to be content with only the milk from our goat. Of course, being just a wee babe, Hannah was very happy with that for some time, but it wasn't very satisfying for a growing and hungry boy! I didn't have anything so wonderful as sweetbreads and pies from the bakery like you enjoy every day. Surely, you can be thankful for that, can't you?"

"I can," an enthusiastic Andy answered, and eventually the other children, including Ollie, agreed.

"Mommy said you had chickens too."

David Harrison smiled, remembering back over half a century of time. "That we did, for a while anyway, until something got in and ate them all in the night."

"What ate them?" Chase asked.

"Something very large!" David exclaimed.

"How do you know it was big?" Merrie asked.

David gave a hearty laugh. "Well, chickens don't die quietly. Neither do they bang around in the night, nor knock boards off the sides of their pen."

The children all stared at him with large eyes now. "Did you hear it?" Andy wanted to know.

"Oh yes. It would be difficult not to hear something like that, living all alone out in the middle of nowhere with a wee babe to keep safe."

"Were you frightened?" Meredith asked.

"To be frank, I was terrified! Remember, I was only a little boy. My mother was missing and something huge was killing one of our few sources of food."

"Did you go out to chase it away?" This was Ollie again, eyes wide with curiosity, asking the inconceivable, though David only looked at him with raised brows.

"Now, Oliver, do you think that would be very wise, hm, to leave my little Hannah baby in the house and go outside to chase such a thing? No! I looked out the window, but there wasn't even a moon to light up the night; I couldn't see a thing."

"Then what wath it?" Andy still wanted to know.

"Or, what were *they*?" David posed the question. "I doubt that one animal could do so much damage to a building or eat nine whole chickens in one night, leaving nothing but a very many feathers on the floor."

All of the children were hopelessly caught up in the suspense of their imaginations as they waited with bated breath for David's next words.

"All that night, I waited inside the house, frightened near to death of what I would find in the morning, but when I finally got up the courage to go out, all I could find were feathers."

"What about the goat?" Annie asked.

"Well, she was alive, but so frightened that, even by morning, she wouldn't come out of the corner she had been hiding in all night. After that, she spent her nights in the house with us. I couldn't take the chance of not being able to feed my baby sister."

"Ew!" Merrie cried out. "That would be messy."

David laughed heartily. "It was, occasionally, but Tilly was good to wait most mornings until she got outside. She was a very good goat that way."

"What happened to her?" Chase asked.

"Well, she started to dry up, and then one day our neighbor, Mrs. Baker, was in the woods and heard Hannah crying. She was almost a whole year old by that time, but there wasn't much to feed either of us by then and Hannah had gotten very sick. Mrs. Baker came to the house and began asking questions about where our mother was and what was wrong with my sister. Then she took us and Tilly to her house. There, she took care of us and put Tilly back with the herd. You see, Tilly was one of her goats originally. She gave her to us before Hannah was born."

"You must have been relieved," Meredith observed.

"Oh, yes!" David laughed. "I was very relieved. After that, we had time to be children again, or at least I did. Hannah never really knew what it was like to be so alone and on your own, but afterwards we had far happier pastimes, like the time we found a duck's nest and raised the eggs until they hatched."

"Mother never told us a story about ducklings before," Melanie stated.

David drew his hand to his chest in exaggerated surprise. "She never told you about Blue Wing?"

"No," the children chorused.

"Well then, let me tell you. Near the Baker's house was a small lake. Mr. Baker liked to fish there whenever he could, so we went often to call him home. One day, we were exploring around the reeds and found a nest of eggs. Of course, being little, we thought they were abandoned, so we brought them home and hatched out five little wild mallard ducklings. Four of them were brown females, but one of them was a male. They were all fuzzy and yellow when they first hatched out, but as they grew older and began to get their feathers, they looked quite different."

"What did the boy look like?" Andy asked.

"Oh, he was a handsome little duck. He had a bright, shimmery green head and a perfect front of soft gray. On his wing, grew a patch of such beautiful, bright blue feathers, that Hannah began to call him Blue Wing. Since she was the one they saw as they were hatching, they thought she was their mother and followed her pretty much everywhere. Eventually, however, they became too big for the house and Mrs. Baker insisted that we put them outside with the chickens. Hannah cried and cried, but Mrs. Baker wouldn't change her mind."

"Why wouldn't she let the ducks stay in the house?" Annie asked.

David screwed up his nose into a grimace. "Well, young'un, ducks don't house-train as well as goats. At least Tilly tried to hold it while she was in the house, but with five ducks waddling all over, well, Mrs. Baker wasn't at all fond of cleaning up after that mess."

"Mother could have cleaned it up," Andrew offered innocently.

"Yes, I suppose; but could and would are two very different things. Remember, she was very young."

"What did she do after that?" Melanie asked.

"Oh, I think you can pretty much figure that out. What do you think she did?"

"I say she wanted to sleep with them, out with the chickens!" Meredith announced. It was, after all, what Meredith would've done.

"You're right, except that Mrs. Baker wouldn't let her. There were wolves in the woods and she had heard about what happened to our chickens. She wasn't about to let Hannah do something so dangerous."

"Then what did she do?" Oliver asked.

David Harrison smiled broadly, and when he did, the wrinkles at the corners of his twinkling eyes seemed to fold over on top of each other.

"She snuck out in the night and went to sleep with them anyway."

"Did the wolves get her?" Chase wanted to know.

David all out laughed. "Well, no, Chase. Not in this life."

"Silly, Chase!" Meredith laughed with the others. "If the

wolves got her then she wouldn't be alive to be our mother."

"She could have run away from them… fast," Chase protested, feeling suddenly embarrassed at the chiding.

"That she might have, lad; you make a good point; but she didn't. Mrs. Baker found out the first morning that little Hannah overslept with her feathered friends and scolded her soundly. After that, she made Hannah sleep in their room until she was certain she wouldn't try it again."

"Did she try it again?" Annie asked.

"No; and then, soon enough, Blue Wing and all his sisters grew up and flew away for the winter."

"Oh no!" Annie gasped. "Did she cry?"

"Now, Annie dear, have you ever known your mother not to cry when she's lost something she's loved as much as that."

Annie giggled at the thought.

"But there's more to the story. Each spring, those little ducks came back to the lake and quacked and quacked until Hannah came out to greet them properly with plenty of bread crumbs. On the third year, just a few weeks before spring, the Bakers got a letter from our Uncle Jason and, before we knew it, we were off on a train to go live in Mapleton. Poor Mrs. Baker and Hannah blubbered all the way there. Mrs. Baker was broken-hearted at losing us, but I think Hannah was more distraught that she wouldn't be there for her babies when they came home. She made Mrs. Baker promise to go out and feed them bread as soon as they came."

"Did you cry?" Oliver wondered.

"Not about the ducks," David announced. "No, as a matter-of-fact; for some reason, I was more relieved that our relatives had found us. I don't know why. The Bakers were as good and as kindly as people come. I was probably more afraid of Jake coming back some day and figured he'd be less likely to find us at Uncle Jason's."

"Who's Jake?" Oliver asked.

"That, my boy, is a story for another time; but you see, you all have very much to be thankful for, even you, Oliver; and that is the secret to living a happy life."

"What's the secret?" Annie asked.

"Counting your blessings and not your troubles."

Oliver looked down. "It doesn't sound all that happy to me."

David looked at him tenderly, remembering the pain of his own losses so many years ago.

"I understand, Oliver. You've known some very sad things, but when you can, try to look at the good things all around you and don't get lost in the sadness. Ask yourself this: If the only things you'll have tomorrow, are the things you're grateful for today, what would they be? Do you understand?"

Oliver nodded an acknowledgement.

"Say," David cocked his head and put a hand to his ear, "is that someone out in the drive that I hear?"

It was true. The sound of the motor car could be discerned, followed by voices, very happy voices.

"I think I hear your father out there; what do you say?"

The children said nothing, but rushed to the door instead to welcome Hannah and Nathan in.

"Welcome home, Nathan," David greeted cheerfully at the door. "I see you're still with us."

"Yes, I was delayed in Idaho. I sent a wire, but apparently it wasn't received. Thank you for helping out around here. I understand you saved our family from a non-functioning stove."

"All's well that ends well," David replied with a laugh and a friendly slap on the back.

And with that, David Harrison waved his jolly goodbyes and left through the door and across the fields toward home. As he walked in the fading evening light, he thought he heard a duck call out overhead, causing him to smile.

Orphans or not, of the many gains and losses in all of their lives, they were alive and healthy, fed and loved. Overall, the years would surely be good to them. Oliver, Annabelle, and Nell were all very lucky to have what they did in a home as good and with parents so kind as Hannah and Nathan promised to be. David was sure they would grow to appreciate it, in time – just as he had done.

Chapter Thirty-two

Barnstormers

May 1919

"It'll be strange being home; don't you think?"

"Maybe," Jon replied; "but it will be nice to get back to a quiet life of farming."

Jason sighed. "Farming hardly seems interesting anymore after all we've seen and done."

"You have a point," his brother laughed; "but what else is there to do?"

Jason and Jonathan Harrison were seated on a train across from each other, looking out the window at the passing countryside. Rarely had they been separated throughout their lives, including the past nineteen months they'd spent in the military, where they had done everything in their power to keep each other safe. Those months had been filled with so much action, fear and glory that neither of them was sure they'd ever be able to process it all.

Now, after their long ocean voyage, they were on the tail end of the train ride headed home. They had boarded in New York and traveled across the entire expanse of the nation to Sacramento, California. Here, the train began to slow for yet another station stop.

"This is our transfer," Jon announced. "We go north from here."

"Hey, look at that?" Jason pointed out the window to a busy airstrip just beyond the town limits. "Why do you suppose they have so many planes out there?"

Jon shrugged. "I don't know, but we have a couple hours until the next train."

The boys looked at each other and smiled before Jason verbalized both their thoughts.

"Let's check it out."

Planes had become something of a passion for the two young men, having dabbled in every possible part of them during the war. They started out in maintenance and repair and ended up flying in combat.

After checking their bags into the station, the Harrison boys briskly walked the remaining distance to the airfield nearby where planes were flying in and out through takeoff and landing routines.

Coming to an unattended group of machines sitting idle, Jase ran his hand along the wing of one and smiled. "Look, Jon, an Aeromarine thirty-nine."

"Yeah, I saw it; but look at this Jenny over here; one-fifty horse-power and duel wing tanks."

Jason immediately left the sea plane behind to inspect his brother's find. "Dual tanks; really?"

Jonathan ran his hand over the wing, inspecting the extra fuel supply. "You realize that's more than four hours in the air between refueling."

"Better than five with a tail wind." Jason held a wet finger to the air and then ran his hands once more over the gleaming metal. At last he stopped to inspect the landing gear. "The tires look brand new," he announced. "Very nice."

Meanwhile, Jonathan checked the mechanics of the secondary fuel tanks. "I wonder if it's new. I don't see any signs of use on this plane at all."

"You boys like her?"

Jase and Jon nearly jumped a foot at the greeting. They had been so engrossed in their inspections that they'd failed to notice the gentleman's approach.

"She's nice," Jon answered, then looking around the premises, he gestured to the rest. "Why so many planes?"

"Surplus," the man replied. Extending his hand first to Jonathan, he took him in a firm grip. "Don Sammons, surplus sales agent. This girl never even made it to a training base."

Jonathan nodded as he glanced inside at the double cockpit, complete with dual controls. "She's very clean."

Looking over at Jason, he let out a laugh. "You boys must be related. I can hardly tell you apart. Either of you pilots?"

Jason barely nodded. "We both are."

"Well then, can I interest you in a plane?"

Jonathan smiled at the offer. "I'm afraid we just came over to admire; could never afford anything like this. I've seen their price tags."

"Were you the type to spend all your wages, or save them?"

"We both saved them," Jason put in, "but we could never afford a brand new Jenny, especially not a 4-H."

"Just how much do you think they're selling for?"

Jonathan let out a long whistle. "If I remember right, they ran well over four thousand."

"Yes," Don agreed. "Closer to five; but the war is over, and now there's a huge surplus that Uncle Sam needs taken off his hands. "I can put you into a brand new Jenny for less than a thousand dollars."

Jason choked on the number as Jonathan shook his head and replied. "I thank you for the offer, Mr. Sammons, but neither of us is in any sort of position to buy one at this time, tempting as it may be."

"Eight-fifty?" the man bartered.

"I'm afraid not."

"Seven hundred," he announced, making both boys stare at him in amazement.

Jonathan was incredulous. "Seven hundred, for this Jenny?"

"Seven hundred and it's yours!" the man declared.

Jon could only shake his head. "I wish I had that much, but I don't; not even close. What's more, we're on our way home and just waiting for our connection."

"Where's home?"

"Oregon, on the coast."

Mr. Sammons looked over at the marine models. "I'm surprised you're not more interested in those."

"They're very nice; we just favor the Jennies."

"I see. How much do you have?" Mr. Sammons pursued.

"I'm not sure anymore; maybe four hundred dollars, maybe four-fifty, but it would take me down to my last cent. It's all at home in the bank."

"Tell you what I'll do; I'll sell you that brand new Jenny for four hundred and fifty dollars, gas tanks filled." Mr. Sammons glanced at his watch. "It's a little after ten o'clock now. You could be home before nightfall and the proud owner of his very own plane!" Mr. Sammons didn't have to look hard to see the gleam in Jon's eyes as he considered it. "Just think of the opportunity ahead of you!"

"All we have left are our train tickets," Jason put in. "We couldn't afford to fill the tanks with all the gas needed to get us the rest of the way home."

"You could sell your tickets back to the station. That would give you more than enough."

Turning aside to his brother, Jason whispered. "Jon, I know it sounds like an amazing deal, and I would love to take advantage of it as well, but where would we land the thing once we got home? Silver Falls is hill country. There are no airstrips."

Mr. Sammons, who was unabashedly eavesdropping on them, butt in. "Were there always airstrips overseas? Every good pilot worth his weight that I ever knew landed in whatever field was available. Are you boys saying that you don't have *any* level fields at home?"

A smile tugged at the corner of Jason's mouth first, and then at Jon's as they both thought of the same place at once - the fairgrounds. There was a stretch of road that could double as an airstrip and a mostly flat field with large show barns at the fairgrounds.

"My money is still at home," Jonathan declared as his last possible objection.

Mr. Sammons laughed heartily. "I think we can work that out. Step into my office and we'll have you both in the air within the hour."

*

Meredith cocked her head to the side and listening as hard as she could. "What's that noise?"

Hannah listened too. "I don't know, but it's getting louder."

Gathering at the front door, everyone with any degree of mobility listened intently as the buzzing sound grew closer.

"Look there!" Andy shouted, pointing out over the ocean.

"What is it?" Oliver asked.

Hannah's eyes grew large as the object came closer to view. "It looks like an airplane! Who do you suppose would be flying an airplane out here?"

The family moved out of the house and onto the bridge to get a better look as they watched the flying wonder close in on the area. It soon swooped down and over their farm, nearly touching the tops of the giant silver maples. Turning in the sky, it circled back around for a second pass, flying over the house once again and then swooping down close to the field.

By now, everyone had come out of their homes to see what the commotion was about. Susie and Grant stood in front of their house holding Mason, while David and Laurel stepped outside their back door. Nathan came from the area of the barn and met his family on the bridge, while Alannah and her children gathered near their fence to get a better view. No one in Silver Falls had ever seen an actual plane before, let alone this close up. It was exciting, to say the least.

They watched the craft fly back out over the ocean and bank to the right, flying toward them once again, just as it had done before. As it pulled ever so low over David Harrison's fields, Susannah handed her baby to Grant and ran out to the field, waving in excitement to the pilots and hollering her recognition of them both.

"It's Jase and Jon!" she screamed.

At the proclamation, everyone else ran into the field to watch the boys turn once again and head back for their second round. This time, they dropped a small object, nearly at Susie's feet. She picked it up, read it, and then shouted to Laurel and David across the way.

"It says they're going to land at the fairgrounds!"

Everything was helter-skelter after that, as the families scrambled for their cars to drive the three miles to town. Susannah and Grant rushed to join Laurel and David, while Hannah hurried to gather her children into the seats of her sedan.

Racing down the lane, she barely paused to check for traffic at the end and then drove as fast as she dared, causing the wind to rush past their faces, blowing everyone's hair into tangles. All the while, the children kept a steady eye on the magical flying machine in the sky.

"They're going out over the ocean again!" Melanie shouted.

The Laynes pulled into town just seconds after the Harrisons and followed them to the fairgrounds. Eventually, they both pulled onto the grass at the side of the road so as to give the plane as much space as it might need. Here, they all jumped out and gathered to watch the landing.

The plane made several passes, checking out the surface before going back out over the ocean. Banking again to the right, they headed back toward land, lower than ever before.

"Here they come!" Andy announced.

"I can't believe it!" Laurel shook her head, her eyes welling with tears. "How did my boys ever manage to fly home in a plane?"

David shook his head. "I just hope they didn't steal it."

"Davy!" Hannah laughed in spite of trying to sound reproachful.

"Well, Hannah, you know as well I do how often those boys have found trouble over the years."

"Oh, stop it," she laughed.

"Here they come! Here they come!" Susie shouted, waving her hands, jumping up and down in excitement.

The plane came lower and lower as it slowed in its descent, then the wheels touched the dirt of the road and it passed by them all in a copious cloud of dust.

Jonathan guided the machine onto the fairgrounds and over near one of the larger barns before they all headed over to meet them.

It was a happy reunion, with hugs, kisses, and handshakes passed all around for the first several minutes, all while the questions began.

"An airplane?" Laurel asked.

Jon shrugged. "It was a deal we couldn't refuse."

"But, an airplane?" his mother asked again. "Whatever do you plan to do with it?"

"Barnstorming. Did you know that the average cost for a ride in an airplane is *five* dollars," Jason added. "FIVE dollars! We could be rich with this."

Laurel shook her head. "But who would pay five dollars to fly?"

"Come with me now, Mother. I'll take you up into the blue sky and you'll never want to come down."

"I don't think so, son. If God had intended us to fly, he would've given us wings."

Jonathan laughed at that, gesturing toward the plane. "But he has; right there, wings and propellers and the most amazing freedom you'll ever know. Doesn't anyone want to go for a ride?"

"For free?" Susie asked. "Or for five dollars?"

"For free, silly," Jason laughed.

"I'd like to go," she replied with renewed enthusiasm.

David laughed. "I would too!"

"As would I," Grant agreed.

"Uncle Nathan?" It was Jason, venturing the unlikely.

"No, thank you. I think I'd better stay on the ground for now. I've read too many reports about crashes in those things."

"Auntie Hannah, what about you? You're up for some adventure, aren't you?"

"Actually, I'm still just trying to get used to the car; maybe at a later time."

"I want to go!"

Meredith had been waiting rather impatiently to be invited and when it began to look as though the opportunity would pass and she might miss out, she jumped in and boldly stated her desire.

Jonathan looked doubtfully at her parents, thinking they would never approve, and Nathan looked stern at first, but then his expression softened.

"I suppose it might be all right at some point, but not today."

At the realization that their father would even consider the possibility, Oliver, Andy and Chase, their hearts pounding from the thrill of anticipation, began clamoring in an attempt to secure a future ride as well.

"Actually, we're hungry as bears at the moment," Jason confessed. "Let's have something to eat, then we'll fill her up and fly everyone around in the morning."

"To The Falls!" David announced. "This is a day truly worth celebrating!"

As they climbed into the various cars, Jonathan managed to squeeze his way into Hannah's sedan.

"Where's Emma?" he asked.

"At home," Nathan answered. "The babies were still sleeping when we left."

Sitting in the back, among a sea of children, Jonathan leaned forward and whispered into his aunt's ear.

"Did you get my letter about her?"

"Yes, Jon," she whispered back; "but it's too soon to speak of such things."

Jonathan nodded his understanding. "Then I'll be patient and wait."

At that, they drove off toward town, the beach, the train station, and then to The Falls.

Jonathan Harrison settled back into the seat, surrounded by his little cousins old and new. It was good to be home, very, very good! His hopes were high and he could hardly wait to discover what the future might bring.

Chapter Thirty-three

Osnabrück

May 1919

Blowing in from the Channel to the French harbor, the spring breezes wafted through the salty air with a warmth foretelling of summer. For days the area had been shrouded in fog, but today, as if by order of decree that all oppression be lifted, the sun broke through bringing with it a feeling of triumph and celebration.

Caleb positioned himself at the dock where droves of soldiers continued to make their way toward the ship in a rush to get home. So many had come on this journey never to return, and these last lucky men were anxious to be on their way to the land and loved ones they had left behind a lifetime ago.

"I'm looking for Hayden Larssen," he asked a group of men passing by. "Have any of you seen him?"

The response was always in the negative, as it had been for all the months that he had tried. He did find one person, once, who had met him, but all they could remember was that he'd gone to the French underground and that was the last anyone had heard of him. Still, Caleb pressed on.

"I'm looking for Hayden Larssen; do you know him?"

After yet another soldier of the thousands he had questioned shook his head, he realized he was going to have to try something dramatically more effective. The masses were quickly departing; there was no way he could personally question the scores of men thronging to get onto the boat. Time was running short. How much longer could he stay, searching in this foreign land? He was, after all, scheduled to be on this very voyage home.

Finally, deciding on one last, extreme tactic, he climbed up onto a large, wooden mooring and with a voice booming as loudly as he could, he called to the crowds around him.

"May I have your attention, everyone? I'm looking for Private

Hayden Larssen. Does anyone know him, or know where he is?"

"I do," a voice came from the crowd. "I know him, or did."

Apprehensively, Caleb climbed down from his perch and approached the young soldier.

"You say you knew him. Is he dead?"

"Not last I knew, but he wasn't in shape enough to travel. We were prisoners together at Osnabrück Camp."

"Where is Osnabrück? What more can you tell me? How can I find him?"

"Go to Münster. It's a ways, maybe two-fifty, or even three hundred miles, but there's a train still running through to it. After that, you'll have to find other transportation to Osnabrück, which is north, another twenty-five miles or so. We had to walk to Münster to get a train out. Private Larssen wasn't strong enough to make the march, which wasn't surprising; he was originally transferred to Osnabrück due to the health problems that have plagued him. Last I heard he was being transferred to a civilian hospital somewhere around there. You should be able to track him down without too much trouble."

Caleb scrawled hasty notes of the most vital information before trying to fix in his mind where he might begin in finding his way to Münster.

"Thank you, young man!"

"Sure; I hope you find him. He was a good man. If he's still alive, tell him Riley says hi."

"Riley?"

"Major Tim Riley, from Nebraska. Good luck to you!"

"Yes, and thank you again."

Caleb waved a farewell and then headed away from the ship, very much against the flow of soldiers, to return in the direction of the train. Osnabrück, Tim Riley. They were two names that he must not forget.

*

The hot June sun shone down upon the heads of all those gathered at the Silver Falls station to welcome Caleb home. The doctor had written a month earlier, saying only that his search had come to an end and he was returning home. An additional wire from a brief stop two nights before informed them which train he would be on and would someone please be there to pick him up.

Of course everyone showed for the homecoming. Most of the soldiers had been back for months now, and regardless of the success or futility of his search, Caleb was the last to return. The entire Layne clan, the Larssens, Harrisons, Sandersons, and Carrolls, as well as many friends and former patients, nearly everyone that knew him, gathered at the station. There they stood, patiently waiting with banners, automobiles, and flags. A grand dinner at The Falls, care of Dane and Janette, would add to the festivities as well. Afterward, Silver Falls would parade him home, hero style, clear to his front door.

Being the final warrior of those who would return, it was all rather symbolic, a sort of rite in this close-knit community, as an end to the end of all the war and suffering and sorrow.

Children and babies were passed around from person to anxious person as they began to grow antsy. Where was the train? It hardly ever ran late! Why would it choose today of all days to do so?

Suddenly, someone called out. "I think I hear it!"

A hush settled over the crowd as the distant call of a whistle sounded out over the countryside, followed by an eventual trail of thick, black smoke in the sky. Cheering and excited chatter broke out over the next several minutes as the clatter drew closer and the locomotive finally arrived. Engine slowing, it squeaked and squealed into Silver Falls, with a pop, hiss and thud at the platform of the station.

After what seemed an eternity of people disembarking, Caleb finally appeared at the door of the train and was met with cheers as he waved to everyone around him, but then he stepped back inside. When he came out again, he was helping a frail, old gentleman down the steps, a tall and extremely thin man, whom no one really knew - at first.

"Hayden?" Emma called out.

Astonished and in disbelief, she hesitated only a moment before handing Henry to the person nearest her. Fighting her way to the front of the crowd, she ran across the platform, throwing her arms around that near skeleton of a soul. Not an old man at all, it was her young, beloved husband who had been lost for so long, and was now found.

"Hello, Emma," he smiled, wrapping an arm around her as he steadied himself against the railing.

"Oh, Hayden, Hayden, you are alive!"

"Well, barely," Caleb commented. "Go easy on him, Emma. You don't want to knock him over."

Most of the crowd stood stunned and silent at the presentation. Caleb had said nothing about finding his son-in-law, and they had all assumed the worst. Surely, had he found him, he would have said something to ease their anxiety and wonder.

"Oh, Daddy, I can't believe you didn't say anything!" Emma censured. "Why didn't you tell us?"

"Don't be upset with him, my darling. We both wanted to be certain I would make the journey home alive before anyone raised your hopes too high."

"He has a long recovery ahead of him yet," Caleb put in. "I tended to him as well as I could before we left, but the travel has taken another great toll."

Elise Larssen was the next eager person to tearfully reach her son, followed by all of his sisters, while a stoic David Larssen stood back, waiting a turn and wiping his eyes.

"Hip hip hooray!" Dan Carroll called out from the crowd.

At the cheer, the rest of the group seemed to come to their senses all at once.

"Hip hip hooray! Hip hip hooray!" they cheered all together.

As the train began to pull away,and they made their way from the platform, Emma led Hayden by the hand to Hannah and Nathan, who were holding two wiggly babies in their arms.

Emma looked up at him with hopeful eyes. "There's someone else you need to meet. This is Henry and his sister, Eliza Mae."

"Cute; whose babies are they?"

"Ours," Emma ventured tentatively, "or at least, I was hoping they would be."

"Ours?" Hayden took a step backwards, questions and surprise filling his face.

"They are orphans from the plague; I've been raising them since they were tiny little things. I want to adopt them, and now that you're home, well... we can." Looking up into her husband's face, Emma begged him with her eyes. "I thought you were dead, Hayden; these sweet babies pulled me through that grief. I love them completely."

Hayden's eyebrows rose high on his forehead. In his wildest dreams, he had not expected to come home to this, nor could he imagine having the strength to deal with a baby just yet, let alone two of them at once.

Sensing the potential disappointment, Caleb intervened. "Maybe in time, Emma. He'll have to get his strength back first."

Hayden stood still in his speechlessness, until he recalled a promise he had made long ago, one that had haunted him daily during his months of imprisonment overseas. Though exhausted from the trip, he held his hand up to stop his father-in-law from saying more, while a gentle smile spread over his hollow face.

"Hello, Henry; Hello, Eliza Mae," he said, touching their little chins. Looking down into Emma's pleading eyes, he whispered. "Then I suppose we will figure out a way to make this work, my love; won't we?"

Taking a deep breath, he steadied himself once more, then taking Emma's hand on one side and Caleb's arm on the other, he stepped off the platform and into the crowd.

It was time to let the past go, look to the future, and to put the war behind him. This was Silver Falls here and now, and he was home, at last.

Chapter Thirty-four
The Church Picnic

June 1919

"Good morning, Hannah, Nathan; you're here early."

Nathan had no sooner pulled his horses to a stop to allow his family out of the wagon than Alannah called out her greeting.

"And you are even earlier," Hannah called back. "What a surprise."

Nathan merely smiled at the salutation. They had come ahead of the crowds to help with the set up, but Alannah was there before them all. Sitting with her children on a large quilt in the churchyard, she was casually soaking up the rays of sunshine before even the reverend could show.

It was early enough to ensure possession of her own favorite picnic spot, near enough to a large mulberry tree to provide shade in the afternoon but, more importantly, it gave her the perfect vantage point to freely observe everyone and everything going on for the day. The only place hidden from her view was a very small area behind the church which held the privy, the one activity she felt certain she could miss.

Alannah followed a similar routine each time for the annual church picnic, and Hannah was happy to join her in it. Some people might have called it being nosy, but Hannah understood; it was just a part of her sister-in-law's natural interest in people that compelled her to seek such a position well ahead of the crowd. Oh, there would be plenty of chit-chat going on about the attendees, to be sure, but it was just Alannah and her fascination with people and their accompanying human nature.

While Nathan unloaded the children and their picnic supplies, Meredith and Andy helped their mother spread the enormous patchwork quilt on the grass. As soon as it was down, Meredith, Melanie, Andrew and Annie settled the littlest children and supplies onto the surface and then got down to the business of teaming up for pleasure and play with Maggie, Ben, and Rose.

Oliver and Chase lingered only a minute before following the older children off across the churchyard as well.

Little Annabelle, hating to be left behind, immediately crawled to the edge, put one hand on the course grass and sat back, looking for another means of escape. Alannah spread her blanket a little further, bridging the gap, after which the child crawled over to Jennie.

Meanwhile, Nell took a seat so near to Hannah that she was in constant physical contact. It was Nellie's way, her own peculiar habit; she hated being separated from family by any distance. Hannah often wondered if it stemmed at all from her experience on the streets of Portland or her months in the orphanage.

"Where's Peter?" Nathan asked. "Surely, you didn't come alone?"

"No, he had to see a few patients before the picnic. It was either drop us off early or all of us come late."

Nathan laughed at the idea. "Can't have that, can we?"

Alannah shrugged. "Not if I can help it. Besides, we knew you wouldn't be far behind, what with your 'anything-less-than-a-half-hour-early-is-late' rule."

Nathan shrugged as he climbed back into the wagon and drove the horses over to the shed and paddocks.

Hannah watched him and smiled. "He does enjoy being early to things," she admitted; "though I think his motives might be different than yours today."

"How so?"

"He volunteered to help the Larssens set up for the event."

"But they're not even here yet."

"True, but they will be soon and, well, he didn't want to be late." She smiled.

Just then the sound of large, lumbering horses could be heard in the distance.

"That might be them now. They have an extra-large amount of goods they're bringing and Nathan said he'd get some tables set up."

"It's sure to be a profitable day for them," Alannah mused, though Hannah shook her head.

"They aren't charging; everything today is free, donated for the benefit of the church."

Alannah looked suspiciously at her sister-in-law. "It sounds like Nathan has been involved."

"No, not at all; it was entirely the Larssen's idea."

"Have they done that well with their business?"

Hannah nodded. "Surprisingly well, and they're so good at it. Everyone at our house very much appreciates their cooking talents."

Alannah smiled. "They could probably run the entire business with your family alone."

"It's true," Hannah admitted. "But until the children are older and able to help more, it's an expense we're willing to take. You can't imagine how delicious their foods are."

"Oh, yes, I can! We order from them too, nearly every week."

As the bakery wagon rolled into the churchyard, the two women waved to the Larssens, after which, Alannah sat back and looked up into the branches of the tree.

"It's a lovely day," she announced.

Their blankets were spread in full sunshine at the moment and she welcomed the warmth. In another couple of hours they would be sitting in full shade. Off in the distance, she watched Nathan as he joined efforts in getting several tables set up. Thinking about the Larssen's and their bakery business, Alannah began to muse further.

"I wonder how much they make. Have you ever heard anything about it? They have minimal staff outside their family, don't they?" Alannah continued to wonder. "Flour and sugar aren't very expensive, especially when bought in bulk."

Hannah smiled. "Hayden is thinking of working with the bakery rather than farming."

Alannah was surprised at that news. "Really? Why?"

"He's had trouble getting his strength back, and with the bakery so profitable…"

"Ah!" Alannah interrupted. "So you do know something about it."

Hannah smiled. "Emma said that last year, after all their expenses, they cleared over four thousand in profit."

"Dollars?! Four thousand *dollars*; for breads and donuts? That's astonishing! How can that even be possible?"

Hannah shrugged and smiled. "They deliver door to door most days of the week and supply the restaurant as well. Our bill alone runs about twelve dollars every month, and that's now. It was even more when we had all the orphans. I'm sure we order a little more than most, but we're still only one family. Think of how many people patronize their business."

Alannah nodded, looking off in the direction of the wagon. "Good for them! I'm glad to see they've finally put their hand to something so prosperous."

Hannah agreed. "They work hard for it."

At the conclusion of their conversation, a car rounded the corner, pulling into the churchyard. It was Helen Daley, driving the good reverend and his children to the picnic. Alannah's brows rose at the sight.

"Carlen came with Helen Daley?"

Hannah didn't respond, but instead watched as they pulled beyond the bakery wagon to park and unload. As the Sanderson boys left to play with their friends, Helen settled little Marianne on her hip, while Carlen hurried to help Nathan and the Larssens with the tables.

"Do you think she is chasing him?" Alannah whispered. Clearly, her curiosity of the situation was far from satisfied.

"Helen helps him now and then. As far as I know, that's all there is to it."

"Still, they look good together," Alannah declared. "They are both so tall and willowy, the perfect picture of a match; well, except that it's Helen. That part seems too odd to reconcile."

Hannah smiled and shrugged. "She's nice enough. Maybe we've just misjudged her a little."

Alannah nodded. "And no one has said that they're even a couple. One car ride to a church picnic isn't exactly a public declaration of love."

Once his chore was complete, Nathan made his way back to the area of his family with a small bag from the Larssen's wagon. Upon reaching the blanket, he handed the goods to Hannah then settled down near her, grabbing Annabelle from the edge and putting her between them.

"The Larssens have Mother's tarts on the wagon. I got enough for all of us."

Alannah smiled as she twisted one of Jennie's dark curls around her finger. "I'm sure we'll all enjoy them. Even Jennie is old enough to have a bite now; aren't you, little one?"

Nathan looked at the little girls. "She's the same age as Nellie, isn't she?"

"A little younger," Hannah volunteered. "Nellie will be two in October and Jennie in February. It's funny how our children have all lined up to be near the same ages."

"Except that you have twice the number we do," Alannah added. "I don't think we'll ever catch up. I'm not sure I even want to."

Nathan laughed at that. "No one said it was a race..."

Off in the distance, a car horn interrupted their talk with two beeps on the road.

"That will be Davy," Hannah predicted. "He loves making an entrance."

In another few seconds, the Harrison's car rounded the corner and pulled into the churchyard, driving down to the end of the stalls and parking behind the wagons. Upon exiting the car, David handed the blanket to Jason and the picnic basket to Jon. Finally he pulled out a loaded satchel and offered his arm to Laurel, as they walked toward the tall tree under which the Laynes had gathered.

"Good morning," Laurel greeted; "mind if we join you?"

"Busy gossiping, I see," David added. "You'd better let her in; the chatter circle won't be complete without her."

Alannah patted the grass nearby "There's plenty of room. Find a place for your blanket and join us."

As the boys spread the quilt and flopped down onto it, Nathan's curiosity at the clinking was roused.

"What's in the satchel?"

"Apple-ginger ale," Laurel smiled, "*and* we brought enough to share."

Alannah laughed. "Yum! By all means, join us!"

"Where's Susie?" Hannah asked.

David looked back toward the road. "They were right behind us; unless Mason fell out of the car again. They need to put that boy in a straitjacket while driving. He's such a bundle of energy and refuses to sit still."

Alannah raised her brows. "He fell out of the car?"

"Just yesterday; fortunately they were barely moving. He dumped right out on his head though. Good thing, I suppose," David winked. "Anywhere else and he might have gotten hurt. He'll have playmates aplenty in this corner of the churchyard. Aren't they all about his age?"

"Pretty close," Alannah answered. "Jennie's a month younger, then Anabelle and Nellie are three and four months older."

"Close enough," David agreed. "Maybe one or two of them will end up married someday."

Alannah rubbed her hands together in exaggerated excitement. "Oh, matchmaking; now we're talking!"

"I think that's our cue to leave," Jon whispered to his brother.

"We'll be down by the food," Jason announced.

Laurel looked at them in question. "Are you boys hungry already?"

Jason turned back and gave a nod in the direction of the crowd.

"Ah, girls," David answered.

Alannah shook her head. "I don't see any girls down there."

Hannah smiled at her. "The Larssen girls are in the wagon."

"Do they all like each other?"

"Jason likes Amelia," Laurel answered.

"Does Jonathan like one of the others?" Alannah pursued.

"No, he's still pining over Emma. I think he's the only person in Silver Falls who didn't jump for joy when Hayden returned."

"Davy!" Hannah reproved.

"Well, it's true enough," her brother declared.

Laurel shook her head. "Not all truth merits being said aloud."

"Surely, he'll get over it eventually," Alannah added, trying to smooth over the situation.

"I don't know," David mused. "He's been secretly crushing on her for the last six years, ever since he met her."

"Met her?" Hannah asked. "Or heard her sing?"

"You might be right with that, Sis. Either way, it's been a very long time. He may just die single – that or from barnstorming."

Nathan nodded his agreement. "The planes seem very unsafe to me."

"That they are," David agreed. "The boys frequently mention crashes they've heard of or seen, but in the same breath they claim it's only the inexperienced pilots who have them. Besides, the barnstorming brings in so much money that they'll not soon be letting it go. During good weather, they easily bring in fifty dollars a week, and for just a day or two of effort."

Alannah's brows rose. "That's amazing!"

David nodded. "One Saturday last month at a county fair, they made ninety-five dollars in one day. Even splitting the profit between them, they'd never be able to earn that sort of money working an hourly job."

"Ninety-five dollars in one day?" Nathan asked. "That seems impossible."

"That's right. It was a long day and they spent nearly six hours each in the air, but who can argue the results. They do love it, though, being up there in the sky."

"Does that mean you'll want an airplane of your own now?" Hannah teased, though David shook his head.

"Someone has to feed the world."

Just then another car rounded the corner revealing Grant and Susie, with Mason safely held in his mother's arms and Hayden, Emma and the twins in the back seat. Then, as if everyone else decided to arrive at once, a steady stream of buggies and motor cars began to pour into the area, parking at the stables, horse and car alike. Alannah brightened at the sight of it. The action was soon to begin in earnest.

"So, back to couples," she mused, continuing to look over the crowd, "we have Jason Harrison and Amelia Larssen, Johnny Layne, Amanda Layne, Melissa Layne… oh, this won't do at all! There are too many Laynes and not enough others. David, you need to tell Jonathan to snap out of it and he can have his pick of the other girls! Who will Melissa marry, or Amanda, or Grace?"

"I think Grace and Mike Van Dynne are sweet on each other," Hannah put in. "Besides, you forgot Emma's brother, Paul, and Maria Larssen."

"Yes, but they're already engaged. No mystery there."

"What about Kirsten Larssen. One of the Layne boys can like her," Hannah persisted.

"It's still so limiting," Alannah complained.

"Well then, don't forget Christian and Annie. Maybe you're focusing too much on the older crowd."

Their conversation was cut short by Jonathan returning to the area with a basket full of baked goods from the wagon.

"They've got Sarah's tarts on the wagon today. I doubt they'll last for long so I snagged one for each of us."

"Good work, son!" David said, slapping the boy on the back as he took a seat nearby. "I imagine even Alannah will forgive you for that good deed."

"Alannah?" he asked.

Everyone burst into laughter as Jonathan merely looked at his neighbor in a state of confusion.

Alannah smiled at Nathan as he tucked a napkin over his own cache of tarts. "Eat up, Jon!" she offered. "They're a great comfort food; and if we're still lonely when those are done we can divvy up Nathan's stash."

"Two batches of tarts?" David asked. "Oh, excellent!" Looking out across the yard he ventured his further thoughts. "I noticed that Helen Daley is pursuing our good reverend everywhere he goes."

"She's been helping him with the children," Alannah volunteered.

"They're not a couple then?" David sounded almost disappointed.

"Not that anyone has heard," Hannah answered.

"It looks like Eliza Mae and Henry are walking," David observed. "How old are they now?"

"Ten months," Hannah and Alannah answered in unison.

"Well, I must say, it's a little comical to watch, with Hayden and Emma hovering over them like that. Are they afraid they'll fall? They're not that far from the ground anyway, you know. Oops, there goes Henry."

Hannah smiled. "Hayden seems to be getting stronger and putting some weight back on," she mused. "I'm glad he and Grant have reconciled their differences."

They were all quiet after that, as they watched the festivities unfold. Reverend Sanderson soon started a game of tug-o-war between several of the boys, while off at the church steps, a group of young girls compared their dolls. Down in the northwest corner, the Larssens stayed busy hours longer into the day distributing delectables, while off to the other side of the church, Grant organized several children into teams for a game of kickball.

It was a lovely day; perfect for a church activity where people could ebb and flow, mingle and mix, as easily as the ocean tides upon the shores. It wasn't long in that cozy environment before the tree fully shaded their blankets and the babies nodded off to their naps, and when they did, as if on cue, Peter finally arrived.

"Sorry I'm late," he offered as he settled onto the blanket near his family. "It looks as if things are beginning to wind down. What did I miss?"

"Most of the day and a glut of Mother's tarts, for starters," Nathan answered.

"Henry and Eliza toddling their way to exhaustion," Hannah added.

Peter laughed at that. "They are early walkers, aren't they?"

"Then there is poor little Hansel," Alannah began. "I've been watching him for hours. He's the only one his age and tries so hard to fit in."

Hannah smiled at that, looking over the churchyard until her eyes at last fell on the lad. "He's had a lot to deal with this past year; poor little tyke. I wish there were more children his age; he longs for love and acceptance."

"Does he now? Hansel!" David called to the boy who was, even at that moment, drifting from crowd to crowd. As he approached with a look of question on his face, David invited him to join their group. "I happen to know that Nathan, over there, has one, last raspberry tart tucked away just for you. Would you like that?"

"Oh, yes, sir!" the boy answered enthusiastically.

"Well then, have a seat and join us."

Nathan patted the blanket near the basket while Hannah retrieved the final tart for the little boy.

"How old are you now, Hansel?" David asked.

"Seven this month, sir," the boy replied.

"How do you like Miss Daley?" he pursued. "Is she a nice babysitter?"

Alannah drew a gasp at David's bold question.

"Oh, yes, sir; and can she ever cook! Fried chicken and mashed potatoes! She always tells me to eat all I want, and then we eat pie every single night!"

That statement turned everyone's heads!

"She cooks for you every night?" Alannah asked.

"Yes, ma'am; she has to work during the day, but she comes to our house after that and makes us dinner and pie every night. On the weekend she makes us lunch and sometimes breakfast too."

Surprised looks passed through the entire group as they listened to Hansel's enthusiastic report.

"She cleans the house too," Hans continued, "and irons our clothes and makes our beds."

"Sounds almost like a mother," David observed.

"Oh, she is! She is just like a mother; she even said I can call her Mother if I wanted."

David Harrison was the only one of the group with enough sense to keep his head on straight after that bit of information.

"Does she spend the night?" he asked in jest.

"Oh, no, sir; she goes home every night after we've all gone to bed."

"Well now, is that the truth?"

"Yes, and Mrs. Layne," he turned back to Hannah, "Chase and Oliver are in the rose bushes."

"Are you tattling on the boys?" David asked.

"No, sir, but they are pricking themselves with the thorns and making their fingers bleed."

"What?!" Hannah asked in alarm, standing and searching the churchyard.

"Over there," Hansel pointed. "They said they want to be blood-brothers, so they are trading blood."

"Why don't you just go get them for us?" Nathan asked, after which Hans was up and off in a jiffy.

"Well now," David announced after the boy had run off, "that was an earful of news."

"There you go, Alannah," Laurel added, "one more couple to complete your matches."

"Apparently so," Alannah laughed, looking over the area until her eyes at last found Carlen's tall frame, and then Helen's, never far away. "They do make a lovely looking couple."

David nodded. "That they do. Odd, but interesting."

Laurel smiled at her husband's outspoken assessment. "Well, it's good to know that Carlen has found someone for those children. I dare say it's been a long year for them all since Linda's passing."

"That it has."

Glancing at his sister, David smiled. She would likely never know all the gossip that had centered around herself and Carlen Sanderson. No one could really bring themselves to tell her. But Carlen had heard it, and Alannah had heard it. David had certainly heard it, and he knew that Nathan had anguished over it. Considering the repercussions, David Harrison heaved a sigh.

"It looks as if his trials just might be coming to a close."

At these words, Nathan rested back on the blanket with his arms behind his head. Looking up through the leaves to the clear blue sky above, he let out a sigh of his own and whispered to himself.

"Thank heavens for that."

Chapter Thirty-five

The Handsome Stranger

July 1919

Hannah's kitchen was usually a cheery place to be, but it was even more delightful when Alannah came to visit. As the several children alternated their play between the house and the yard, their mothers finished preparing dinner, all the while visiting and catching up on the daily rituals of life.

Hannah paused to enjoy a breeze coming through the screen door. "It's a perfect day outside; should we make it a picnic for them?"

Reaching for the pitcher of lemonade and a slice of sweetbread, Alannah nodded her agreement. "They would like that, and it would be less mess to clean up inside. When is Nathan going to be home?"

"He said he'd be back no later than five, and it's…" Hannah stretched to see the clock around the corner in the front room, "nearly that now."

Grabbing a large basket from the top of the icebox, she began packing the sandwiches and cookies inside. Pouring lemonade into a couple of bottles and corking them closed, she added a few more cups and napkins. Finally, she set a tablecloth on top of it all, latched the top closed and took it to the front door.

"Maggie, Melanie," she called out, holding the picnic basket aloft. "Make sure the sandwiches are eaten first and the cookies saved for dessert."

"A picnic!" Several of the children squealed in delight as the older girls came to retrieve the basket.

"There's a cloth to sit on inside," Hannah continued. "See that the children eat up and be sure to share the lemonade."

The girls skipped back to the yard with the basket between them as Hannah returned to the kitchen to finish preparing Nathan's dinner and continue the conversation there.

"The lemonade is really good," Alannah said as she puckered her lips at the after-bite.

Hannah only smiled and pushed the sugar bowl toward her. "You can add more sugar if you like."

"No, really; it's perfect; I like it a little tart. So, are there any last items you want to discuss before Nathan gets home?"

Hannah looked out the window and shrugged. "I can't think of anything and, look, there he is now."

As Nathan walked up the path and through the kitchen door, Hannah could see from his expression that something was troubling him.

"Hi; you're home right on time."

Nathan nodded. "It looks like the children are enjoying their picnic."

"What's not to enjoy?" Alannah mused. "Blue skies, fresh lemonade, sandwiches, and cookies."

"It does sound good."

"What's wrong?" Hannah asked as she set a plate before him. "You were so chipper when you left this morning; you seem kind of down now. Did things not go well at the bank?"

"No, the bank is fine."

"What is it then?"

Nathan shrugged. "Probably nothing; Helen had a caller at the bank is all. He said his name was Mr. Crandon. He showed up at the end of our meeting and asked her out to dinner."

"What!" Alannah and Hannah both gasped the response in unison.

Alannah shook her head in disbelief. "But I thought she was serious about Carlen."

"We all did," Nathan agreed.

"And maybe she is," Hannah put in. "Surely, it was nothing."

Nathan heaved a heavy sigh. "He kissed her when they met, Hannah. And she left work early, right after he showed up, arm in arm to the restaurant."

"Oh, poor Carlen!" Hannah mourned. "I'm certain that he's grown to love her. Oh, will his trials never end?"

The three adults were quiet for a while after that, each lost in their own respective thoughts, until Alannah finally broke the silence.

"They are such a handsome couple and the children seem to really like her. It would be a pity if it doesn't work out."

Hannah nodded her agreement. "I thought it strange at first, but they really do get on nicely together."

Nathan sighed. "Well, Hannah, as you said, perhaps it was nothing."

"Of course, kissing a man in public and then taking his arm for a stroll is never something to take seriously." Alannah's tones dripped with rebuking sarcasm.

Nathan looked at her sadly. "Unfortunately, there's nothing to be done about it."

Alannah still struggled to make sense of the whole situation. "Wasn't she just baptized last month?"

Hannah nodded, deep in her own thoughts, as she reached for the sugar, stirring a little more of it in to sweeten the lemonade. When that was done, she cut three pieces of cake and, forgetting about the sandwiches altogether, passed them around the table, eventually taking a seat and joining the others in their quiet and solemn musing.

Outside, they heard the children's voices rise in excitement, followed by a knock at the front door. Nathan left to answer it and they were all a little surprised by what came next.

"Carlen, come in; we were just talking about you."

"I thought I felt my ears burning." He smiled as he came through the front room and then into the kitchen. "Hello, Hannah, Alannah. How are the local ladies doing today?"

"Please, have a seat," Hannah offered. "Who's watching your children?"

"I brought them with me; they're presently in the yard with the rest of the group, being fed lemonade and cookies, I believe."

Alannah smiled. "That sounds about right; there are playmates galore out there."

"Yes, and actually I have some errands to run in town. The boys asked if they could come here to play. I was wondering if you would mind keeping an eye on them for a little while."

"No! I mean, you can't do that! I mean..."

The words had jumped from Hannah's panicked lips before she could stop them and she scrambled to think of how she could cover for the awkwardness that followed. Only one topic dominated her thoughts, and that was how to keep Carlen from witnessing Helen's date in town with the handsome stranger.

The minister looked at her in confusion. She had always been so generous with him, never balking at the occasional opportunities to watch Marianne and the boys. It had been a while since he'd asked and he could hardly understand her refusal now.

"Alright," he hedged; "I suppose I can take them with me."

"Oh, no, no!" Hannah scrambled to think of more to say. "I can watch them; I was just hoping you might stay and visit for a little while before you left. Please, sit down with us," she insisted. "Can I get you some cake, or there are sweetbreads on the table and I just made some fresh lemonade. Surely, you can spare a little time to visit with us, can't you?"

"Thank you; I suppose I can stay a few minutes," Carlen took a seat at the table as another awkward silence followed, and the adults all tried to think of something more to say, more than the taboo topic which consumed their thoughts. Consequently, it took a minute before anyone spoke.

"You know," Nathan began, "I was wondering if you might check out a new horse I bought and tell me what you think of him."

Carlen looked at him in surprise. "I suppose I could, but you are the horseman, Nathan. I don't know what I might have to say that could amount to anything worthwhile."

"I'd love to hear your opinion on him just the same," Nathan replied. "He's right out here in the barn. Come and see; Hannah can save that piece of cake for you while we're out."

Carlen rose from the table, and as they headed out the kitchen door, Nathan looked back with an apprehensive grimace and a shrug.

"Well, that's stretching it," Alannah laughed, "the horse trainer asking a minister for his opinion on a horse."

"I think it's up to us," Hannah moaned. "I'm sure Nathan's hoping we'll come up with something before they get back. How can we delay him long enough to ensure he won't run into Helen?"

Alannah shook her head. "I don't know. How long do you think she might stay at the restaurant?"

Hannah shrugged. "An hour, maybe two? Nathan walks that distance in less than forty minutes; it surely wouldn't take Carlen any longer."

"For Nathan to get home and Carlen to get to town would be barely more than an hour," Alannah began to estimate, "which means we'll need to delay him for at least one more to be safe."

They didn't have much time to think past that as, presently, they heard the men walking back up the path toward the house.

"Really, Nathan," they overheard Carlen say; "you don't need to give me the horse. I'm sure our old gelding will last a while longer."

"Give him the horse?" Alannah laughed. "Boy, he went all out to make that convincing, didn't he?"

Hannah was just setting more cake and sandwiches on the table as both men came through the door.

"Here you go, Carlen; please make yourself comfortable and enjoy a piece of cake."

Looking around at the group with the first hints of suspicion, he slowly took a seat and lifted his fork, as if unsure what to do next.

"Did I miss something?" he finally asked. "Not to give any offense, but you are all acting a bit odd today."

Alannah took a deep breath, raised her finger and then ventured her thoughts. "Actually, I had a question about your sermon on Sunday."

Hannah and Nathan looked at her, not having a clue where she was going with it.

"Past or Sunday future?" the reverend asked.

"Past," Alannah smiled. "You spoke on the doctrine of baptism. Do you really think it is essential for everyone?"

"Yes, of course," he replied. "That is what our Lord said. Why do you ask?"

Alannah toyed with her fork, poking at the layers of frosting and cake. "Well, I have a confession to make; I have never been baptized."

Carlen sat back, clearly stunned at the news. Alannah had attended church since well before his arrival in Silver Falls; he had no idea there might have been such an unresolved matter. Her name was on the church records with Peter's through the payment of their offerings and there had been nothing to suggest that her membership could be remotely in question.

"Are you sure?" he asked.

"I can vouch for it," Hannah agreed. "She's never felt a burning need."

"Or a sure belief," Alannah continued.

Carlen looked around at the adults again. So this was it, he thought to himself. This was why they were acting so strange. Alannah wanted to discuss baptism and they were trying to keep him here for that. Though his business in town was s pressing, he thought he could spare a little time to address her concerns and see where the situation might lead. It was, after all, very important.

"What seems to be holding you back?" he asked. "Do you mind if we talk about this now, or would you rather wait and speak in private?"

"Oh, now is just fine. I've beaten the topic to death with Hannah; and Nathan knows it as well. I've just never really felt the need and, well, I don't know that I believe it is truly necessary."

"Why is that?"

As Carlen became engaged in the conversation, Hannah and Nathan breathed a rather large sigh of relief. Alannah had saved the day and come up with something, an all important topic, to delay his trip into town. Hannah was a bit amused that she had brought up baptism... and Alannah thought that Nathan had resorted to desperate measures?

"To be frank, I have a hard time believing that it's fair. My sister, Lily was, by far, the better of the two of us, and yet she was never baptized; what's to become of her for it? According to your sermon last Sunday, God won't let her into heaven, because she died before she had any opportunity. I don't think that's fair at all; it's why I've never been baptized. If she can't get into heaven, then what right do I have going there before her? Reverend Blistroe even told me that she would burn in hell for all eternity and that I would burn right along with her if I wasn't baptized."

Carlen shook his head. "None of us has the right to make those judgments, Alannah, not Reverend Blistroe or anyone else."

"Is there a doctrine on the matter?" she asked.

"Not a finite one, at least not that I'm convinced of."

"Ah," she declared, picking up on the discrepancy "so then you have doubts as well."

Carlen looked chagrined, before glancing around the table to see the ready expressions at each seat. Drawing a deep breath, he knew he'd have to explain. "There are a very few points of doctrinal philosophy that I haven't been able to entirely reconcile with the scriptures."

Alannah smiled. "Surely, you can offer your opinion."

Carlen looked at Hannah a little helplessly, though she only looked back with her own questioning eyes.

"What *is* your opinion?" Hannah asked.

"Well," Carlen cleared his throat uncomfortably before giving in and explaining himself. "I believe that God is not only just, but merciful. Any situation that is completely unfair would have to be covered by his mercy. The question of Lily, in my mind, goes hand in hand with the other children in the world who have died without baptism. Or, for that matter, even the question of heathen nations; if He is Father to us all, then surely, in his mercy, there would be provisions made and exceptions to the rule if a person has had no opportunity to obey. It is a very great division in the religions of our day. Why would he choose to save some and not others?"

Alannah nodded. "Calvinistic predestination."

Carlen looked at her in surprise. "You're familiar with the Calvinist creed?"

"Mrs. Stotts was Calvinist and preached to me often, but I never believed it, at least not that part of it. What do you think?"

"I suppose we all have to decide what we will believe, but if we always seek after mercy, kindness, and the truth, and are not afraid to find it, then I don't believe God will turn us away."

"Do you believe in hell?" Alannah asked.

"Yes, I suppose I do; but again, I don't believe we are qualified to judge who will go there."

Alannah continued to ask question after question, oftentimes straying far from the points of predetermined church doctrines, all keeping Carlen quite on his toes in an attempt to answer her many varied concerns.

Hannah was actually impressed at the depth of her philosophy and searching questions. She and Alannah had discussed religion from time to time and they were each aware of the other's levels of belief, as well as the doubts, but she had never heard her carry on such a compelling argument, one that required hard answers to justify even their minister's faith. Leave it to Alannah though; she wasn't afraid of anyone when it came to such things. She would rather ask and cross-examine until all of her concerns were answered satisfactorily than to let anyone sweep an unresolved matter under a rug of blind faith.

In this case, however, as the clock chimed at six, she began to relax and breathed an involuntary sigh of relief. She had managed the diversion for nearly an entire hour. Surely, Helen and her mystery man would be done with the restaurant before Carlen could reach town and see them.

"I do say, that hour went by far too quickly; I really should be on my way," Carlen announced, as he stood, preparing to leave. "But I would encourage you to think about baptism, Alannah. It isn't like Lily; you have the choice and opportunity."

Alannah only smiled and walked with everyone else to the front door. As they stood on the porch, momentarily checking on the children, a car turned off the road from town and into the driveway.

"Drats!" Nathan whispered under his breath. It was Helen's car and he could tell, even from a quarter mile away that there was a man in the passenger's seat.

"Well, that's a bit of luck," Carlen announced. "It's Helen."

The group of adults stood quietly on the porch, three of them not sure of what to say or do next, until Carlen spoke again.

"I see Charlie is with her," he continued on.

"Charlie?" Nathan asked. "You know him?"

"Well, know of him. I knew he was meeting Helen at work today; I was hoping to meet them both in town, but it appears they may have tired waiting for me."

At those words, Hannah laughed. "I suppose we'll find out sooner or later, but just who is he?"

"Charlie Crandon, her brother."

"Crandon? Daley?" Alannah asked doubtfully, though Carlen only smiled.

"Yes, it's her older brother from her mother's first marriage. He's the only family she has left and she… well, I'm getting ahead of myself. Come on; we can all be introduced."

The car soon arrived at the hitching post where the occupants got out.

"Stunning!" Alannah whispered again as she saw the reverend and Helen together.

Soon, Helen was introducing them both. "Charlie, this is Carlen Sanderson, my fiancé."

"Yes," Carlen confessed, turning to his friends, waving them over; "and this is my soon-to-be brother-in-law, Charlie Crandon. Charlie, these are my good friends, Nathan and Hannah Layne and their sister-in-law, Alannah."

"It's good to meet you! Nathan," he said, extending his hand for a shake, "I understand you're also Helen's employer."

"Yes, I guess that's true."

"I suppose we should be off then," Carlen announced. "There's much to talk about tonight. Hannah, thank you for your willingness to watch the children, though I guess it's not necessary any longer." Turning to Alannah, he gave a smile and nod. "You'll think about our discussion, won't you?"

Alannah gave only an acknowledging nod, trying with great difficulty not to betray herself.

"Hansel, Chris; come children and bring Marianne, it's time to go."

"Mommy!" Hansel shouted out and waved, as Christian picked up his little sister and made his way toward the car. Coming through the gate, Carlen took the baby from his arms and helped them all into the back seat.

Soon, they were driving down the shaded lane, beneath the giant maples and toward the main road that led to town on the north and to church on the south. Stopping at the end, they turned left and headed out toward Parish Road.

Below a beautiful, blue sky, dotted with high, puffy clouds, Nathan stood near the hitching post and shook his head.

"Hannah, I will never meddle again; will you make sure that it is so?"

Shaking herself from her speechlessness, his wife shook her head. "Who could have known?"

Alannah laughed at the both of them before turning back toward the door. "I do declare, you're both a couple lightweights. I'll be making no such promise for the future. Life is far too interesting to bear it in silence!"

Calling her children, to gather them for home, Alannah turned again to Hannah and Nathan. "Congratulations to the reverend, but I'm certain it won't be the last time we'll all play the fool." Thinking again, she laughed. "You know, he is lucky to have Helen; she is something of a savior for the whole family."

Nathan nodded thoughtfully. "And Helen is lucky to have him. I don't think I've ever known a better man."

"He is, truly, a saint," Hannah mused.

"Saint Carlen," Alannah agreed. "How many times have we called him just that?"

Nathan looked thoughtfully down the lane where they had just gone, nodding his agreement. "I'm sure it won't be the last."

The End

About the Author

Rebecca Woods lives a quiet life in the Midwest, where she enjoys farming with her family, and creating stories from history.

Saint Carlen of Silver Falls is the 5th volume in the award-winning Silver Falls series. For more information, you can view her author page at facebook.com/pages/rebecca-woods.

Books in the Silver Falls Series:

Hannah of Silver Falls

Angels & Promises of Silver Falls

The Rising Winds of Silver Falls

Nathan of Silver Falls

Saint Carlen of Silver Falls

Made in the USA
Charleston, SC
18 August 2016